THE DRAMA CONTINUES...
BOOK 2

ONE *Still* AIN'T *Enough*

THE SALACIOUS SEQUEL BY
MO FLAMES

FLAMES
ENTERTAINMENT

ONE STILL AIN'T ENOUGH

Dedicated to Darnell, Linda, Myron, and Kevin.

I hate that you aren't here to see I've finally published book two, but I know you're all smiling down on me.

Miss you, love you, and I mean it.

Author Note

Dear Beloved Readers,

Thank you for purchasing and/or downloading this book. This work of art contains explicit language, strong sexual content, and certain topics that might be sensitive to some readers.

This is book two in a three part series . . . The Enough Series. It is highly recommended that you read, *One Ain't Enough* before reading this book, as it picks up where book one left off.

Keep in mind this is a fictional story, so things that you may find unrealistic or perhaps unrelatable, may be real and relatable to someone else. I hope that you enjoy the drama that continues with this unforgettable cast of friends, lovers, and enemies.

Contents

How did I get here? It was the burning question in the back of Desiree's mind as she grappled with the realization that everything happening to her was a direct result of her own careless actions—letting Troy live in her heart and head rent free, her failed marriage to Jamal, and the whole time wading through an ocean of secrets and lies. None of it ever should have happened. Then there was Derrik. She'd complicated everything even more by letting him out of the friend zone. Yet here they were, caught up in a complicated affair that made all thoughts of her marriage and other relationships dissolve into thin air. A forbidden love was only the beginning of her story . . .

CHAPTER

1

Oh shit! Of all the people to be on the same plane with her, why did it have to be him? Desiree's eyebrows furrowed as she asked, "What are you doing here?"

He stepped back, looked around the cabin, and responded sarcastically, "I could've sworn this plane was heading to LA, which means I'm going home."

Desiree smiled sheepishly. "I know that. It's just that I wasn't expecting to see you.

"Well, I had business to handle with a client." He looked around again. "You here alone? Where's your husband?"

She waved her hand dismissively. "Yeah, he's not here."

"Hmm, I see. Since he isn't, could I get a better greeting? Perhaps a hug?" He opened his arms. She unfastened the seat belt and stood to embrace the tall, well-built man. He pulled his lower lip into his mouth and lowered his eyes. They caressed her body with lusting, invisible fingers. He flashed a mischievous grin.

"Aaron, what are you—"

Her words were lost when he wrapped his arms around her and swooped in to steal a kiss. Then he nuzzled his face in her hair, his hot breath tickling her ear.

He whispered in a deep, husky voice, "Look, Desiree, I understand. It's not every day that you run into the man you've been fucking on the side, especially when he's supposed to be on the opposite side of the country." She felt her cheeks grow warm as he squeezed her tighter. He pulled away and frowned. "Why are you so tense? Is everything all right?"

Desiree glanced over his shoulder at the people inching by to get past them. She rotated her neck and whispered, "First of all, you're not the man I'm fucking on the side. You know how much I hate that word. We don't *fuck*. And I'm fine. It's been a busy week and an even more chaotic weekend. I have a lot on my mind with this new merger I'm managing."

Just then, one of the flight attendants approached, instructing them to take their seats. Aaron motioned for Desiree to move over to the empty seat next to her.

"But that's somebody's seat."

"Okay, and you can move when they get here."

Desiree wished the person were there already or that Aaron would take his ass to his own row.

"Go ahead. Scoot over."

She didn't know who Aaron thought he was, demanding her to do anything. She really wasn't in the mood. Then he flashed a full, pearly-white smile, exposing deep dimples in both cheeks. She cut her eyes, blew out a short breath and moved into the vacant window seat. Once they sat down, Aaron began probing her. He wanted to know why she hadn't contacted him in the previous month. Her annoyed expression said it all, and before she could respond, he stopped her.

"I know what you said, but I thought we were friends. You can still call. Or you mean to tell me things are so good between you and Jamal that you conveniently forgot about me?"

Desiree wasn't about to admit that her husband wasn't the reason she'd forgotten about him, or that he wasn't the one she'd been preoccupied with anyway. She responded coolly, "I've just been busy."

"That busy?"

"Yes, that busy." And it was the truth. The new merger she'd been assigned to demanded more time than she was used to. Unlike previous projects that had her traveling to LA or out of the country, this one required her to be on-site in Atlanta. Before Aaron could question her about anything else, she asked him about the client he'd been there to work with over the weekend.

"It was Samuel Pryce, and it's still under negotiations, so I'm not supposed to discuss anything about it, but you know him. They're planning another takeover. He had us holed up in the Westin all day, and I didn't have any free time. Otherwise, I would've stopped by the office, called, or texted."

"Aaron, you know that would've been too risky."

"Yeah, but that didn't stop you before."

She felt her cheeks warming again.

"Relax, Desiree. I told you I know how to play my position. Now tell me, why didn't you let me know you were going to be in LA?" He smiled, revealing his dimples again. "Or were you trying to sneak up on me?"

Aaron Moretti was an undeniably handsome attorney she'd met the year before during a major acquisition she'd been in charge of. He'd headed up the legal team for one of the clients. When she traveled to LA, the two would meet for cocktails and dinner to discuss progress made during negotiations. In the final days of the acquisition, they ended up getting closer than she'd intended.

He interrupted her thoughts, "Well, were you?"

"This was a last-minute trip. I didn't find out until late yesterday." She lied, "Once I got settled in, you know I would've called."

Desiree knew why Aaron was persistent in wanting clarity on their status. Initially, their interactions had been cordial and professional. But naturally, as they worked closely together for so many months, they began sharing intimate details about their personal lives. Things weren't going well for her and Jamal, and Desiree wanted a man's perspective. She didn't see the harm, so she started confiding in Aaron.

When she considered everything that happened between them afterward, she knew it was the opening Aaron had been waiting for. Desiree's thoughts took her back to the night of their eventful encounter.

After a long week of intense meetings, the staff met up for drinks. Hours later, Desiree and Aaron were the only two remaining after the rest of their team had left. Rather than letting her take a cab, Aaron offered to drive her back to the hotel. When they arrived, he hastily jumped out, and Desiree noticed he had given his keys to the valet before opening her door. It wasn't until they were in the lobby that

Aaron spoke. "I think you've had too much to drink tonight, Desiree. I'm going to make sure you get to your room safely."

"Trust me, I'll be fine, Aaron. Thank you for making sure I made it here safely. I'll see you in a couple of weeks. Have a good night."

Desiree walked away, but she felt him close on her heels with each step. Finally, she stopped and tried to turn around. He grabbed her arm and pulled her close. Before she could speak, Aaron covered her lips, gently sucking her lower lip into his mouth. Then his tongue slipped past her teeth and tangled with hers. The slight hint of Louis XIII Cognac on his tongue mixed with the wine on hers made an intoxicating, delicious flavor. She pressed her body closer to him. He sucked slowly and gently, but hard enough to make her knees buckle. When she realized what was happening, Desiree raised her hands to his chest and pushed him away. "What do you think you're doing?"

Aaron ignored her and bent his head to kiss her again. She turned away. He grabbed her chin, forcing her to face him. He flashed a mischievous grin, showing his dimples.

"No. We can't do this," she whispered.

"Oh, yes we can."

"Aaron, I'm married, and you have a—"

He smothered her protest. This time, their kiss lasted longer, and Desiree didn't put up much of a struggle. Minutes later, they were fumbling around in the darkness of her hotel room.

"Where's the light switch, Desiree?"

"I-I . . . uh . . . I don't know. I can't see," she giggled.

She didn't think she'd had that much wine over dinner, but combined with her rushing adrenaline, it was enough to make her feel tipsy. Her inhibitions were gone. They were replaced with a horny desire and confidence that she would never get caught.

After kissing and fondling, they managed to turn on the lamp a few minutes later. Desiree backed away from him until she felt the corner of the bed against her legs. She sat down and moved to the middle of the bed. She released the button and unzipped her skirt. He finished pulling it down her legs. She spread her thighs apart, and Aaron quickly positioned himself between them. He slowly unbuttoned her blouse, and she seductively let it slip off her arms. He traced the edges of her laced bra, slipped his hands behind her back, and unhooked it, exposing the supple mounds.

He bent forward, cupping both breasts. His tongue produced wet circles around her areolas. He sucked until they pointed at attention. Desiree released his dark hair from its bun, ran her fingers through the long, soft curls, and pressed his head closer. He reached for the top of her panties. After sliding them over her feet, he spread her legs apart and bent forward, burying his face between her thighs. Desiree's body responded almost immediately. He continued to play with her button as juices trickled down his chin. He exposed more of the tight, pink flesh, and his thick tongue slid in and out. He repeated the movements slowly then increased the tempo.

Desiree moaned, "Mmm, don't stop!" Aaron pushed his tongue in deeper as she held on to his head tightly. "Yes, right there! Yes! Yes!"

He didn't stop until the sheets were drenched. Finally, he pulled away long enough to remove his clothing. Desiree heard the condom wrapper open. He returned to the bed and positioned himself between her thighs. She felt a smooth digit glide over her clit. He rubbed gently, keeping her aroused. Her legs opened wider, welcoming his finger play on her swollen button. His next movements were slow, but when he finally entered Desiree's cavern of heat, she gasped.

He bragged, "Bet you didn't think I'd be working with all this."

She didn't. Men like him came with the "small dick and no work" stigma attached. However, he'd surprised her with his oral skills and well-endowed package. She held on to his forearms. His girth stretched her, and he began to move inside her. The sensation in her abdomen was so intense it sent chills through every cell in her body. She convulsed from his slow, deep strokes. He watched in satisfaction as she experienced the first orgasm.

"Your cum face is sexy as fuck, Desiree. I want to see it again."

Her eyes flew open when his hands tightened around her neck. Fear flashed through her mind. The last time she experienced being choked was at the hands of her ex-boyfriend, Troy. Desiree's eyes bulged in fright. She panicked and started to squirm.

Aaron stared deeply into her eyes as he spoke gently, "Shhh, Desiree, I need you to relax. Trust me. I'm not going to hurt you. Not ever. I just want to you to experience the next orgasm with a little breath play. Will you allow me to give you that?"

His bold eyes raked her soft skin, promising pleasure. Aaron pulled out almost all the way, then plunged deep. He continued stroking slowly but with more force. His grip around her neck tightened, and it did something to her. He added more pleasure, as promised. She couldn't believe he was turning her on that much. The lust between them exploded. She stared into his eyes as he delivered another stroke. Then her body went taut. Her vaginal muscles tightened, and liquid fire streamed through her body.

"Fuck!" he growled. He was going to lose control. He relaxed the grip he had on her neck and took a moment to gather his composure. Desiree didn't want him to stop. She was so close, so desperately close to releasing. She grabbed his ass, then lifted and rotated her hips. Aaron matched her slow motion. Her moans, coupled with his grunting, increased with the wet noises that filled the room. It wasn't long before he felt her walls clutching his thick muscle again. Then he pushed her knees back and sped up his rhythm. Stroke after stroke, he pummeled away.

A wild orgasm ripped through Desiree, then another. Her entire body shuddered, her head tilting back in exploding ecstasy. "Yes! Yes! Oh my god, yes!" she shouted.

Aaron gritted his teeth against the oncoming sensation and couldn't hold back any longer. His body jerked hard, every muscle tight, as he filled the condom. As he regained control of his breathing, he rested between Desiree's thighs, nestling his head between her breasts. Desiree savored the moment of lust while running her fingers through his long, damp curls.

She should've been ashamed, but she wasn't. It was no secret she was having issues in her marriage. She'd been sharing intimate details with Aaron and asking him for advice, and he'd used it to his advantage. They carried on the affair for a couple of months—that was until he complicated everything. Desiree knew it was time to cut things off when he confessed he had feelings for her and announced that his relationship with the socialite was over. She tried to shut him down by saying she wouldn't leave Jamal, but Aaron countered her logic. He told her that her marriage was a sham, and it wouldn't last. He'd been right about both.

"Did you hear me?"

"What?" she snapped.

"Desiree, what's going on with you?"

She rubbed her forehead. "I just told you. It's one of my toughest mergers. I can't even begin to explain how it has me stressed out."

"Excuse me. You're in my seat."

They turned their attention to the petite woman standing in the middle of the aisle. Aaron got up and began speaking with her. Desiree watched as he pointed toward a seat two rows in front of them. The woman appeared happy since she was still getting a window seat.

Shit! It hadn't occurred to her he would also have a seat in first class. When he sat down, Desiree grabbed his arm. "Aaron, before you got on, I was trying to get some rest. Why don't we catch up after we land?"

He smiled. "Yes, of course. Let's do that."

She returned the biggest smile she could muster. He pulled out his laptop and began working. As she pressed her head deep into the headrest, Desiree silently thanked her lucky stars he didn't object.

Still, she knew Aaron was the least of her worries. She'd left her biggest troubles standing in the middle of her living room.

Derrik was ready to get it over with. It'd been stressful hiding his relationship with Desiree for the past few months. But now Jamal was no longer a factor, and there was no other reason to delay the inevitable. Troy was going to find out at some point. This was the logic behind Derrik's decision to tell him. It was time for them to come clean and deal with the backlash. But there was one problem: moments earlier, he and Troy had watched from Desiree's living room window as she backed out of the driveway and sped away.

Derrik understood the seriousness of what they'd done, and he knew Desiree was apprehensive about telling Troy. On more than one occasion she'd expressed concern about how Troy would react once he found out, and Derrik reassured her that he would handle it if things got out of hand. But now with the revelation that she'd betrayed him as well, it was clear to Derrik why Desiree bounced.

Troy's irate tone brought Derrik back to the room. "So you was fucking my girl!"

Derrik whipped his head around and met Troy's penetrative glare. He laughed, "*Your girl?* How, when you're married to Mia? Or did you forget about that?"

"That ain't got shit to do with what you did!"

"Man, how many girls have we passed around? No, how many have you fucked behind my back knowing I'd been with them? How is this any different?"

Troy clinched his jaw tight, his nostrils flaring as he stared back at Derrik. Of all the low things his best friend could've done, Troy never saw it coming that he'd sleep with Desiree. He'd broken the guy code. That was inexcusable. "Nigga please, them bitches don't even count. They knew we was fucking with them like that. If you wanted Desi, why you ain't say nothing? It's 'cause you foul as hell and dead-ass wrong. You knew how it was with her." Troy pointed a stiff accusatory finger at him.

Derrik held his hands up. "T, come on. You weren't thinking about Desi until you saw her."

"And when I did, I decided we was getting back together! She was different. She was special to me."

"Really? If she was so special, why'd you put your hands on her?"

"The fuck you say?"

Derrik didn't care at that point. He wanted to check Troy for what he'd done to Desiree years ago. He'd never spoken up in her defense, and he needed to get it off his chest. No time was better than now to put it out there. "You heard me. You lied knowing damn well you did more than 'smack her up.' Then you discarded her like trash. A good woman, T. She's beautiful, ambitious, loving, and kind. She didn't deserve how you did her."

After Derrik's words sunk in, Troy snarled, "Motherfucka! How the fuck you gon' tell me 'bout her? I know, I was with her first!"

Derrik usually diffused volatile situations with his boy, but this was the opposite. He meant what he said, and he felt strongly about it. "You might've been with her first, but you didn't want her. Not the way I do. You sure as hell didn't treat her right. The whole time you were cheating on her. You were fucking around with Kim, Mia—shit, everybody. The hell you thought. You know how this works. One man's trash is another man's treasure. I told Desi a good man was going to find her, and that man is me."

He saw the pulsating muscle in Troy's jaw. That meant one thing. In all the years of their friendship, they'd never fought one another. Derrik realized he needed to de-escalate the situation and fast. He took a couple of steps back. "Are you fucking serious? I'm not about to fight you," Derrik said, taking another step back. He moved to the left when he saw Troy closing the distance between them.

"Hold up. Nigga, was you fucking her back then?" Troy's patience was gone. He squared up.

Derrik threw his hands up as if surrendering. "No! For real yo, chill! You need to calm the fuck down! I know you're pissed but what is fighting going to solve?"

"Me teaching your ass a lesson. You shouldn't have fucked my girl!"

"She's not your girl!"

"I don't believe you did this shit! I should crack your motherfuc—" Troy stepped back and swung. Derrik ducked, but he didn't move out of the way fast enough. Troy dropped his shoulder and slammed into Derrik's chest, causing him to stumble backward and fall onto the coffee table. Shattered glass flew everywhere. "Get up! 'Cause I'm kicking your ass for this shit!"

While scrambling to his feet, Derrik cut his left hand. "Fuck!"

Wham! The hard punch connected with Derrik's jaw, sending him backward again, this time into an end table. He knocked the lamp over, breaking the glass base. Stunned for a moment, Derrik staggered. The coppery taste of blood filled his mouth. He cradled his chin, checking to make sure it wasn't broken. He stretched his jaw before spitting blood onto the hardwood floor. Out of his periphery, he saw Troy roll his shoulders back and swing again. Derrik moved to the left and threw a right hook, landing a brutal blow underneath Troy's left eye.

Troy stumbled into the other end table, knocking that lamp over. More glass shattered across the floor. Troy touched his face. His eyes widened at the sight of the blood on his fingers. Troy swung and missed. Derrik narrowed his eyes and delivered another right, sending Troy backward again. Derrik followed him and tried to land a left punch, but Troy weaved and bobbed, taking a few steps back.

Chests heaving, they stood in a face-off. Then they ran into each other like two angry rams. Troy tried to head butt Derrik and missed. Derrik gave Troy an elbow to the gut. He doubled over. Derrik took a step back and as he inhaled a deep breath, Troy charged forward, pushing him back into the wall. Derrik landed several blows to the back of Troy's head before he heard Hodges.

"Boss!"

Derrik ignored him. The adrenaline coursing through him kept him pumped. He wanted Troy to feel what Desiree felt that day years ago when he beat her and left Derrik to clean up the mess. They exchanged several punches before Hodges and two other bodyguards broke them apart and restrained both men.

Blood dripped from Troy's lip as he spat, "I shoulda known your trifling ass would do something like this. You was always after my sloppy seconds."

Derrik laughed, "Never that nigga! Desi wanted me just as much as I wanted her!"

"She don't want you! You see she came back! I bet she did this shit just to get back at me," Troy refuted.

That stung. However, Derrik knew this was a game for Troy. He shot back, "What's the point, T? Who are you kidding? You don't really want her! How long before your ass runs back to Mia?"

Troy attempted to yank away from Hodges and the other bodyguard, but it was no use. The seven-foot-tall, husky man and his partner, who also towered over Troy, pinned him against the wall. Troy turned his head towards the bigger man. "Let me go, Hodg' man," Troy demanded.

"Nah, I can't do that, T."

The other bodyguard kept his forearm against Derrik's chest but didn't have to hold him back. The fight was over. Only their heavy breathing occupied the space around them. It was then that Derrik noticed the destruction of Desiree's living room. He dropped his head, ashamed that he let things get out of control. He'd told Desiree months ago that once they crossed the line, there would be no turning back. Standing there in that moment, he thought perhaps Desiree had predicted correctly. He wasn't so sure that he and Troy would remain friends after this. He'd done the unforgivable for a woman who might not even want him as he believed. Derrik lifted his head and his eyes met Troy's hostile gaze. As much as he wanted to say it, the words were stuck in his throat: *He was wrong.*

CHAPTER

2

"What are you doing?"

Aaron flashed a mischievous grin and cupped Desiree's chin. He pressed his lips against hers before she could turn away. His tongue darted between her lips, and he wrapped an arm around her waist, bringing her closer.

Desiree felt the bulge against her thigh as his other hand moved down to her breasts. She withdrew from his lips, pushed him away, and stepped back. She spoke in a breathless whisper, "Aaron, no . . . goodness, I knew I shouldn't have let you come up here."

"You're right, you shouldn't have."

Just as Aaron was about to swoop in again, her phone rang. It was the perfect opportunity to put some space between them. Desiree quickly sidestepped him and hurried over to the bed to retrieve her phone from her bag. She locked her gaze on the name and face displayed on the screen. She'd snapped that photo on their first weekend together. As she sent the call to voicemail, her heart ached.

"Is that Jamal?" Aaron asked.

It was Derrik. Desiree's stomach twisted into knots. Her mind was going in different directions despite her attempts to keep focused on one thing. She held on to her phone and walked over to the window.

"Hey, I asked if that was Jamal."

She lied, "Uh, yeah, it was." She rubbed her forehead. "Let me send him a message. No, I need to call him. Give me a minute."

"That's cool. I need to use the head and make a call too."

Desiree waved him off, not bothering to turn around.

By the time he closed the bathroom door, her phone rang again. This time she didn't hesitate to answer. "Hey, what's up, Bri?"

"Don't what's up me. Girl, why didn't you call me when you landed?"

"I'm sorry, Bri. I was gonna call. I've just been dealing with some distractions from work." She thought about Aaron, the distraction from work. Desiree had never told Brielle about him. It wasn't that she didn't want to. But he was just a short fling, and he wasn't even supposed to be there. Brielle's next words made her forget about Aaron.

"Have you spoken to Derrik?"

"No, not yet. I just missed his call. When we hang up, I'll call him back."

Before Brielle could say anything else, Desiree grumbled, "Ugh, why in the world is Jamal calling again? I have over ten missed calls from him alone. Hold on, okay?"

She switched the calls and responded dryly, "What, Jamal?"

"Are you that angry with me that you can't return my calls?"

"I'm in LA and—"

"Figures," Jamal retorted. Then he heard Desiree sucking her teeth. "I didn't call you for all of that."

"So, why are you calling, Jamal?"

"Why are you coming at me so nasty?"

"I'm not. I'm keeping it short and not so sweet. What do you want?"

His tone sounded genuine. "You probably don't believe me, but I really tried. I know the way we left things—"

"The way *we*? No, sir, the way *you* left things. Remember I put you out after catching you in your lies."

The genuine tone disappeared. He huffed, "Desiree, what the hell did you expect to happen? A man has needs. You stopped fucking me!"

"And you wonder why. Look at how you talk to me."

"You know damn well I never talked to you like that until you stopped treating me how a man is supposed to be treated by his wife. You've been out here pursuing your career and doing whatever you wanted for a while. I put up with more than the average man would. Do you think you were right in how you treated me? Yeah, well I met a woman who knows how to treat her man. You should feel some type of way."

"What!" Desiree glanced at the bathroom door. She didn't need Aaron hearing their conversation. She lowered her voice as she scoffed, "Jamal, do you hear yourself? Why would I feel some type of way about y'all? Does she know that you're on the DL—no, gay?"

"I don't know who called you with that bullshit, but I'm not gay!" Jamal sighed heavily. "You know what, Desiree, I didn't have any intentions of calling to talk about us."

"Yet here you are. All in my ear about it."

"You hadn't returned my calls. I've been trying for the past twenty-four hours. It's obvious you haven't heard about Rico."

"No, I haven't. What's up with him now?"

"Desiree, it's been all over the news. They found him in his apartment over the weekend. They haven't finished investigating, but they're saying it might have been a robbery gone bad."

"Goodness, is he going to be all right?" Desiree knew she couldn't have heard Jamal's next words correctly.

"He's dead."

She backed away from the window in horror, just managing to make it to the bed. The phone slipped from her hands as she heard Jamal's voice echoing from it.

"Desiree? Desiree!"

Aaron was exiting the bathroom when he noticed her crying. "What's wrong?" he asked, sitting next to her.

She shook her head.

"Desiree, please, talk to me. What's wrong? What is it?"

She grabbed his arms, holding on tight. In between sobs, she replied, "I can't believe this . . . my friend . . . he's gone."

Without warning, he picked up her phone. "Hello, who is this?"

Desiree heard Brielle's sharp response. "Excuse me? Who the hell is this? And where is Desi?"

"I apologize for not introducing myself first. My name is Aaron, and I'm a friend of Desiree's. She seems distraught from whatever you just told her. Is there anything I can do?"

"Yeah, you can tell her to call me when she pulls it together."

Desiree snapped out of her stunned state. *Shit!* She couldn't believe Aaron picked up her phone. There would be some explaining to do, but she would deal with her best friend later. Her heart ached with the loss of her other friend, Rico. She couldn't believe she would never see him again.

"I'm sorry for your loss," Aaron offered.

She sniffled, "Goodness, Aaron, this is so surreal. I just saw him last month."

"Do you know what happened?"

Desiree began to cry again as she shook her head. He rubbed her shoulders and kissed her forehead as she sobbed. After a few minutes, she calmed down long enough to tell him what Jamal had shared about Rico. "I have to call Bri back. She didn't mention it, so I doubt she knows."

"Look, if you need me," he paused and grabbed her hands, "I'll make arrangements so I can be with you on the ride back. You shouldn't be alone."

Desiree suddenly remembered the mess at home. She removed her hands from his grasp and gave him a weak smile. "No, Aaron, you don't have to do that."

"It's no problem."

"It's sweet of you, but there's no need. I'm going to be fine. Thank you."

"Seriously, if you need me, I'm there."

She needed to get him out of her room. "Right now, I need to pull myself together so I can get to the office. Carolyn's going to be upset I came over here and didn't get started on anything. Let me go get ready."

Aaron tried to convince her to skip going in to work. He felt her manager would understand the extenuating circumstances, but Desiree insisted on going. She needed to keep her mind occupied. Once Aaron left, she took a long, hot shower.

After getting dressed and calling for a car service, she saw the notifications for three missed calls. They were from Troy.

Desiree shut her eyes. She knew better than to believe in fairytales. Yet, she'd tried to play one out with Troy. She could still hear the words he said to her the night of the party: *"I know I messed up . . . You were the one for me. Desi, I love you."* Just thinking about it, she became enraged. Until the video, she'd foolishly believed there was a chance for them. The ghastly scene with his wife replayed in her mind. Without a second thought, she called him back. It took a few rings before the call connected.

"Hello? Troy?"

There was silence on the other end. She took the phone away from her face to see whether he had hung up. Seeing the call was still active, she placed the phone back to her ear.

"Pfft, now you wanna call a nigga."

"Yes, do you have a minute? We need to talk."

Troy spat, "You right we do. Where the fuck you at?"

"I think it's best we handle this over the phone."

"You think it's best?" He hesitated for a moment then lashed out, "Your ratchet ass got busted fucking my boy, and you bounced. I started not to answer your ass."

Desiree flinched, taken aback for a moment, but then she remembered how arrogant, rude, and disrespectful Troy could be when he was angry.

"Oh, don't get quiet on me now. You bitches always think you can play the game. Wanna tell me why you played a nigga like that?"

Desiree shouted, "First of all, you will not talk to me like this! I'm not ratchet, nor am I a bitch! You played *me*! How could I have been so naïve? You didn't love me! You didn't give a fuck about me! You lied to me. I knew I never should've believed you."

"What you talking about, girl? I ain't lie to you," he argued.

"All that stuff you said at your house, that night at your party. It meant nothing. You were beating on her, Troy!"

He sucked his teeth.

"You were! And I know the moment you got angry with me, you would have beat me again too."

He wasn't going to explain that his wife set him up. And he didn't know why Desiree was still holding it over his head about what happened years ago. She wasn't going to deflect and get out of what she'd done. Troy dismissed everything she said. "You think I'm stupid, Desi? This ain't about that past shit I did to you, and it ain't about my wife. You knew I was trying to make things right. It was supposed to be about us. Wanna tell me how that shit happened with you and D, huh?"

Desiree thought about the previous months she'd spent with Derrik. It happened because he was loving and kind and treated her like a queen. She'd felt a level of happiness with him that she had never felt with Troy, even after almost a year together. "I don't know what you want me to say. I can't explain it. We didn't plan on falling for each other. It just happened."

"Shit like that don't just happen. Y'all motherfuckas was always together. He said y'all was doing business deals. I shoulda known." Troy mumbled something incoherent.

"What?"

"Nah, fuck this!" he spat vehemently. "You need to make this make sense for me. You did this shit while we was together?"

"No!"

"Then how long y'all been fucking?"

Desiree sighed with frustration, "Troy, why does that even matter now?"

"It matters! You was *my* girl, and you fucked my boy! What kinda shit is that?"

Then it hit her. Troy wasn't going to hear anything she said. He didn't want to. She had to accept the fact that the man on the other end of the line was self-centered and egotistical. She sighed again. "This was pointless."

"You know what? You right. *This*, trying to fuck with you was pointless, and it don't matter no more 'cause I know you did this stupid shit to get back at me. You're just like your miserable-ass friend. It's all good. I ain't sweating it for real. Y'all can keep fucking around 'cause I ain't that pressed for yo' ass!"

He ended the call. Desiree stared at the phone. Deep down, she knew she never should've called him. He'd done enough hurt with his words and hands. She was

26

done talking to Troy. Without thinking about it too much, she blocked his numbers then scrolled through her call list. She was about to make the next call when a notification popped up that the car service had arrived. She decided to wait until later. Desiree wouldn't be able to handle another verbal attack, especially if it came from Derrik. She sent him a text that she would call later. She called Brielle once she was in the car.

Desiree was thankful Brielle didn't press her about Aaron after she shared what Jamal told her about Rico. Brielle did some digging online and found the article about Rico's murder. Desiree explained she would have to call Jamal for more details after she got off work. Like Aaron, Brielle advised her not to go into the office, but Desiree maintained that she did not want to sit in her room all day. She'd rather work and keep her mind busy.

When Desiree arrived at the office, it proved difficult to concentrate on anything related to work. While her colleague began outlining the specs of another project, she stared out at the Wilshire Grand Center from the window of the large conference room. The Charlton offices occupied the forty-second floor of the Aon Center with a direct view of the tall skyscraper and the rest of the LA skyline. She needed to pay attention to the presentation, but she couldn't focus. Desiree's mind was elsewhere. Rico was dead. She would have to return home to pay her respects, and that meant she would have to face the consequences of her recklessness sooner rather than later. Her gaze wandered to the rooftop bar, Spire 73. She could drown her sorrows in several glasses of their strongest cocktails. But that wouldn't be smart considering her biggest dilemma: an unplanned pregnancy.

What should I do? She wasn't certain of her next move, but she knew time was of the essence. She needed to make a decision.

CHAPTER
3

Minute by minute, the anger ate at him, nibbling his nerves raw. Troy gripped the steering wheel tighter. His knuckles were sore, but that discomfort was nothing compared to the rage he felt inside. He glanced in the rearview mirror. Remnants of dried blood stained his right cheek. Troy touched his cracked and puffy bottom lip. The biggest tell-tale sign that he'd been in a fight was the small gash and reddish-purple bruise underneath his left eye. His forehead creased as he thought about everything that had transpired since the weekend.

In a matter of three days, his entire world had flipped upside down. It started when his wife, Mia, exposed his abusive behavior to the public. Apparently, that wasn't enough damage for her to inflict, so she'd blackmailed him for millions of dollars of endorsement money. It was clear to Troy that Mia's goal was to leave him and empty his bank account in the process. When Troy thought he couldn't get screwed over any worse, there was Desiree and Derrik's betrayal. He never saw it coming. If it weren't for Derrik's bodyguards breaking them up, they would've destroyed Desiree's living room. And his foot would've been a permanent fixture in Derrik's ass.

"The nerve of these motherfuckas!" Troy shouted as he arrived at his destination, putting the Range Rover in park. He snatched the black grocery bag from the front seat and stomped towards the townhome. It was a strategic purchase he'd made while sidelined with his knee injury. He'd planned to use it as an investment property. It was never supposed to be his home. He still couldn't believe Mia snatched the rug out from under him. Troy slammed the front door shut and made his way to the kitchen. He put the bag on the island and went to the bathroom to clean his face.

When he returned, he took a small tumbler from the cabinet, filling it to the brim. He threw his head back. "Ow!" He ignored the stinging from his lip and poured another. Knocking back that glass in seconds, he poured a third and wasted no time gulping it down. Troy bent forward, resting his elbows on the cool countertop, his chin between his palms. As he assessed the situation, his eyes darted around the spacious kitchen. It reminded him of her. She'd picked it all out—the entire upscale luxury design from the quartz countertops to the top-of-the-line stainless steel appliances. She'd chosen the color scheme and selected the decor and furnishings throughout the house. The complete interior design of the townhome was Mia's concept. He'd let her handle it so she could add the work to her portfolio.

Troy groaned. He didn't want to be there. He straightened his back and dug in the pocket of his joggers to retrieve his cell. His thumb slid across the screen. He hovered over Mia's name for a second and decided against sending the call. Instead, Troy snatched his keys from the counter and left in a hurry.

An hour later, he sat in front of the house he shared with Mia. Troy remembered her excitement when their realtor brought them to view the new construction. Mia wasn't excited about the home's countless amenities. Nor was she focused on having an office and a walk-in closet the size of a bedroom. She'd stood in the middle of the living room and announced she couldn't wait to fill the eight-bedroom mini mansion with his babies.

"Fuuuck!" he said aloud.

Derrik had told the truth. Troy was first attracted to Desiree, believing she was the one. His feelings changed when he met Mia. Despite how much he enjoyed being with Desiree, he found himself straying right into Mia's arms. There was always something about her that drew him back again and again. They were drawn to each other like moths to a flame.

The night of the party, he'd told Desiree he would bring her up on stage and announce they were going to be together. That was the arrogant, cocky side of

30

him talking. Troy changed his mind when he glanced over at Mia. She kept those almond eyes on him and batted her eyelashes. She parted her lips, twirling the tip of her tongue. He knew that look. His mind went to all the things he would do to her afterwards. Little did he know that just a few minutes later, Mia would embarrass him. That reminder made him exit the Range Rover with a quickness.

He slid the key in the door, and, to his disappointment, it didn't turn. Troy rang the bell. He waited a minute and pressed the button again. When she didn't answer he resorted to banging on the door. "I know you're in there, Mia! Open up!"

He finally heard her voice from the other side of the door. "What do you want, Troy?"

"Come on, baby, open the door please. I need to talk to you."

"Go away, Troy!"

"For real, baby, I got hurt fighting. Please, Mia, I need you."

A minute passed before he heard the locks disengage. Mia's mouth dropped open. She'd never seen him in such a state. She stepped outside. Her eyes swept over him. Troy was still fine as hell. It was as if the gash under his eye and the bruising on his face added to her husband's sexiness. He wore a white sleeveless hoodie that exposed his muscular arms and tattoo sleeves. The gray joggers hugged him in all the right places, especially in the crotch area. He rocked a pair of crisp, white Christian Louboutin sneakers. The Creed cologne he always wore hit her nostrils when she took another step towards him. She touched the side of his face. He flinched. She was careful not to irritate the gash. "Wha-what happened?" she managed to stammer out.

Troy mumbled, "I don't wanna talk about it."

"But you were fighting. Who and why?"

"I said I don't wanna talk about it!"

"Fine." Mia pursed her lips and tossed the loose hair over her shoulder. She'd seen him arrive on the security cameras. She'd had a feeling he'd show up. That's why her first item of business had been to change the locks. She wasn't going to come to the door at all. Yet, there she stood on the receiving end of her husband's rudeness.

"Yo, why the fuck you do this, Mia!" he bellowed, causing her to jump.

She took a step back across the threshold and issued a caution with her index finger. "Troy Xavier Harris, do not yell at me! You better be glad I even opened it. Yell at me again, and I will slam this door in your face!"

"Really, my whole name?" he asked, ignoring her threat about the yelling.

"Yes, because you need to know I'm not playing. Don't think for one second I didn't do any of this without just cause. You had it coming."

Troy stared at her for a moment. He blew out an impatient breath but responded without raising his voice, "Wanna enlighten me on what the fuck has gotten into you?"

He tried to listen as Mia insisted that he left her no choice. For the past year, she'd tolerated his blatant disrespect of their marriage. She couldn't take the constant verbal and physical abuse anymore. She was tired. Unlike the other instances, this time she was going to stand up to his bullying once and for all.

Troy didn't bother addressing her feelings. "You got some fucking nerve, Mia. After everything, this is how you do me. Me?"

"Look at how you've treated me, Troy! Do you really think I enjoy you talking to me sideways and hitting on me?"

"Okay, my mouth is reckless, but so is yours." He shrugged. "And I know I can get a little rough sometimes."

"A little? Troy, you leave bruises!"

"Mia, you have light skin. I smack your ass and it goes from red to black and blue."

She shot him a dirty look. "You know what the hell I mean. Do you even remember what you said to me? You said if I wanted to leave, I'd leave with absolutely nothing. I'd walk away exactly how I came into this marriage. Do you know how that made me feel? After all the shit you've put me through?" Mia held up her fingers as she recited, "From your trifling-ass family to the lying, the cheating, verbal and physical abuse. I still held your ass down."

Troy saw the tears pooling in her eyes. She didn't dare let them fall. Mia kept her voice steady as she continued, "When your knee blew out, I didn't recognize the man you became. You thought your career was over, and I thought our marriage was too. I've always been your biggest fan and supporter, Troy. But instead of

32

allowing me to help you through that difficult time, you started taking everything out on me. I thought I could deal with your outbursts, but your anger multiplied in ways I couldn't imagine." Mia paused shaking her head. "Angela told me to leave before you killed me, but I stayed, knowing that your shoves would turn into slaps, and those slaps would turn into punches. One night you choked me until I was unconscious. I woke up realizing I hadn't died but thinking maybe if I did, you'd realize what you'd had."

For a brief moment, his eyes met hers, and there were unspoken words between them that neither of them had to express. Troy couldn't argue about any of Mia's claims. She was absolutely correct. He'd pulled them into a dark space when he feared his career was over. He was often enraged and so full of bitterness and self-pity that he was unsatisfied no matter what she said or did. Still, Mia was a devoted wife who did everything she could to care for her husband. That was something he could never deny. As he stood there looking at her, he realized that she possessed an inner power he'd never really acknowledged before. She'd demonstrated the same prowess that night at the party and later in the lawyer's office. He hadn't seen this side of his wife before. She was invincible. He realized and respected that she was going to be a force to be reckoned with from now on.

Finally, Troy reached out and rubbed his hand down her face, "You know, you're so beautiful."

Mia swatted his hand away. "Troy, I'm being serious."

"I am too. I ain't used to seeing you like this. I ain't gon' lie, it's sexy as fuck." He stuffed his hands in his joggers and sighed. "Mia, how long we gonna do this? We already know how this is gonna go."

His arrogance infuriated her. "You're not coming back in here," she declared.

"Why not? I don't give a damn what y'all had in that paperwork. This is my house, and don't forget you still my wife, Mia." Troy scolded, "This shit you did wasn't cool. I know I fucked up. But why you tryna mess up what we got?"

Mia squeezed her eyes shut. He didn't get it. No woman should have to endure what she'd gone through. She wanted the man she fell in love with, but he'd abused and disrespected her yet again, and she could no longer ignore it. She opened her eyes. "I'm not trying to mess up anything. You did that, Troy."

His forehead creased. "What you mean? I ain't mess shit up."

"Yes, you did, and I'm done."

"No, you ain't. Despite this stunt you pulled, you ain't going nowhere."

While she attempted to explain things weren't the same anymore, Troy pushed the door out of her grasp. He took a step inside. As he shut the door behind him, his eyes bore into her. Her heart began to beat faster. She took a step back and held her hands out in front of her. "I can't do this anymore, Troy."

"Will you cut the bullshit, Mia! You did all this for what? Clout? All you doing is fucking up everything we done built. Does Maxwell know about this? I highly doubt it. You know he ain't with his family's name being associated with drama. Ain't that what you told me? Did you think about that in your grand scheme of things to fuck me over? Do you really wanna keep this charade up?"

She ignored his question about her father. "This isn't a charade, and I don't need clout, Troy. I did this because, because I'm tired. You can be kind and loving one minute, then you're mean and nasty the next. Look at how you're acting now. That night you said you hated me—" Mia's voice wobbled. "I guess you really do."

"Dammit, Mia, you said it first," Troy contended. "Like I said, your mouth is reckless too. I was already pissed about something else, and then you pushed me like you always do."

He heard Mia suck her teeth. He realized his plan of getting her back wouldn't work if he kept up with his caustic criticism. Troy switched to a more apologetic tone. "But baby I don't hate you. You know I love you."

Mia's mouth set in a hard line. She folded her arms across her chest.

Troy blew out a long breath. "Dammit, I hate it when we beefin'. Please, don't be mad at me, baby." He took a step towards her.

She wasn't about to let Troy pull a Jekyll and Hyde on her. If she didn't stick to her guns, they would fall back into the same pattern. This time she meant what she said. "Don't, Troy. I mean it."

"No, you don't. I know what my girl wants." He opened his arms wide. "Mia Symoné Harr—"

She held her hand up. "Nah uh, nope! Don't even go there."

"You called out my whole name a minute ago. Now come here, Sym."

He knew she loved the way he said it. He only called her by that nickname when he was in the doghouse. She'd heard it all before and knew better. Mia released a sigh.

"What?"

"I don't . . . I-I just . . . you don't get it. You crossed the line, Troy. I don't think I can forgive you this time."

Troy saw her attempt to stifle the tears shimmering behind her eyes again. He closed the space between them and embraced her. She let out a loud sob. He squeezed tight as her body trembled against his. Troy knew he had trouble keeping his hands to himself. Maybe this was the last straw, but he didn't want to lose her. He couldn't. He whispered, "Sym, you're right. I was out of line for what I did. I never meant to hurt you like this. I'm so sorry."

"You need to go," she blubbered.

"I ain't going nowhere, Sym. I gotta fix this."

"But you can't!" she screamed against his chest.

He kissed her forehead and held her tighter. "I can and I wanna make it better. Will you let me?"

Troy released her and cupped her face between his big hands. Mia didn't want to lose control. She couldn't let Troy weasel his way back in. His eyes continued to penetrate hers. Her mind screamed no, but her heart was tormented. She truly loved this man. Her vision blurred as the dam of tears broke. She looked away. His thumbs wiped the tears from her cheeks.

"Look at me, Sym."

She kept her eyes focused on the wall behind him.

"Baby, please." Troy pleaded.

Mia's red-rimmed eyes found his hooded, brown eyes. *Why does he have to be so damn fine?* She shook her head. "No, Troy. I can't let you—"

Troy's mouth was on hers smothering the next words. There was a brief pinch, but he ignored that pain. It was replaced by an ache to feel her soft, plush lips. He tasted the salty tears as his tongue slid inside, filling her mouth as it opened to his kiss. Their tongues tangled and fought a silent battle in the warmth of her mouth. Troy's hands slipped behind her neck to angle her mouth for a deeper kiss that went on for several minutes—unbroken, slow, and sensual. Mia moaned as the thickness of his manhood expanded against her belly. He reluctantly broke away.

Their eyes locked as he bent and gripped Mia's ass, lifting her from the floor. She clasped her hands behind his neck and wrapped her legs around his back. He made the short trek down the hall to his office and set Mia down on the top of the desk. Troy stared at her for a brief moment. She moistened her lips. He leaned forward, ravishing her mouth. His kiss pushed all thoughts from her mind and set off a wild need in her.

She tugged at the bottom of his shirt. He helped pull it over his head and went back to claim her lips. She ran her hands across his chest, squeezing both nipples between her fingertips. He pulled away from their kiss and groaned, "Symmm."

Mia smiled, lifted her shirt over her head and threw it on the floor. She gazed back at him seductively, tossing her long, black tresses. She ran her fingers through the thick mane, teasing it so that it partially covered her eye.

"You're so fucking gorgeous. I love when you wear your hair out like this, Sym."

She blushed. Troy reached behind her back, unclasped her bra, and pulled the straps to her elbows. Mia slipped her arms out, and Troy tossed the bra to the side. He squeezed her breasts together alternating between them, licking, nibbling, and sucking. He slid his hand inside the waistband of her sweatpants. She lifted her hips, and Troy eased them off. He ran his fingers along the edge of the laced material before ripping off the sopping thong.

Troy knelt down. Mia scooched to the edge of the desk and spread her thighs. His tongue swiped across her drenched lower lips. He separated the plump folds of skin hiding her love button. He suctioned her clit into his mouth and slid two fingers inside her moist, hot cavern. Mia gasped and shuddered. Troy twisted his fingers upward, teasing her G-Spot, then eased them out and pushed them deep. He repeated, in and out, in and out, stroking her pussy into a stream of liquid fire. While fingering her, Troy added his tongue, flicking back and forth and swirling it around the swollen nub. His skillful tongue demanded a response. Mia gripped his head, pushing her hips closer. She grinded her pussy into his face, and he devoured her, alternating between sucking, licking, and slurping until she came undone.

"Trrrrrroy!"

"You taste good, Sym." He lifted his head, revealing his face glistening in her juices. Troy's eyes never left hers as he stood up. She redirected her attention to his crotch. His erection was stiff as a board, stretching the jogger material. It appeared as if he were going to bust a hole through the front. Mia couldn't resist her husband's well-endowed package. She leaned back on her elbows and gave him the come-hither look while biting into her bottom lip. Troy shoved his joggers and boxers down and kicked them off. He pushed her knees up and nestled himself between her thighs. His engorged helmet teased her entrance, rubbing without penetrating. He coated his thick head in her wetness. He needed to feel her, but he had to take his time. It had been several weeks since they last had sex. Mia was noticeably tight.

Troy eased a couple of inches inside. He withdrew slowly. She reached down and guided him back in. He couldn't hold back any longer. He plunged into the wet heat, filling her completely. He moaned, pulled out again, then drove deep. He stretched her walls to fit. Her muscles gripped him.

Mia threw her head back. "Oh Troy! Yessss!"

"Damn, Sym! Your pussy . . . fuck! It feels . . . shit . . . sooo good." Troy said in between strokes.

Lifting her hips, Mia met him thrust after thrust. He pulled her closer and sucked her bottom lip into his mouth. Mia caressed his smooth, bald head as they shared another rough, deep kiss. Body to body, mouth to mouth, they moved together as one.

Troy pumped harder, losing himself deep inside her heated core. Her body thrummed in response. She raked her nails across his back. The powerful sensations throbbed below her waist. Mia's pussy held him in a vise-like grip. Her orgasm came in rippling waves. He gritted his teeth as he fought his own release. Troy felt his balls tighten. He gripped her ass, thrusting one last time. His body tensed, and he poured his seed inside, her pussy milking him of every last drop.

After regaining control of their breathing, they dressed in silence. Troy thought no other woman had ever felt so good. Perfect. Not even Desiree. He watched Mia's eyes with curiosity. Her gaze dropped to the floor as she swallowed the sorrow her eyes couldn't hide. His arms snaked around her body, and he hugged her tight.

"Sym, I'm so sorry for pushing you to do this. Baby, I love you more than you could ever understand."

Mia wiggled free from his arms and wiped her face. "No, you need to leave, Troy."

"What? After we just made up? You want me to leave?"

"Yes. And we didn't make up. We had sex, Troy. This always happens when we fight. I can't, not this time."

Mia stepped to the side and headed out of the office. She was almost at the front door when Troy grabbed her hand and spun her around. Their eyes met. He searched for a clue, but Mia's expression was blank.

"What the fuck, Sym? I told you I'm sorry. You really kicking me out?"

"Please, Troy. I don't need you clouding my judgment with your dick and empty promises. I've made up my mind, so yes."

She pulled away from his grasp, and he didn't stop her. Mia opened the door and looked past him. "You need to go."

He didn't move. Troy couldn't believe she wasn't letting him stay. "Mia, you know this ain't hardly over. I'mma give you some time to think about it."

She noticed he'd resorted back to using her first name. "There's nothing to think about. I've made up—"

Troy took an aggressive step forward. He replied as if what she wanted didn't matter. "A week at the most." He walked out the door and declared, "That's what I'm giving you to get the fuck over this."

CHAPTER
4

"Angela, sweetheart, can I come in?"

She didn't answer. Jamal knocked on the door again before opening it. Angela was curled in the fetal position, holding a picture to her chest. She'd been in bed since the night they learned of her brother's death. The only time she left the room was to relieve herself. She was too distraught to do anything else. He moved to the edge of the bed and sat down next to her. She pressed the picture closer to her bosom.

"Can I see?"

Angela reluctantly held it out, but she didn't allow him to take it from her grasp. Jamal inspected the picture briefly. He couldn't find any resemblance between them except their curly hair. It was as though she'd read his mind.

"We have different fathers," she mumbled. "My dad left after Mamá got pregnant with our baby brother, Junior. Tré stepped up to be the man of the house. He shouldn't have had that responsibility at ten years old, but Mamá needed help. At the time, I was two years old, and Junior was just a baby."

Jamal knew Angela had two brothers and was close to her mother. However, she spoke of them rarely, if at all. In the three years he'd known Rico, their paths had never crossed. Rico sometimes made comments about what he'd do if he caught a man near his sister, but he never said her name, so Jamal never saw a reason to ask about her. He never suspected that Angela was one of the younger

39

siblings Rico mentioned he helped raised. Nor did he put it together that Rico was the older brother Angela was referring to. She called him Tré but never Rico. His eyes swept over the picture again. Even though he should've said something, Jamal couldn't bring himself to tell her that he'd known her brother.

She whispered, "This was one of the last pictures we took together." Then she cried out, "Why him, Jamal? He didn't deserve this."

He pushed back the hair covering her eye and wiped her face with a tender caress. "It's going to be okay, sweetheart."

She bit back tears of grief, cradled the picture, and shook her head. "No, it's not. It's never going to be okay."

"They'll do everything they can to find out what happened. You know that, don't you?"

"He-he-he's not coming back and-and-and I—" she paused before wailing.

Jamal held her close as she sobbed, knowing there wasn't much he could say to make her feel any better. Once she calmed down and her sobs became sniffles, he let go to grab some tissues from the box he'd set beside the bed.

He wiped her face as he spoke in a gentle tone. "Angela, it's been days. You're still wearing the same clothes from the weekend."

"You think I care if I smell, Jamal!" Angela snapped back.

"Sweetheart, that's not what I meant. I'm sure a hot shower will help you feel a little better. Why don't we put on some pajamas? Please, let me help you."

Angela nodded reluctantly and placed the picture on her pillow. Jamal lifted her from the bed, carried her into the bathroom, and helped her undress. He started the shower, then guided her into the tub before removing his clothes and climbing in behind her. She allowed him to bathe her body thoroughly. She tried to smile and feel happy that her man was at her side. Still, her heart ached for her brother. After getting her dressed, he detangled her wet curls and pulled her hair into a ponytail.

Angela sniffled, "I forget that you're a doctor."

"Even if I wasn't, I still would've done this."

"Thank you."

Jamal smiled and went over to the dresser. He returned to her side with two medicine bottles. She'd had a rough couple of days dealing with anxiety attacks, so he'd decided to prescribe antidepressants to keep her mood swings under control.

Angela blew her nose and looked at him with bloodshot eyes. "What are those for?"

He stroked the side of her face. "To help with the anxiety. Trust me, Angela, everything is going to be fine."

"Okay," she said through a sniffle.

He watched as she took both doses. Then he hugged her and explained he needed to take care of some things in the office. As he began to walk out of the bedroom, he heard Angela mumbling. He turned around. "What did you say?"

"Close the door."

"But I won't be able to hear if you call me, sweetheart."

"I want the door closed."

He did as she requested. Jamal stood on the other side of the door and pressed his forehead against it. His fingers slid down the door as if he were caressing Angela. *I'm so sorry, sweetheart. I never meant to hurt you in all of this. How was I supposed to know?*

In his heart, he knew it would be the hardest thing he'd ever have to do, but he had to keep calm if he wanted things to go his way. Instead of going to the office, Jamal went to the living room and tried to relax, but his thoughts took him back to that night. He headed toward the kitchen. Rather than getting a glass, he took the bottle out. He gulped down a few swigs of the cognac, then he went back to the living room and sat on the couch, staring at the dark screen of the television. It wasn't long before he drifted off into a fitful sleep.

Moments later, Jamal opened his eyes. Rico stood in front of him, naked. Jamal rubbed his eyes, thinking it had to be an illusion, but Rico was still there watching him. Jamal asked Rico how he got there. Rico didn't respond. Instead, he smiled and motioned for Jamal to follow him. Jamal's eyes wandered from Rico's broad shoulders down to his tight ass as he walked over and climbed into a golf cart. *I'm dreaming. I have to be,* Jamal thought to himself.

Rico waved for him to get in. Jamal looked around and realized he had no idea where he was. They weren't on their golf club's putting green. Unfamiliar with their surroundings, he decided it'd be best to join Rico. When he settled into the cart, he glanced over at Rico in disbelief that he was sitting there in the nude. Rico pressed his foot on the pedal. Jamal never knew the carts could go that fast. They hit a bump that lifted Jamal an inch off his seat. He tightened his grip around the steel bar of the cart's frame. "Whoa! I think you should slow this down a bit," he suggested.

Rico didn't respond. He turned to face Jamal, and the corners of his mouth lifted into a full smile, revealing all of his teeth.

"Where are we going?" Jamal asked.

Rico nodded and looked in the opposite direction. Jamal's eyes followed his. In an instant, they were standing in Rico's bedroom. Jamal inhaled a sharp breath. Before he could say anything, Rico shoved him back. Jamal stumbled and landed on a chair that wasn't there moments earlier. In a quick move, Rico was on him, and next thing Jamal knew, he was handcuffed to the chair. "Hey, get these off of me!" he shouted.

Rico finally spoke. "Who the fuck do you think you're playing with, Jamal?"

"You can't do this."

"No? You don't get it, do you? This is all for us. I got tired of waiting on you. This was my golden opportunity to help you see the light. You didn't need them. I'm everything you need."

Jamal writhed, and the handcuffs dug into his wrists. He spat, "I told you I'm not a fucking fag! Why do you keep testing me?"

"And I told you I would do whatever it took."

Rico moved closer with a bowl filled with strawberries, bananas, and whipped cream. He placed them next to Jamal and revealed the gag ball. It was then Jamal realized the tables had turned. This time, it would be him dying at Rico's hand.

"Don't do this," Jamal begged.

Rico moved in closer and whispered, "You're mine, Jamal. We're in this together . . . forever."

Suddenly, Rico's swollen face flashed before his eyes.

"Shit!" Jamal exclaimed as he sat up.

He got up from the couch and went back to the kitchen. He grabbed a glass from the cabinet. Panicking wasn't going to solve anything. He had to relax. The police officers said there was foul play involved, but he didn't understand how they could have come to that conclusion.

As he filled the glass, Jamal noticed his hands were trembling. He carefully placed the bottle on the counter. He lifted the glass to his mouth and drained it within seconds. All of a sudden, his eyes grew big. *The handcuffs!*

Jamal filled a second glass, guzzling it just as fast. He ignored the burning sensation rising in his chest as he poured another glass. Sweat beads began to form across his forehead. After returning the bottle to the cabinet, he went back to the living room. He sat down and closed his eyes.

Jamal had watched enough of *The First 48* to know the crime scene investigators would look around Rico's body first. He'd made sure to put on gloves before he touched anything. He'd been careful to remove the handcuffs and chair without disrupting the position of Rico's body. Thankfully, Rico was a neat freak. His house was spotless. Still, Jamal had wiped everything down. From their drinking glasses to the bowl with the fruit, he'd made sure to remove any signs he'd been there. He thought about their virtual connection.

Months before, in a drunken state, Rico shared that he kept a notebook with usernames, passwords, and other personal details. Jamal didn't have to search long for the notebook. He logged into Rico's online accounts. While he deleted the communications between them, he found there were other men that Rico talked to and was intimate with. Jamal knew Rico was lying when he said he'd only been sleeping with him. There were at least five other men Rico had slept with in recent months. Jamal intentionally left those conversations, believing it would lead the police to look for one of them.

When Jamal opened his eyes, a crooked smile formed on his lips.

I have nothing to worry about.

CHAPTER

5

"Ahem?"

Brielle turned her head in the direction of the door and stepped back from the man's embrace. "What the—Derrik?"

"Uhh, my bad. Sorry for interrupting." Derrik glanced at the tall man who wrapped his arm around Brielle's waist and drew her in closer. Derrik looked at her. "Could I talk to you . . . in private?"

"This is my friend Derrik. Derrik, Justin. Love, can you give me a few minutes to talk to him? It won't be long. Right, Derrik?"

"This will only take a few minutes."

She could kick Derrik's ass for interrupting them. Brielle returned her attention to the sexy man in front of her. Justin groped her thick ass, squeezing as he tongued her down. Derrik averted his eyes and blew out a long breath to remind them he was still in the room. With reluctance Brielle withdrew from Justin's mouth.

She stroked the side of his face and said, literally gasping for air. "I'll meet you at your house as soon as I'm done here."

Justin spoke in a rich, husky tone. "Okay, Peaches, I'll be waiting."

When Justin made it over to the door, he paused to stare Derrik in the eye. Although Justin was lighter in complexion, both men were matched in handsome features, height, and build. He gave Derrik an upward nod. Derrik returned the gesture, hoping it was clear that he and Brielle were just friends.

Once Justin left the room, Derrik grinned at Brielle. "*Peaches?*"

She blushed. "Shut up."

"So is he your new boo?"

"Maybe. I'm working on that," she replied coyly. Then she squinted. "The fuck?" Brielle hastily moved over to Derrik and examined his face. There was discoloration and swelling underneath his right eye. She looked down at his hands. His knuckles were bruised, and one hand was wrapped in a bandage. Brielle reached up to touch his face but yanked her hand away to cover her mouth. "Oh shit, y'all fought?"

Derrik nodded. He moved around her and slumped down in the armchair facing her desk. "Sorry to pop up unannounced, but since you didn't call me back the other day, I decided to just come by. Desi's texted me, and I've been back to her house, but I know she hasn't been there. I can't catch her at work either. Is she at your house?"

She didn't answer his question. Instead, Brielle asked if he was okay. Derrik ignored her question. "I know you heard me, Bri."

"You know I can't tell you, but she needed to get out of town to sort everything out."

He let out a sigh of frustration. "So she's not even in town."

She sat down in the chair next to him and turned it to face him. Brielle knew Desiree was wrong for leaving the way she did. But in her friend's defense, the embarrassment of it all really was too much. All of a sudden, Brielle started chuckling.

He frowned, "You find this shit funny?"

"Well, no, and then again, yeah. Desi getting caught in this bs—that part ain't funny. Knowing y'all were fucking and Troy found out is though. You have to give me the rundown on what happened after she left. From the looks of it, y'all was scrapping. Please tell me you fucked him up."

Derrik shrugged. "He doesn't look any better, that's for sure. I'm not sure if he's able to open that left eye."

Brielle clapped her hands. "Hell yeah! You whooped his ass!"

Derrik explained that they each had taken serious blows from the other. It was the ass whooping he'd been wanting to give Troy for years. "I probably would've stayed on his ass if Hodg' and nem didn't pull me off of him."

CHAPTER 5

"Wait, they were there too? Why didn't y'all jump him?"

"Nah, there was no need for that. And yeah, they were there because I never go anywhere without my bodyguards. You won't always see them, but they're watching my back. They knew when Troy got there, and they saw when Desi bounced. It was the noise we were making in the house that made them come check on me."

Derrik thought about the amount of damage they did to her living room. He told Brielle he needed to hire a cleaning company. The large hole in one wall would need repairing. He would also need to replace the coffee table and lamps they broke.

She opened her mouth. "It was that bad?"

He nodded.

"What happens now?"

Derrik shrugged. "Not sure. But I doubt things are ever going back to normal. What can I say? We both got played."

Brielle wasn't going to let Desiree mess up the best thing for her, and she wasn't going to allow Troy to ruin what they started—not if she could help it. "I know how everything might seem right now, but I know Desi didn't play you. This is all his doing, Derrik. That man is a manipulating liar. Did you know he was harassing and stalking her after he saw her at your office?"

Derrik raised an eyebrow. "What do you mean?"

Brielle told him how Troy called Desiree nonstop and made up the lie about the foundation. She did her best to explain how Troy conned Desiree into believing his wife was there when she'd gone to his house to pick up the paperwork. He'd apologized about his past wrongdoings to play on her emotions. Brielle paused to see how Derrik was processing everything. "I take it she didn't mention any of this to you?"

"No, Bri, she didn't."

"You have to believe she wasn't doing this intentionally. And I'm not making any excuses for her, but he was her first love. You knew this going in. Do you remember that day she dropped the charges against him?"

Derrik nodded.

"We both know they never had closure, not properly. He dissed her like she wasn't shit, and she couldn't let his sorry ass go that day. And let's not forget about how she was still checking for him that night at the party I threw for her promotion."

His expression didn't change. She saw the hurt in his eyes as he mumbled, "Yeah, once again, I stood by watching her choose another man over me."

Brielle knew there wouldn't be any damage control that could spare his feelings, so she spoke truthfully. "She was trying to move on, Derrik, especially after hearing he'd married Mia. Jamal was, well, you know, a rebound if anything."

"I guess," he said with defeat in his tone. Derrik relaxed in the chair and made a steeple of his fingers. He might have broken the guy code, but he knew Troy didn't deserve her. Neither did Jamal. He looked at Brielle. "I wish she would talk to me so that I can hear her side of things."

"Give it some time, Derrik. This is embarrassing for her. She had to risk losing what she had with you and face the truth of who Troy really is. Derrik, she feels stupid for making the wrong choice."

"Yeah, that makes me feel better," Derrik grumbled.

Before Brielle could respond, Derrik's phone rang. He looked at the name on the screen and abruptly rose from the chair. "Uh hey, I need to grab this."

"Yeah, sure, go ahead."

She picked up Derrik's reaction from the call and for a moment thought it was Desiree. Brielle watched as he moved to the other side of the room. She got up to go back to the other side of her desk.

"Hey, what's going on? . . . Yeah, I've been busy . . . What? . . . You're where? When did you—you know what, never mind . . . I'll be there." He checked his text messages, frowned, and turned around. "Hey, Bri, I gotta run. Something's come up that I need to take care of."

She stood up. "Is everything okay?"

"Yeah, I'll catch up with you later. When Desiree calls, tell her I'm not that mad where we can't talk about this."

Brielle nodded. "Of course."

Without another word, Derrik left her office.

CHAPTER

6

Derrik made it across town to his house within an hour. While he was with Brielle, Hodges had sent a text that he had an unexpected visitor. One of the other bodyguards on his team stayed behind while Hodges went to handle it. Derrik walked into the foyer and called out, "Khloe! Where are you?" His voice echoed throughout the downstairs area.

Her voice came from the direction of the kitchen. "I'm in here."

He placed his phone and keys on the granite countertop as a petite, curvy woman sashayed from the other side. She came to a halt next to the wide island in the kitchen's center. She was short in stature, no more than five-foot-one. The Prada sandals she wore brought her to average height, and her skin-tight dress left nothing to the imagination. The front dipped low, revealing cleavage. Her voluptuous breasts threatened to spill out. The bodycon dress had a thigh-high split that stopped above her upper thigh, exposing the area next to her panty line. He could tell she wasn't wearing anything underneath.

After inspecting Khloe from head to toe, his eyes roamed up and met her seductive gaze. She bent her head, and the lengthier side of her asymmetrical bob shielded her left eye. The chic hairstyle elongated her neck and accentuated her facial features. With her bronzed skin, slender face, Hollywood lips, and high cheekbones, Khloe was a stunningly attractive woman.

"Hello, Derrik," she purred, tossing the hair away from her eye.

Khloe Dillon was the CEO of Dillon Ventures, a successful and reputable venture capital firm. It was one of the few Black-owned investment firms in the Boston area, where Derrik was originally from. In his junior year of college, he was awarded a coveted internship at her company. His hard work didn't go unnoticed. By the time his internship was over, he was invited to come back during his senior year. It was then that their paths crossed. Derrik was working with one of Khloe's investment officers and shared his business plans for after graduation. Unbeknownst to him, Khloe was nearby eavesdropping. He remembered getting the call from her assistant that she wanted to meet with him.

His nerves were on edge meeting with the CEO, but he had nothing to worry about. He wasn't in any trouble. She conveyed an interest in Derrik's desire for entrepreneurship. After he expressed his goals, Khloe took him under her mentorship and taught him what she'd learned through the years. He soaked up the information like a sponge. In turn, he showed her a few hacks and helped with acquiring a couple of new firms to co-invest with. Khloe felt that the best way to reward his hard work was to help him get started with his entertainment company. The portfolio she gifted was more than enough to launch Derrik's business venture and any other venture he wanted to dabble in. He wasn't sure how to thank her, but Khloe showed him how he could repay her for everything.

Of course, she taught him more than the girls he'd dated in the past. Equipped with a vast knowledge on many things, she had the upper hand. Initially, it shocked Derrik to find out her age. She didn't look a day over twenty-five. Yet, Khloe was seventeen years Derrik's senior. His age didn't put the brakes on Khloe's hidden intentions. At twenty-three, Derrik jumped at the opportunity. He enjoyed reaping all the benefits and attention from a beautiful, wealthy, older woman. After Derrik graduated and relocated to Atlanta, he and Khloe remained in contact, especially after his company's successful launch. Unknown to the world, Khloe Dillon was Derrik's silent benefactor—she had been for the past seven years. And with her standing in the middle of his kitchen dressed that way, he knew there was more than business on her mind.

He was about to respond when she rushed over and touched his face. With gentle fingers she traced his bruises and held his bandaged hand, her eyes filled with concern. "My beloved, what happened? Were you fighting?"

"Yeah, but it's nothing I want to talk about." He lowered his eyes. "Why are you dressed like that, Klo?"

"You don't like it? Since you had me waiting, I figured I would put on something comfortable."

"I had you waiting? I didn't even know you were coming here. And you call that comfortable?"

"Why, yes."

"Knock it the fuck off. I know what you're up to."

Khloe clutched her chest and batted her eyes. "Whatever do you mean?" She reached down, massaged his crotch, and gave a gentle squeeze.

Derrik moved her hand and repositioned his package. "Klo, you didn't bother calling or texting. I don't do surprise pop-ups."

"Yes, I know. But you don't have to worry about me popping up if there's nobody here for me to catch in your face or your bed."

He spoke in a stern tone, "Respect my house, Klo. Don't let this shit happen again."

She wrapped her arms around his waist. Derrik looked down. She batted her eyes again and blew a kiss.

He bent forward and kissed the tip of her button nose. "Are we clear?"

She nodded. "It won't happen again."

"Now what is this visit about?" he asked.

"A friend of mine called at the last minute and told me a couple of major players were going to be involved in this deal and said I should get in. I hadn't decided because I wanted to share it with you. There are some documents for you to go over. I put them on your desk." She rubbed the front of his jeans again. "But can we look at that later? Right now, let's pick up where we left off."

He backed away and frowned. "You've been in my office?"

"You act as though I've never been in there."

"But you have no business being in there if I'm not here," he chastised.

Khloe nodded and responded in her soft voice, "Okay I'm sorry, but relax, my beloved. I put the folder on your desk and that's it. I didn't touch anything else or go through your stuff."

Derrik thought about the picture on his bookshelf. He and Desiree took it at a fundraising event he'd hosted the year before. When things got serious between them, he moved it from a private box of memories to where he could look at her face daily. It was obvious Khloe hadn't noticed. He would've gotten more than an earful if she had.

"Where is Hodges anyway? He was supposed to be here."

She chewed her lower lip as she looked seductively at Derrik. Before answering, she massaged his biceps. "Gone."

"Where, Khloe?"

"Please don't be upset with him. He's had a thing for my assistant for a while. I brought her along, and since she wanted to hang out in the city, I asked him to show her around."

"He knows better than to leave my house without anyone here," he grumbled.

"Well, he didn't. You saw your other guys were out there, but I did tell them once you arrived to make themselves scarce. We need our privacy."

Khloe eliminated the distance between them again. She hugged him tight and pressed her face against his firm chest. "Hmm, you have no idea how much I've missed you, my beloved."

He clasped his hands behind her back and rested his chin on the top of her head. Derrik and Khloe were supposed to have a friends-with-benefits arrangement. But lately his sole focus was Desiree. He'd spent the past couple of months trying to build the relationship he'd always wanted with her. Derrik never considered his on-again, off-again relationship with Khloe and how it might put him in a predicament. Although he shared a special bond with Khloe, Desiree had his heart. But her backtracking and sleeping with Troy threw everything into a tailspin. He wasn't sure what to think or what would happen now. His phone sounded an alert and vibrated. Before he could pick it up, Khloe did.

"You know better. Hand it to me."

She ignored him and attempted to view the message. Derrik snatched the phone away. He glared at her before taking a look himself.

It was Desiree.

Hey Derrik. Can you talk? – Desiree

Fuck! Derrik glanced at Khloe. Even though his phone had a privacy screen, he still took a step back as Khloe raised her eyebrow, cocked her head to side, and shot him an impatient stare.

"Hang on, Klo. I gotta respond to this." Derrik rushed to key in his reply.

Not at the moment, baby girl. Can I hit you back when I'm free? – Derrik

He scrolled through his messages and emails as he waited for Desiree's response. He didn't look up at Khloe, but he could feel her eyes burning a hole through his hand. His phone chirped again. Khloe's eyes became thin slits.

Yes, of course. I'll be up for a while. Just call back when you can. – Desiree

Derrik slipped the phone into the pocket of his jeans and peeked at Khloe. She crossed her arms. "Is this somebody new, or is it Marley with her insecure ass trying to sniff around again?"

"Come on, Klo. We've been doing fine for months now. Don't start this shit."

"Well, is it?"

He wasn't up for her pressuring him about the text. He needed to change the subject. Derrik motioned for her to follow him as he pivoted to leave the kitchen. "Now tell me what this new venture is all about."

She responded to his back. "I really think you're going to like this one. Another holdings company wants to do a major takeover. He's a heavy hitter in utilities, retail goods, transportation, and financial services."

While she provided the details of the companies involved, Derrik made his way to the home library. The room was over a thousand square feet in size with bookshelves on each wall. Derrik took a seat on one of the plush couches sitting in the middle of the large room. Instead of sitting, Khloe remained standing to wrap up her summary about the venture with the business conglomerate.

Derrik's raised an eyebrow as his eyes swept over her body. "And this particular one you had to see me face-to-face to discuss?"

"I could've texted you." She lowered her gaze and leaned over, speaking in a sultry tone, "But we have unfinished business, Mr. Carter."

She stepped back and pulled the dress to the side, exposing her freshly waxed pussy. Khloe propped one of the heeled sandals on the coffee table. She sucked two fingers while watching Derrik's eyes on her. She withdrew the fingers covered in saliva and pushed them into her pussy. He relaxed back into the pillows and watched the performance.

She squatted lower, opened her legs wider, and worked them in and out. She bent her head, and the lengthier side of her asymmetrical bob covered her left eye. Her seductive gaze never left his as she fingered her pussy. It was turning Derrik on to watch her pleasuring herself. Khloe's moaning grew louder. He adjusted the crotch of his jeans to relieve the tension on his growing erection. Her fingers glistened from the silky nectar beginning to leak out. The scent made its way to his nostrils.

"I want a taste," Derrik confessed.

She withdrew her fingers and stuffed them in his mouth. Derrik enjoyed the sweet-flavored cream, sucking her fingers clean.

She giggled, "You're so fucking nasty. I love it!"

Khloe hoisted the dress up to her waist and sat on the wooden table. She opened her thighs wide and pressed the middle digits against her clit. As she increased the speed of the circular motion on her button, cream oozed from her pink opening.

Derrik moved from the couch to the floor and positioned himself right in front of her pussy. He bent forward and spread her lips wider. He slid his tongue inside, twirling it around while she rubbed. With the help of his tongue fucking, they brought her to an orgasm fast.

"Oooh, my beloved . . . yes, right there . . . that feels . . . oh shit! I'm about to . . . oooh!"

Khloe's thighs shook as she unraveled. He licked with ferocity, lapping up the juices. When he finished, he kissed her fat pussy lips and murmured against them. "Damn, Klo. You always taste good."

She sampled her fingers. "You're right. I do." She licked the tips of her fingers and whispered, "Fuck me, Derrik."

Khloe massaged her clit while Derrik yanked his shirt and jeans off. He pushed his boxers down, and the thick, veiny muscle sprang out. She licked her lips at the sight of him. Derrik's chiseled body was a masterpiece. He helped Khloe up from the coffee table over to the couch. She leaned back, spreading her knees, wanting and welcoming every inch of him. He positioned himself between her thighs and rubbed his manhood against her pearl. Hot, sticky cream leaked from her opening. Derrik eased his heavy erection into the slippery heat. Khloe held onto his forearms as he worked his hips to loosen the snug fit. He finally stretched her, pumping and grinding his pelvis into hers. She rocked and rotated her hips to receive his long, deep strokes. Her knees trembled as another orgasm took over.

He leaned forward, nuzzled against her cheek, and groaned in her ear. "Damn, I felt that Klo."

Pleasure rippled through her body, making her legs shake uncontrollably. He threw them over his shoulders and gripped her ass. His pumps increased, sending Khloe over the edge. The heat rose and radiated through her abdomen. Their eyes connected when her walls spasmed around his dick again.

"Fuck!" he growled.

"Derrrrik!" She didn't want to run, but he had a huge dick. She put her hands on his thighs and tried to slow him down, but he knocked them away. Khloe writhed wildly beneath him, tossing her head from side to side. Derrik kept pounding until every muscle tensed. His back stiffened, his dick pulsed, and he spewed a load into her. After a few moments, he withdrew from Khloe and eased her quivering legs away from his shoulders. She wrapped them around his waist.

He leaned in and gave her a peck on the nose. "That was good as always."

"Well, you'll be getting good and plenty of this whenever you want."

Derrik stared in confusion as Khloe announced, "Until this venture is underway, I've decided to stick around." She sat up and teased his lips with a kiss. "Besides that, something's telling me I have to protect my vested interest."

"What vested interest?"

"You."

CHAPTER

7

Jamal woke up earlier than usual and decided to make breakfast. Right before he planned to go in to wake Angela, she dragged herself into the kitchen, making her way to the small breakfast bar on the far side of the room. The aroma of frying eggs and fresh brewed coffee attacked her senses. She mumbled good morning as she sat down. Jamal flipped the egg whites a final time. He turned the range off and faced her.

"Good morning, sweetheart!"

Angela grimaced and rubbed her temples. "Ugh, shhhh. Not so loud. Okay, Jamal?"

"What's the matter? Headache?"

She nodded.

"I bet I know why. You drank two bottles and passed out without touching your food. Good thing I made breakfast. You need to eat something."

She waved dismissively. "No, I'm not hungry."

"Angela, you really should try to—"

"I said I'm not hungry," she snapped.

"Okay then, how about a cup of coffee?" Jamal offered.

"Yeah, I guess."

It had been a week since Rico died. She wasn't lying in bed all day anymore, and the medication seemed to be helping with the anxiety attacks. However, her patience was shorter. Everything irritated her. Jamal was sympathetic and did what he could to help her cope with this new normal. He handed her the cup and began munching on his breakfast sandwich. He attempted to make small talk about his upcoming day at the office. When she didn't show any interest, he asked about her plans for the day.

"Are you going to your mom's?"

Angela's headache eased with each sip. Her man not only knew how to cook, but he could make a mean cup of Joe to cure hangovers. She took another sip, savoring the flavor of cinnamon. It was delicious.

"No, Mia's coming over. I know I wasn't much for company when she stopped by last week, but I'm missing her. We have to catch up on what happened with Troy and this reality show she might be featured in. I think it's supposed to air in the winter."

Jamal furrowed his brows in disapproval. "I hope you're not getting any ideas of wanting to join her."

"No, absolutely not. That's Mia's thing."

"For the record, I don't want my woman involved in any drama behind some reality show. They ruin relationships. There are certain things the public shouldn't be privy to."

Angela nodded in agreement. "You don't have to worry about me. I have no interest in being a housewife of Atlanta."

"Good," he said, getting up from the table. After washing and putting the dishes away, he noticed the time. "Dammit! I have to get out of here now if I want to beat the traffic."

Jamal quickly left the kitchen to grab his bags from the office. Angela met him in the hallway. He kissed her forehead before moving to her lips. They shared a short embrace. When he released her, Jamal's watchful eyes remained on her for a moment. "Angela, remember what I said. Everything's going to be okay."

"I know, babe."

He didn't move. He caressed her shoulders and kissed her forehead again. "I'll call you later. I love you."

"I love you too. Now go before you're stuck on I-85."

Angela closed the door behind him. By the time Jamal opened the door to his Audi R8, he saw she'd pulled back the curtains and blinds. She waved at him. He smiled, returning a wave. He began backing out of his space. The honking from a horn startled him. Jamal slammed on the brakes. He looked in the rearview and immediately recognized the woman shaking her head back at him. She pulled into the parking space next to him. When she got out of the white Mercedes G-Wagon, he let his window down. "My bad, Mia. I wasn't looking when I backed out."

She nodded. "It's all good. Glad you heard me."

They exchanged pleasant goodbyes. This time Jamal ensured his path was clear before leaving.

"Goodness, was he in a rush? He was about to back right into my shit," Mia said as she approached the walkway leading up to Angela's condo.

"As a matter of fact, he was. He's running late and was too busy waving at me." She looked over Mia's shoulder. "Hmm, I see somebody's putting their new fortune to use. Did you really need a G-Wagon, Mia?"

Mia smiled, looking satisfied with herself. "Yes, I did."

Angela invited her girl in. Even though Mia had settled for a casual look in her maxi dress and sandals, she still gave high-end fashion vibes. Her hair was out of the bun and hanging loose. She was gorgeous and glowing. Angela couldn't wait to get the scoop. They went into the living room and sat on the gray, plush sofa. The women shared a tight and friendly embrace.

Mia grabbed her hands when they released one another. "How are you holding up? I know this has been hard on you."

"I still can't believe this is even happening, Mia. Never in a million years did I think my family would experience anything like this."

Mia squeezed her hands. "No one ever does."

Angela saw the past week as a nightmare she was forced to stay awake and live through every day. She didn't want to talk about it. Instead, she changed the subject, asking Mia for all the details of what happened after the party. From the looks of her new ride, it was evident that she'd accomplished getting Troy's money. Angela wanted to know what her girl was up to now. Mia released Angela's hands and smoothed down the front of her form-fitting maxi dress as if it had wrinkles.

"Come on, girl. Tell me everything." Angela urged.

Mia gave her a shortened version of how it went down with Troy and their meeting with the lawyer. In the end, everything had worked out in her favor. By the time she left the lawyer's office, she had the house, most of the cars, and the status of a millionaire. "I even changed the locks."

"That's great, Mia. It was time for you to get out of that toxic marriage. You can focus on your goals and dreams now. Are you thinking about opening your interior design company? And what's up with this reality show?"

"He came by later that day."

Angela cocked her head to the side. "He begged, didn't he?"

She nodded. "Of course."

"Did you let him in, Mia?"

She nodded again. She didn't look in Angela's direction, but her face said it all.

Angela's eyes widened, and her shocked expression turned to a look of disbelief. "You fucked him, didn't you!"

Mia whined. "I couldn't help it. He'd been in a fight. And he was looking and smelling so good. Then he started calling me Sym. I just needed one more time, Ang. I put him out after that."

Angela shook her head.

"I'm not going to let him back in. I can't do this with him anymore."

"And we've been down this road before. Do you really believe that, Mia? Do I need to remind you about last month?"

"No, you don't. And we have not been down this road. My plan worked. I'm walking away from him rich. I'm not letting him come back."

Angela raised an eyebrow. She snapped her fingers. "This is the same look you had in the aftermath of that last big fight y'all had. You forgave him and let him come back."

Mia knew that this time was different and that she was done with Troy's lies and abuse. But she decided to change the subject and tell Angela about the other big news in her life: Mia's agent, Tanya, pitched her story to the B&B network to join the upcoming reality show, *Wives in Football*. After word got out about what she'd done at the party, they felt she would be a good fit. By the end of the week, she would have a camera crew following her and chronicling her daily life. Mia would be on television by winter if she could come up with enough dramatic content for the show.

"Which brings me to an idea I have, but I need to know you're okay with me doing this. I think it would be helpful to the police."

Angela frowned. "Okay with you doing what?"

Mia explained she wanted to bring the camera crew to Tré's homegoing service. Angela thought of Jamal's warning about her friend's intentions.

"Mia, I don't think—"

She didn't give her the chance to finish. "Look, killers are sadistic. They always want to watch the aftermath of what they've done. I have a feeling he or they will be at the funeral."

Angela sat back. It was hard enough to accept her brother was gone, but to have their family's tragedy broadcast on a national television show felt like too much. Her mind raced with the idea of her brother's death being under the spotlight. She looked at her friend with uncertainty.

Mia could feel her apprehension. She put her hand over Angela's and squeezed. "Your brother's murderer is out there, Ang. The police will do their job, but there's nothing wrong with giving them a little help along the way. They want and need it. Somebody knows something about what happened."

She wanted justice for her brother, but she didn't want too much attention on her family. The murder had already made the local news. They didn't need any further exposure. "Mia, I don't know if my family can take all of that. We're private."

"Are you kidding me? Look at how most people bring murderers to justice. They do it by getting the media involved. Do you even remember how *America's Most Wanted* got started? If it wasn't for what's-his-face, you know the host's son getting kidnapped, those families he helped would've never had justice. Don't allow them to get away with this. Perhaps you'll save someone else's brother, dad, or son. You owe this to Tré."

Angela sat in silence allowing Mia's words to sink in. After a minute, she spoke, "I'm still in shock. I feel so helpless."

"I'm sure your whole family is in shock. Doing this you won't feel like that. I know we'll be doing a great service alerting the public to this killer."

Angela nodded and stood up. "Hang on. I'll be right back."

She went to the bedroom and sat on the bed. Her heart was racing. It felt as though the room was spinning. Angela looked down at her hands. They were shaking. She turned her palms up and watched as the sweat beads began to form. She rubbed them on the sides of her sweatpants. Her eyes went to the prescription bottles on the nightstand. Without hesitating, she grabbed them, took a couple of pills, and sat down. After a few minutes, she returned to the living room.

"I was just about to come in there and check on you. Everything okay?"

"Mia, I . . . you know what . . . wine. Right now, I need a glass of Cabernet Sauv to take the edge off. Just a glass, okay? Do you want one?"

"This early in the morning?"

"Girl, it'll be brunch soon, and I know it's five o'clock somewhere."

Mia scoffed, "Goodness no, I can't. I have a meeting with Tanya in a few hours. I need to be on point for that. I'll take a bottle of water."

"Okay, be right back."

Angela didn't heed the warnings on her medicine bottles. She believed the wine helped to better numb her emotions. She popped the cork and poured until the large glass was full. She gulped the contents in the glass. She refilled the glass and repeated. Angela poured another glassful. After drinking half the contents, she started to put the wine away but looked back at the half-empty glass. She filled it to the top. She returned the now almost empty wine bottle to the fridge and grabbed a bottle of water for Mia.

Before walking out of the kitchen, Angela sucked in a deep breath and exhaled slowly. Her heart rate seemed to slow down, and she didn't feel the anxiety that had overcome her moments earlier. She went back to the living room feeling weightless. "Here you go."

Mia picked up on the shift in Angela's mood. "Angela, you shouldn't be drinking while you're grieving like this. You think it helps, but it's just covering up your pain."

"Girl, stop it. I'm fine. You know I can hold my wine. There's no reason for me to harp on this situation. Tré is gone, and I have to learn how to cope with him not being here. That's what Jamal said."

Mia opened her mouth, but Angela continued, "Seriously, Mia, I'm good. Like you said, they're going to find out who did this to my brother. Now, why don't you tell me exactly what you're planning. His funeral is next week. You're going to bring the cameras, right?"

Mia stared at her briefly, then nodded, "Yes, in addition to the details of what happened, maybe we can share a little about who he was. You could help with that. Tell me some things about Tré so people will know the kind of son and brother he was."

Mia stopped when she noticed Angela wasn't paying attention. She was rotating her wrist, looking at the liquid swirl around in the glass. She noticed Mia staring, so she smiled back before turning the glass up. She placed it on the table and looked at her, giggling. "No lies! There's nothing like a little wine to help lighten the mood."

CHAPTER

8

It had taken Jamal almost an hour to get through traffic, but he made it to the office in time for his first patient. His day and client flow proceeded as normal, smooth and without issues. After his last appointment, he returned to his office to write up some notes. As he finished, his cell rang. He looked at the display and frowned. It was Desiree.

"Hey, umm, how are you?"

Desiree sighed. "I'm better, thanks."

"I'm sorry I didn't call back. It's been busy the last couple of days, but I got your message. I'm not sure what happened. Rico's sister hasn't been able to tell me much except they don't have any leads or suspects. His memorial service is next weekend. Are you planning to come?"

"Yes, could you send me the details?" Desiree asked.

"Of course, I will."

"And I'm sorry for how I acted, Jamal. You didn't deserve that under the circumstances. How are you holding up?"

Jamal knew he needed to play the part of the grieving friend. He replied in a quiet, yet steady voice, "I'm okay. I don't think it's quite hit me yet that my boy's gone, you know? I'm still processing this shit. It all seems so surreal."

"I know. Same here."

An awkward silence filled the air. Jamal didn't feel like talking about Rico. He needed to get Desiree off the phone. "Listen, I'm still at the office, and I need to get the rest of my notes in the system before heading out. I guess I'll see you next week."

"Yeah, okay then. Later."

The second he ended their call, his office manager buzzed him. "Dr. Edwards, there are two detectives here to speak with you."

Instantly, his skin felt hot. His stomach somersaulted as if he were in the first drop of a rollercoaster. Seconds passed. He grabbed the water bottle sitting on his desk and gulped down half of it. Then he took a deep breath before responding, "Okay, I'll be right there."

He knew the police would talk to the people closest to Rico. He thought of everything he'd seen on television, but he knew nothing could prepare him for what he was about to face. Jamal slowly made his way to the front office. He finally reached the door and took another deep breath. The door to the lobby felt unusually heavy. Jamal pushed it open.

"Hello, Dr. Edwards."

"Yes, hello."

"I'm Detective Wallace."

With bags under his eyes and lines creasing his face, he bore the distinctive look of a man in his late fifties to early sixties. He wore a brown sports coat, shirt, and khaki dress slacks. His brown loafers looked worn down, but not from running after criminals, Jamal was sure.

Wallace nodded in the direction of his partner, a younger, taller man sporting a stylish navy coat, dress shirt, tie, suspenders, and slacks. His brown Stacy Adams looked similar to the ones Jamal wore. He nodded in response. "And I'm Detective Green."

Wallace continued, "I hope we're not keeping you from any of your patients."

Jamal kept it cool. "No, not at all. We've seen all of our patients for the day. I was finishing up with writing some notes in a few files. How can I help you?"

"Do you mind if we spoke in private?" Wallace asked.

"Sure, of course. Let's go to my office."

CHAPTER 8

The detectives followed Jamal to the back. Although he moved at a steady pace, his heart began to beat faster and louder. He was certain they could hear it. Jamal knew he needed to relax. They reached his office, and he waited until they were inside before closing the door behind them. "Could I get either of you a bottle of water?"

"No, I'm good. You, Green?"

The younger detective nodded, "Yes, I'd like one. I've had my cap on soda for the day."

Jamal grabbed a bottle from the fridge in the corner of his office. He sat down at his desk, watching as both detectives reached into their coat pockets for little notepads. Green was quick to let him know that the reason for their unannounced visit was to obtain information regarding Rico's death.

Jamal consented, "Yes, of course. I'm happy to help however I can."

"First, could you give us your full name, please."

"It's Jamal Devon Edwards, the third."

"And how did you know Mr. Alvarez?"

Jamal recounted how he and Rico had met at the golf club three years ago.

Green continued, "And when was the last time you saw Mr. Alvarez?"

"Uhh, yes, it was a few weeks ago. We were up at the golf course."

"Ok, how long were you there, and when did you leave?" Wallace asked.

"Rico and I spent most of the day up there. I want to say we got our game started right after noontime. He had an allergic reaction to this fudge shortbread my wife made, and we had to go to the ER."

When the detectives asked Jamal his whereabouts on the night Rico died, Jamal was able to gather his scattered thoughts and maintain his composure. He disclosed that he'd been with Angela for a little while before he went to the hospital, where he stayed for most of the night. He'd gone home but left and went back to Angela. He also revealed that Rico called, but they only spoke for a few minutes.

"Did you speak to him again after that?"

"Yes, the other night. We spoke for a few minutes before I went to the hospital. We were going to catch up and hang out, but he canceled because he had a date."

"With whom? Do you have her name?"

Jamal shook his head. "No, I don't know. He didn't say. When I went to the gym the next day, he didn't show up. I called. I even left a couple of messages and sent a few texts. I didn't think it would be . . ." He let his voice trail off. Jamal took a deep breath and sighed, "I didn't think it would be this."

Wallace asked, "Is there anything else you can think of? More specifically, is there anyone who would want to hurt Mr. Alvarez? Did he have any enemies?"

Jamal shook his head forcefully. "No, Rico was cool with everybody. I can't imagine anyone wanting to kill my friend."

The detectives finished the interview, gave him their card, and asked that he contact them if he thought of anything else that might help in their investigation. Jamal walked the men to the front. When they left, he went back to his office. His body sank into the chair. He looked down at his hands as they trembled. Suddenly, he thought about what he'd said to Rico. *When they find you, they'll rule your death an accident.*

Now, he wasn't so sure.

CHAPTER
9

"I'm glad you got me out of there. I needed an escape. Khloe's been on me since she got here."

Hodges snorted.

"You think that shit's funny, Hodg', but it's not. Khloe won't stop at nothing to keep my dick up in her. And I meant to say something to y'all asses the other day. You know she shouldn't have been in the house by herself. You let her assistant cloud your judgment."

"My bad, Boss."

"She uses her womanly charms to get what she wants. I won't deny it. She's been using them on me for years, and her assistant is pretty. I see why you like her."

Hodges grinned from ear to ear.

"Hey, man, I won't get in your way with that, but please make sure Khloe stays out of my office and plundering around the house. According to her, they're going to be here for the next week, maybe two, and this isn't like before. Despite what happened, you know things are serious with Desi now. I've tried to let Khloe down easy before, but . . ."

Hodges shot Derrik a disapproving look. Over the years, Derrik had learned his bodyguard wasn't a man of many words. Still, he knew exactly what that look meant.

"Okay, okay, you're right. I haven't tried hard enough. What do you want me to say? Khloe's been around since the beginning. She's partly responsible for why I even have BlakBeatz. I just told you she uses her magic. It doesn't help that she's fine as hell, and the sex is fucking amazing. She's that older woman my mother always warned me about."

Hodges looked at him and surprisingly, he said a mouthful. His baritone voice was low, and the Louisiana accent came through strong. "Listen, Boss. My mama said be careful 'bout women like her. She's smart, really smart, and cunning. Most men would be intimidated by her power and knowledge, but not you, and she loves that 'bout you. I see that. She's beautiful, yeah. But Khloe? She dangerous, Boss. She Creole, and my mama said them women will fuck around and get a root put on your ass. Women like that don't go away quietly. Never."

Derrik nodded. "That's why I got to get her out of my house—no, Atlanta. And before Desi gets back."

They'd missed each other's calls over the last couple of days. Derrik knew Desiree was likely avoiding him. She'd told him that she would call later, but it had been hours and nothing. He looked at his phone then glanced at Hodges. The expression on the bodyguard's face reminded him of someone sucking on a sour lemon. He ignored it. "Where are you taking me, anyway?"

"Some party my friend is working. You need more guys, and he's been wanting to get on with us. I figured you could meet him."

Derrik noticed they were heading into an upscale neighborhood in Brookhaven, an affluent area twenty minutes outside of Atlanta. It was only minutes away from his home in Buckhead, and he'd once considered buying property there as well. Derrik looked down at his phone again. He'd decided to send another text, but before he could finish, Hodges took the phone from him and placed it on the middle console.

"All right. She'll hit me back when she can."

The two remained quiet for the rest of the ride. Once they reached their destination, Derrik followed Hodges into a newly constructed tri-level townhome. The entrance led into a massive living area with an open concept and high ceilings.

Another guy around Hodges's height and build approached them. Hodges introduced Derrik to his friend.

"Derrik Carter! What's going on, man? Nice to finally meet you. I'm Nate." He extended his hand.

The men exchanged a quick handshake. "Nice to meet you as well. Hodg' thinks you'll be a good fit for us. If you're free, let's catch up tomorrow. Tonight, I just want to hang out and enjoy myself."

Nate's Louisiana accent was as thick as Hodges's, but he had a boisterous voice, the total opposite of Derrik's bodyguard. "That's what I'm talm 'bout! Well, this is where it's at tonight, no doubt. These guys are partying until the morning. Any friends of mine are welcome." Hodges nodded as Nate continued, "The guy they're throwing this party for is somewhere around here. You might know him. He plays ball for the—"

Just then, a man appeared, carrying a woman who was hardly able to stand on her own. She collided with Nate as soon as he came to a halt in front of them.

"Hey, uhh Nate, this one needs a ride home."

"Or a toilet," she hiccupped.

The man pulled a bag out. She buried her face inside. Each of the men grimaced when she started vomiting.

"Let me take care of this. Y'all go 'head and enjoy. The food and drinks are over there. The guys made sure there's plenty of entertainment, as you can see. Y'all know how these athletes do."

In the middle of the living area were dancers from some of Atlanta's elite adult entertainment clubs. They were twerking, popping their pussies, making their ass cheeks clap, and giving lap dances. It was then that Derrik recognized a few faces. He nudged Hodges and nodded in the direction of a group standing near the kitchen. His bodyguard gave him a look and shook his head.

"Hodg' man, I promise, I'm good. We ain't doing no more of that."

Hodges held up his hands in surrender. Derrik led the way over to the men huddled together. By the time he reached them, one of them turned around and greeted him.

"Ayyyy! Yo, it's Derrik Carter in the mothafuckin' hizouse! What's good, yo? How you been, D?" They clasped hands and shared a brief hug.

"Good. Ain't nothing but the same ol' same ol'. You?"

"All is right with the world. Our team is back together."

"Yeah, uhh so, where is he?" Derrik looked around.

The guy shrugged. "Lemme ask. Hey, have any of you seen Troy?"

Another guy yelled across the room, "Yo, do y'all know where Troy went?"

"Man, he upstairs with that Jamaican chick that's been on him all night. I don't know if you want to interrupt him though." The guy winked and started laughing.

The men began exchanging daps and hi-fives. One of guys handed the group some shots and got everyone in on the chant, "That's our dawg and he's back! Troy! Troy! Troy! Troy!"

Derrik ignored what the guys said and made his way upstairs. Before he knocked on the door of the master suite, he motioned for Hodges to hang back.

"Hey, what's up T? Can I come in?" he shouted through the closed door.

The nerve of this bitch ass nigga, Troy said to himself as he emerged from the bathroom. He grabbed the glass of Hennessy from the nightstand. He took a sip and responded dryly, "Yeah."

Derrik walked in and came to a halt when he noticed Troy's angry expression. He saw that the darkening around his left eye was still there. He didn't want to fight again, but he'd happily give him a shiner in the other eye too.

"The fuck you doing here?" Troy snarled.

"I honestly didn't know this was your party. Hodges knew one of the bodyguards. He brought me. If you don't want me here, I can just leave."

The two men stared at one another for a moment. Troy was still pissed about what his boy had done, but he wasn't about to let him fuck up his plans. As if Derrik heard his thoughts, his eyes darted over to the girl lying in the middle of the California king-sized bed.

"She sure as hell ain't going nowhere," Troy said.

"She doesn't have to. But do you mind? I wanted to talk to you for a sec."

Troy retorted, "I don't know what else you have to say to me." He walked over to the side of the bed and sat down.

Derrik moved over to the oversized ottoman across the room. As soon as he sat down, Troy started shaking his head. "You know that shit you did was fucked up, right?"

"Look, T, I'm—"

"Nah, don't say shit. It ain't nothing to say."

He nodded, deciding to keep his apology. "All right."

"Yo, I can't believe you, D. You supposed to be my boy. How long have we been friends?"

Derrik shrugged. "Since we could hold a football."

"You like a brother to me, yo," Troy mumbled.

"You are my brother."

"Regardless of what we did with them other bitches, brothers don't do this kind of shit," he snapped back.

"You're right, T, but apologizing or saying that I didn't mean it would be a lie." *Shit! Did I say that out loud?* He watched as the muscle in Troy's jaw twitched. Derrik cleared his throat, "What I meant to say was I'd be lying to you if I said I don't have real feelings for her."

"Whatever yo."

"I know this wasn't right, but it's hard to explain. We didn't plan on falling for each other. It just happened."

"Yo, you sound just like her ass."

"Y'all spoke?"

"Yeah, she called," Troy said flippantly.

Derrik's heart sank a little hearing she'd spoken with Troy instead of him. Yet, with the girl lying in his bed, he knew Desiree wasn't as special as he'd claimed. It was no shock. Still, he was curious about his friend's actual motives. He needed to know if Troy was truly interested in Desiree.

"Did you really want her back, T?"

"What difference does it make? She was down to fuck, so I went with it."

"Come on, T. A fuck? Really? We came to blows over this shit."

"And I should still be on your ass for not saying nothing and fucking her behind my back."

Derrik ignored his statement and huffed, "You said she was special."

"Yeah, keyword here: *was*. Honestly, D, I never got over that shit she did to me. She let her lonely, jealous-ass friend set me up in that situation and got me locked up."

"Man, you put your hands on her."

"Nigga, it was a slap."

Derrik glared at him, but Troy wasn't fazed. He continued in a dismissive tone, "All right maybe I did choke her a little, but she bruises easy just like Mia's ass. I guess you think it's okay when they slap and throw shit. Ain't no woman gon' disrespect me, D."

Troy had a skewed perception of gender roles in relationships. He'd grown up in a different household than Derrik. Regardless, he knew better than to touch a woman.

"Yo, you out there on this one."

"Nah, you out there, D. Women need to know their places. And it wasn't just that. I ain't think I could trust her. Now I can see her and Mia on some vengeful shit. Ready to destroy a nigga 'cause shit ain't going her way. Who's to say Desi and that trifling-ass girlfriend of hers wouldn't have hemmed me up again?"

Derrik shook his head. He didn't have an answer. He certainly didn't want to think about Desiree choosing Troy over him.

"Man, D, I hope you ain't thinking she's worth fucking with. She tried to play both of us and got caught. I'm telling you. She used you to get to me. It's the oldest fucking trick in the book. Your ass shoulda known. But I'm done with all that. I'm about to get it poppin' with this honey. She came to hook your boy up. Now, you can sit there if you want and watch. Hell, you can even join in."

He slid back to the middle of the bed, and on cue, the girl moved over Troy. She released his half-swollen pole and started giving him a blow job. "Ahh, yeah, that's it. Suck this dick!"

Derrik got up and exited the room. He walked past Hodges, mumbling under his breath. He hated Desiree played a game with them. He dialed her number, hoping she would pick up. Five rings later, his call went to voicemail.

"Hey, we've been doing this phone tag game, and I've tried to be patient. But I'm sick of it. Stop avoiding me. It's time *we* talked."

CHAPTER

10

"So, how was your flight?"

"It was just fine considering I slept the entire way." Desiree placed her bags against the wall in the entryway and turned to embrace Brielle.

"I'm so glad you're back."

"I wish I could say the same," she said as Brielle let go.

"Yeah, I know, this sucks about Rico."

"Not just because of him."

"Right. I know you weren't expecting to come back this soon."

"No, and I need to decompress. With everything that's going on at work, this clusterfuck of a situation with Derrik, and now Rico's death, I'm starting to feel overwhelmed."

"Do you want some tea? The water finished boiling right before you got here."

"Yes, that sounds good."

While Brielle went to the kitchen, Desiree took out her phone and sat on the oversized loveseat. She took the soft throw blanket hanging across the back and snuggled in the corner. She'd told Derrik she would call after she settled in, but as soon as she started to, she decided against it. She recalled the tone in his voice message. He'd sounded pissed. She knew they would have to talk eventually, but she wasn't quite ready yet. Desiree placed her phone on the table and was burrowing into the chair when Brielle reappeared with two large mugs.

"Here, I didn't sweeten it too much. We have to watch your weight."

Desiree took the cup of tea. "Real funny, Bri. You know full well I like my tea sweet," she complained.

Brielle sat in the armchair across from her. "Well, we're not adding any unnecessary pounds to that hourglass figure. I can see a little pudge already."

"You don't see nothing, heffa."

Brielle laughed. "Seriously, how are you feeling? Fatigue, morning, or evening sickness?"

"No, nothing. I actually feel the same. It's crazy. I wouldn't have known if they didn't tell me, or I didn't finally notice I hadn't gotten my period."

Desiree's phone rang. Her eyes went to the display. She knew Brielle's did too. Desiree picked it up and answered casually, "Hey, Aaron."

Desiree didn't make eye contact with Brielle, but she could feel her suspicious eyes watching. Aaron was checking to see if she'd made it there safely.

"Yes, I got here not too long ago. I'm hanging out at my girl Brielle's house."

He had the nerve to say he was getting ready to jump on the next plane to be there with her, and she only needed to say the word. Did he forget she was still married? Desiree needed to get him off the phone.

"No, Aaron, I already told you that wouldn't be ideal . . . Yes, when I find out from Carolyn what our plan will be, I'll let you know then . . . All right, sounds good . . . Yes, thank you . . . No, I appreciate you checking up on me . . . Okay, bye."

Desiree looked up to see Brielle staring her down, her head tilted to the side and her eyebrow raised. "So uhh, would you like to tell me more about this *Aaron* character?"

"Nope. There's nothing to tell." Desiree took a sip from the cup. "Hmm, this is pretty good. Maybe you're right. I didn't need that much sugar." She tried to steer Brielle into talking about the tea, hoping she would drop it about Aaron. "Which brand is this? I'm going to have to get it."

"Some shit from Trader Joes. What else don't I know?"

She didn't take the bait. There was something to tell, and Brielle wanted her to spill it. Desiree tried to stick with the story that Aaron was a lawyer she knew from work, but Brielle reminded her that he was in her hotel room last week. Desiree tried to explain they were assigned as collaborative partners on a merger and acquisition last year and had to work together to get things finalized on it.

"Hmm, a *collaborative* partner. A sexy, deep voice like that. He sounds like he is foine as hell. Y'all worked on getting things finalized all right. What else, Desi?"

"That's it. There's nothing else, Bri." She couldn't mask the smirk on her face.

"Desi!"

"Okay, there was this time after work when everybody went out for drinks. We ended up in my hotel room. But—"

"I knew it! That man sounds like he can lay some pipe too. Why didn't you tell me about him? I thought you weren't getting any dick after you stopped having sex with Jamal."

"I wasn't. It was short lived, so there was nothing to tell. Really, Aaron ain't nobody."

"No, he's somebody. I know you, chick. You don't let any ol' kinda dick get near Carmen. Come on. Gimme the dirty deets on this one."

Desiree giggled, "Fine." She recounted how they'd met and gave Brielle a short summary of her few escapades with Aaron. Desiree told her how he ruined the affair once he started pestering her to leave Jamal. She honestly thought Aaron was good only on paper. They had certain things in common, but she sensed something was off about him. She couldn't pinpoint it, except that Aaron was clingy as fuck, which irritated her.

"He's hella fine, Bri, and the sex was pretty good. He would've been great dick on demand, but I couldn't deal with him being all clingy and stuff."

Brielle chuckled. "You see how long Derrik's been waiting to tap that. It's called having that 'good power-U.'"

"Shut up." Desiree waved her off. "I had to tell him that I still loved Jamal and we were going to try to make our marriage work. That finally got him to leave me alone, and I thought I wouldn't have to see him again, but then he showed up on my flight. Like what are the chances?"

"Uh-huh. What are the chances?" Brielle responded sarcastically and sipped her tea.

"Why did you say it like that?"

77

"You mean to tell me before me or Jamal called, y'all wasn't about to get busy?"

"No, Bri we weren't. How can I think about sleeping with him at a time like this? Did it conveniently slip your mind that I'm pregnant?"

"My bad, you're right."

She sighed, "Another reminder why I wasn't ready to come back. This whole ordeal has me out of sorts."

"You're out of sorts because you need to talk to Derrik. He knows that you're back, so he's going to stop by sooner or later. Hell, I told you he came to my office looking for you. And for the record, I hate being in the middle of all this drama and scandal. He thought you were playing him for a sucka. I told him Troy conned you with his stupid-ass foundation. Although I'm still baffled by how you even fell for that bullshit and went to his house."

Desiree rolled her eyes.

"Well, you did and that was a dumb-ass move, Desi. Look at what it's caused."

"I know," she sighed. "And Bri, there's more. It's why I'm nervous about talking to him."

Brielle gave her a look. "Lord girl, what are you about to tell me that your unsupervised ass has done now?"

She raked a hand through her hair. "I'm pretty sure Troy told him."

"Told him what?"

Desiree took her time recounting what happened the night of the party when Troy approached her while she was alone. He'd promised her they could start over and have a real chance at a life together. Desiree couldn't explain why she'd believed him. She confessed with embarrassment, "I was about to break things off with Derrik. I was going up on stage with Troy to announce that we were getting back together."

"What! With his wife *and* Derrik *and* your husband right there? Oh, you really lost your damn mind over this asshole."

Desiree nodded. "I can admit it. I did in that moment. But when we spoke—"

"Wait, you spoke to him? When?" Brielle interjected.

"Last week when I got to LA."

"You're a glutton for punishment."

"No, I'm not," Desiree retorted. "For your information, after his wife played that video of him attacking her, I accepted right then and there that Troy would never change."

Brielle held her hands out. "Then why did you bother calling him?"

"I wanted to know why he lied to me, Bri. He was about to have me looking stupid again, and I was pissed. Of course, it went over his head. He said I was trifling for sleeping with his boy. He called me a ratchet bitch and claimed he wasn't that pressed for me."

"His ass is lying. He was pressed. He was big mad his boy got that good pussy now. Fuck his ratchet, hoe, bitch ass. Seriously, Desi, I hope you're truly done with Troy. He doesn't deserve any more of your energy, not ever."

Desiree nodded quietly.

"Now, what are you going to do about Derrik? It's time to stop being a punk and talk to him."

"I'm not being a punk. I've been thinking about his feelings. I don't want to hurt him more than I already have. Think how devastating it would be for him to try to start a life with me only to find out this baby isn't his. That would be fucked up and so unfair. He doesn't deserve that, does he?"

Brielle came over and knelt in front of Desiree, grabbing her hands. "No, he doesn't. I'm sorry for being insensitive. I know this can't be easy to deal with."

Desiree leaned back in the loveseat and pulled her hands away. She instinctively cradled her belly as she thought about the unborn child she carried. She wasn't going to tell Derrik about it. Not yet. That would have to come later.

"No, it isn't, Bri. I know I need to talk to him, and I will. In the meantime, I guess I should get home. I need to check on it since you said they trashed my living room."

"And I also told you Derrik hired someone to clean it up. I went by to check, and everything's in place. They even repaired the hole in the wall. He was waiting for you to get back to replace the coffee table and lamps."

"Goodness, I still can't believe they fought."

"I don't know why. Hell, I wish we could've seen it. Derrik said he put a whooping on Troy that shut his eye. I know his red ass was black, blue, and purple.

I want to tag his ass just once myself. He's been asking for it for years, but I am happy that Derrik handled it for me."

"God, you're so hateful. I didn't want that to happen between them. It's what I was afraid of. I knew Troy was never going to be okay with this."

"Of course not, but you can't help who you love, and Desi, that man did not love you the way Derrik does. And I'm not hateful. You know I can't stand Troy. Never could. It's not like y'all were ever going to be a happily-ever-after story. We know Troy wouldn't have been able to keep his hands to himself, and his abusive ass would've had Derrik blacking his eye anyway.

Desire agreed, but she struggled with knowing the two friends fought. Their friendship was likely over, and it was her fault. Brielle reassured her that it wasn't. She also reminded Desiree that Troy wasn't thinking about her all these years until he saw her, and even then, it was only to have sex.

She released a deep sigh. "I just wish it were different."

"That you picked the chocolate one instead, I know."

Desiree nodded. "Yes, I really do."

"You haven't lost him. Not yet. But all of this avoiding him is immature. It's time to be an adult, Desi. Call him. Like right now. And good idea, you should go home because I need your ass outta here. Justin's coming over."

"Huh? Why did you ask me to come chill with you and now you're putting me out? I figured I could stay the night here." Desiree pouted.

Brielle peeked at her Apple watch and cussed. "He texted while I was in the kitchen. I got sidetracked when Aaron called and then we started talking about this. But, yeah, I'mma need your ass to bounce. He should be here in a minute. It'd be different if he weren't staying over. Girl, we talk a lot of shit. I don't need you hearing it."

"Trust me, I'm not trying to hear it either."

"Girrrl, that man is going to make me forget about having anything on demand or reserve."

The doorbell rang. Brielle smiled big and almost ran to answer it. Desiree made it to the foyer in time to witness Justin Walker, a tall, tawny-beige, well-built specimen enter the house. He bent forward, grabbing Brielle's ass with both hands, and gave her the sloppiest of kisses. When he finished, her girl gazed back up at him, completely mesmerized. If it were her, Desiree would've been just as caught up. She couldn't deny how attractive Justin was. He turned his head in her direction and smiled before waving.

"Hey, Desiree!"

She waved back, "Hey, what's up, Justin?"

He returned his attention to Brielle. His Caribbean accent and deep voice sounded as sexy as the rest of him. "Peaches, you didn't tell me she was here. Am I interrupting y'all?"

Brielle glanced over, and Desiree mouthed, *'Peaches?'* Brielle crossed the hall, yanking Desiree by the arm. She gave Desiree the eye and ushered her over to where the luggage sat. Brielle responded to Justin over her shoulder, "No, love, you're not interrupting anything. Desiree just stopped in to say hello. She was getting ready to leave."

"No, I wasn't, *Peaches.*" Desiree whispered.

Brielle hissed, "Shut up, heffa!"

It took everything for Desiree not to laugh. Besides, Brielle's pinch kept her from it. "Ouch!"

Brielle glanced over her shoulder and smiled at Justin. "Love, you can go ahead to the living room. I'm going to walk Desi out."

He nodded in her direction. "Good to see you again, Desiree. I didn't get a chance to thank you for hooking us up." He clapped his hands together and revealed a smile as big as Brielle's. "Thank you and have a good night."

"It was all my pleasure. I'm sure y'all will have a good night too." She stifled a giggle.

He winked at Brielle and disappeared behind the wall.

Desiree began wheeling her luggage out. "It's you who needs to give me the dirty deets, *Peaches!*"

Brielle went to the door and opened it. "Get out and get out now."

Desiree laughed harder as she wheeled past her. She definitely needed to know why Justin gave her that pet name. Brielle followed her outside. Desiree didn't stop teasing her while they loaded her bags in the car.

81

"You're worried about why he's calling me Peaches, but your ass needs to be calling Derrik so y'all can make up. You can have your legs in the air by midnight by your baby daddy."

Desiree opened her mouth to protest.

"Call him."

"Look, I'm calling him now. See?" She held her phone out.

Brielle waved and began heading back towards her house. "All right, call me when you get home, diva. Love you!"

"Love you too, diva!"

Desiree climbed into her Mercedes AMG coupe and ended the call before Derrik could answer.

CHAPTER

11

Troy yawned and stretched before sitting up in bed. He picked up his phone from the nightstand. The corners of his mouth turned up into a full grin once he saw the notifications on the display. He scanned a couple of texts and emails confirming several meetings in the upcoming weeks.

"That's what I'm talking about! They're not playing with your boy!" he exclaimed, jumping from the bed.

His knee locked up. "Ahh fuck, come on!" he hollered. "Not today." He moved to the middle of the bedroom and did a few repetitions of the exercise the rehabilitation specialist taught him. After a fourth set, he started to feel the muscle loosening up, but there was a lingering pain Troy couldn't ignore. He limped towards the bathroom. He opened the medicine cabinet and stared at the bottle for a moment. He didn't want to take the prescription medication, but the pain in his joints was unbearable. The thump radiating through his knee made Troy unscrew the cap and pop a couple of the capsules.

Then he climbed into the six-jet stream shower and turned it to the hottest setting, making sure the hot water focused on his aching knee. Troy stood there for what felt like an hour until the pain dissipated. By the time he emerged from the shower, his hands and toes were wrinkled.

As he dried off, his nose caught a faint trail of what smelled like bacon. He threw on a wife beater and a pair of sweats and stepped into the Nike slides he kept by the door. He wasn't taking any chances, so he went into the nightstand drawer for his Glock, grabbed his phone, and quietly made his way out of the room. When he reached the staircase, he noticed the scent was even stronger.

He wanted to believe Mia had come to her senses and realized what she was doing to them. Perhaps she wanted to surprise him with breakfast. He wasn't so sure since she hadn't returned his calls. When he made it to the bottom step, he slowed his movement to stealth mode. He placed his back against the wall and peeked into the kitchen where he saw two girls preparing breakfast. He recognized one of them right away: the Jamaican honey pot from last night that made sure his nuts were completely drained. Troy slipped the piece in the back of his pants and came into the entryway.

"Umm, ahem."

He startled them. When they realized it was him, they looked at each other, giggling. They turned to look back at him and flirted with a greeting in unison, "Good morning, Troy!"

"Good morning, but uh, can you tell me how y'all got in here?"

The Spanish girl spoke up first, rolling his name off her tongue, "Trrroy, we never left. She said stay, so we cook breakfast for you, sí?"

The Jamaican girl nodded and pointed to the island, "'Ave a seat. Wi nearly finished."

He lowered his eyes. Troy would never allow a woman he barely knew to stay the night, let alone have access to his home. It was an awkward moment as they stared at one another. He went over to the other side of the kitchen and placed the Glock in the drawer. When he turned around, the Jamaican girl had a smirk on her face and winked.

"Last night was wild, yeah mon?" She was the lone dancer he'd kept at his side for the entire night. There was something intriguing about her, and he was drawn to it—her bodacious ass, of course! Just as he was about to smile, his eyes widened. He knew after the number of drinks he'd consumed, his judgment and the actions that followed were questionable. She'd offered him a pill. Troy objected, but she convinced him after proving a few of his teammates were doing it too. She promised it would enhance the sexual experience between them. She wasn't exaggerating about it being a wild night. She reminded him of his wife—she was uninhibited about sex, allowing him to do whatever he wanted, so long as he was satisfied.

Troy shook his head, "Yo, that shit you gave me."

"Yeah mon, yuh irie?"

"What?"

She chuckled, "Are yuh okay?"

"Yeah, I mean no. Is that shit gonna come up in a piss test?"

He didn't allow her to answer as panic settled in. "Shit, it's gonna come back dirty. I can't have nothing fucking this up!"

"Eh, relax, Troy." She quickly made her way over to him and began caressing his arm. She spoke softly, reassuring him. "Everyting will be fine, I promise, yeah. No worries, mmmkay? I'll make sure it won't. Now let me finish cooking for yuh, yeah mon?"

He stared down at her for a moment. She smiled and continued softly caressing his arms. Troy began to relax. "Shit, I am hungry," he confessed.

She flirted, "Wi 'ave more than anuff for yuh to eat."

A pulse shot through his dick. He watched as she purposely tossed her natural, wavy tresses over her shoulder and sashayed to the other side of the kitchen. Her flawless skin looked as though she'd been dipped in honey. He noticed she was wearing one of his t-shirts. It stopped right above her plump ass cheeks, exposing shapely thighs and long legs. He pushed down on the bulge growing in his lap and shifted his position on the bar stool.

"Excuse me, y'all know who I am. Can you give me your names?"

She kissed her teeth and spun around, "Oooh, yuh forget me so soon afta the night we 'ave, eh? Tuh!"

"Girl, stop. You know how much I had to drink. I'm surprised I'm not hungover. Cut me some slack. What's your names?"

She smiled. "I'm Sadé. Dat my gyal Carla."

"*Sadé*," he repeated.

"And Carla," the Spanish girl repeated.

"I heard her, Mami."

She beamed at his endearment for her. Carla was voluptuous as well, but while she was easy on the eyes, Sadé had his complete attention with her exotic features and physique. He could tell she hadn't altered her body the way Carla had done. Sadé's breasts and ass were authentic. He couldn't help thinking of how much her figure matched his wife's. His insatiable appetite included food, but he wanted more of the island beauty.

"How long before breakfast is ready?" he asked.

Carla responded, "Not long. Want a drink, Papi?"

"Yeah, a shot of Henny. I know I'm gonna need it."

Sadé turned to peek at him. Troy winked. She returned a sly smile, knowing what he meant by his statement. Carla was oblivious to their exchange. She poured his drink before sashaying back to the other side of the kitchen next to her companion. The girls finished preparing the meal and brought over a plate filled with grits, eggs, sausage, bacon, and pancakes.

"Damn, y'all wasn't playing. But, how come I didn't get some authentic Spanish or Jamaican food?" he asked, chuckling. "I know both of y'all asses ain't from here. Them accents thick as fuck."

Sadé rotated her neck. "It ain't like yuh got what wi need to trow down in chere, anyway."

He laughed at her feistiness and strong accent. "Good point, sexy." Then he stuffed his mouth before holding up the fork and saying in between chews, "Doubt I'd eat any of that shit anyway. I'm funny about eating certain things."

Sadé licked her lips, "Are yuh now, eh?"

He laughed again, "Let me finish this. I'm gonna make sure you find out exactly what I enjoy eating."

Sadé came over with a pill and another shot glass filled with Hennessy.

He gave her a stern look. "I ain't doing that again."

Carla looked at her and shrugged. Both girls popped theirs. Then Sadé began coaxing him. "Come on, Troy yuh know how it was last night."

"Girl, I'm not tryna fuck up my career behind this little pill. Go 'head, yo."

Sadé took his hand, cupped a handful of her breasts, and squeezed. She bit into her bottom lip as she squatted on top of his knee and started a slow grind. Troy watched her hips, but he could feel the plump lips rubbing against his thigh.

She purred, "Truss me, yuh won't. I'll make sure of it, mmmkay? Let's just 'ave fun yeah, mon? I thought wi celebrate yuh, no?"

Carla came up behind Sadé and wrapped her arms around her waist. "Aye, Papi, you'll need it to handle both of us, sí?"

Troy's eyes lit up as he thought about what that meant. He shook his head and held his hand out. Sadé placed the small pill in his large palm and handed him the shot of Hennessey. He hesitated for a moment. She smiled and gave him a nod of reassurance before affirming again, "Truss me, I got yuh."

He threw the pill and shot back. Then he stared at Sadé and spoke in a serious tone, "I'm telling you Sadé, I'mma fuck you up if my piss comes back dirty."

She gave him a peck on the cheek and sashayed away with Carla right on her heels. Troy couldn't believe the island beauty was peer pressuring him into doing more wild shit, but he was down for it if she was going to make sure his urine came back clean. He enjoyed his breakfast as well as their company. When he finished, Troy left them to make a call while they stayed and cleaned up. About half an hour later, he made his way back into the kitchen. They met him at the island breakfast bar in the middle. He reached for Carla first. She giggled like a schoolgirl when Troy lifted the t-shirt revealing a two-piece G-string set. He pulled it over her head while Sadé assisted by unhooking her friend's bra. He marveled at her voluptuous breasts. He squeezed and juggled them.

"Hmm, now these I can get used to holding on to. Y'all can come over to Papi's house anytime!"

"Aye! Aye! Yes, Papi!" Carla exclaimed.

Then Sadé pulled off her shirt, revealing double D's. She unhooked and threw her bra to the side. Troy released Carla's breasts to give Sadé the same attention. While he massaged her friend's breasts, Carla began tugging at his sweatpants. She gasped in amazement when she released the thick, heavy, brown muscle. It bobbed up and down. Troy purposely made it pulse.

"Oh, mi Dios, you didn't tell me Papi had this much!"

Sadé snickered.

Troy's ego inflated. He massaged the full length of his dick and asked, "Can you handle all of this?"

She dropped down to her hands and knees. He hoisted Sadé onto the island. While Carla started to work on his dick, he ripped Sadé's thong off and spread her thighs wide. He dipped his head low, kissing her moist lips. She leaned back, moaning. He licked them open, revealing the bright pink, wet meat. Her scent turned Troy on in an instant. Even though he was full and satisfied after breakfast, he began devouring her pussy as if he were still hungry.

"Yes!" she cried out.

"Fuck!" Troy grunted the moment he felt the back of Carla's throat.

"You like that, Papi?" she asked, licking the tip.

"Don't stop."

He pushed her head back to finish what she started. Then he shoved two fingers deep inside of Sadé and worked her tight opening while sucking on her clit. She slid to the edge of the island to meet his finger strokes. Troy flipped his fingers upward to stimulate her G-spot. He pushed them in and pulled them out as his thumb rotated on her swollen clit. Carla continued to deep throat his dick while he brought Sadé to an orgasm that drenched her friend's face.

"Yessss!"

He needed to get inside of Sadé's honey pot. "Come on," Troy said as he eased Carla off his dick, now up like a missile.

He escorted the women from the kitchen to the guest bedroom down the hall. He went to the end table and took out a strip of condoms. Then he instructed them both to get on the bed. "Play with each other."

The girls kissed, licked, and teased one another. Troy watched them as he rolled the condom on. He came to the side of the bed and pulled Sadé to the edge. She spread her thighs wide. He didn't hesitate to penetrate her tight space in a long stroke.

Sadé hissed, "Ffffuck!"

"Sit on her face," he commanded Carla.

She took a squat on her girl's face. Troy went deeper, while watching Sadé lick her friend's pussy. That turned him on to go harder. He delivered a hard smack to Carla's ass.

"Oww!"

Her ass wasn't as fat as he liked, so he switched positions and put Sadé on all fours in the doggy style. He instructed Carla to lay on her back so Sadé could eat her pussy. Then he held Sadé's ass cheeks apart and thrust into her.

She pressed her palms against his thighs. "Shhhit!"

"Nah uh! Don't run from me." He spoke through each stroke, "You wanted . . . this . . . dick. Now . . . take . . . it."

He gave her a hard slap on her ass that made the right cheek jiggle. He rubbed the left cheek and delivered another hard slap that made Sadé knees buckle. Troy pulled her ass closer and pushed her back down into a perfect arch. He drove deeper, slapping his balls against her ass.

"I wanna see you make her come, Sadé," he commanded.

Troy continued to jackhammer away at Sadé's pussy while watching her suck Carla's clit. When he saw Carla squirt, he almost lost it. He pulled out for a moment to regain his composure. He walked over to the desk on the other side of the room. Troy motioned for them as he sat down. The girls wasted no time making their way over to him. He made Sadé sit on the edge of the desk and pulled Carla to sit on him.

"Eat her pussy, Carla. I wanna see you make her come too."

She spread her girl's lips apart and slid her tongue deep inside, licking at her walls.

"Oooh, Carla," Sadé moaned.

"Damn! Y'all really know how to please Papi."

A few minutes later, he could feel the sensation rising in his abdomen. He didn't want to stop, but Carla's up and down motion was becoming too much. Watching her eat Sadé out and her ass bouncing against his thighs was bringing him to climax and fast.

"I'm about to come. Shit!"

"Wait, Papi, no!" Carla shouted.

Carla got up, and Sadé hopped of the desk. Both girls went to their knees. Sadé quickly eased the condom off and popped his dick into her mouth. She began working it with her hands just as he erupted. Troy's body went stiff. Then he jerked as the girls shared licking up the milky fluid that shot from his dick.

"Ahhh shhhhit! Wait! Stop! Stop! Urrrrgh." He convulsed and held on to both girls' heads as they continued sucking his dick, draining him of all his cum.

The girls giggled, wiping their mouths as they pulled away.

"You good, Papi?" Carla asked.

At that moment, he reflected on his life. His football career had not yet ended. Even though Mia remained upset and kept him in the doghouse, he had two beautiful women at his feet, ready to fuck him any way he wanted. Nothing could make him any more content.

Troy rubbed his head and chuckled, "Yeah, Mami, I am. I really am."

CHAPTER

12

"Hey! Wait a minute! What are you guys doing? Not here. Set up over there and right there, please. Tanya, make sure they set up cameras over there as well," Mia instructed.

"Why? I thought we were good in those areas."

"I need to be sure we capture everyone. You never know, we might record the scumbag here. You know what kind of ratings that would bring in?"

Tanya frowned. "Do you think this is a good idea, Mia?"

"Of course. This is a great idea. Where else in here do you think we can get a good angle?"

"I meant filming today. Do you think it's appropriate?"

Mia waved her off, "My girl is looking for her brother's killer, and one thing I know from watching *Criminal Minds* is that they're always around the victim's family as if they didn't do it. The killer could be right under our noses today. I want to be sure we put it out there."

"This isn't *Criminal Minds*, though."

"Pretend it is then."

Tanya ran a hand through her short, auburn curls. She decided against disagreeing with or questioning Mia further. "You guys heard her. Get those cameras set up over there. Yes, over there, and keep one close to where the family will be seated." Then she spoke to a lone cameraman, "You and I will follow Mia."

Before she could walk away, Tanya grabbed Mia's arm gently and pulled her to the side. "Mia, are you sure Angela will be okay with all of this?"

Mia blew out an impatient breath. "Yes, Tanya, I'm sure. Will you just relax? Look, I discussed everything with her the other day. She talked to her mom about it, and her mom is fine with it. This might flush out some information on her brother. When people get on camera, they start running their mouths. Give folks five minutes of fame, and you get all the dirt on everybody. Trust me, we're going to get something."

"All right then. We did a soundcheck, and your mic is good. Everybody's in place and ready to record once everything gets started."

"Okay, we should be good to go then. You know what? Let me say my spiel now. Wait, how's my hair?"

"You look flawless, Mia."

"Of course, I do."

Tanya grumbled under her breath as she signaled for the cameraman to come over. "All right, Mia, we're ready in five, four, three, two, and go."

"Today is difficult. I'm mourning the loss of a beautiful soul. My best friend's brother, Ricardo Trevor Alvarez, who was affectionately known as Tré to his family and Rico to his friends, is being laid to rest today. He was murdered, and we need to bring his killer or killers to justice. We know they are still out there. If you have any information on his murder, please share it with the Atlanta police. The Alvarez family is asking that you come forward with any information that might help. Thank you." Then she bowed her head as if to shed a tear.

Tanya held her hand up. "Okay, Mia, that was awesome. Wow, you're natural in front of the camera."

She beamed as she tossed her bone straight, jet black, hair over her shoulder. "Ha! Tell me something I don't know. You already see how it's been working out for me so far. Let's go sit down before the masses get in here. I heard it's going to be crowded. Trust me. This playboy had a lot of hoes. I expect most of Atlanta to turn out for this one."

Tanya opened her mouth in shock but held her tongue. She followed Mia down the aisle to their seats. Mia instructed the crew to start recording as soon as the funeral-goers began filing into the sanctuary. She then turned to Tanya to talk about her plans for their next taping.

Meanwhile, outside of the church, Brielle pulled into a parking space near the front. "I hate funerals," she mumbled.

Desiree sighed. "Yeah, me too."

"Let's hurry up and find somewhere to sit before it gets too crowded," Brielle said, shifting into park.

They entered the sanctuary and moved toward the front middle rows. Desiree quickly scanned the room to see if she could locate Derrik, but the mega church started filling up quickly. She bowed her head, pretending to look in her program. Brielle raised a brow.

"What?"

"Nothing." She didn't know who Desiree thought she'd be fooling, attempting to disguise herself with a hat and veil. She couldn't blame her girl for trying, though. Just then someone caught Brielle's attention. "Will you look at who's here with cameras."

"Unbelievable. How tacky can she be? Did she even know Rico?" Desiree asked.

"I don't know. That crazy bitch probably just wants some extra attention. Tasteless for sure bringing her camera crew up in here like that."

A few minutes later, the pastor approached the podium. "Family and friends, we are gathered here today not to mourn the loss of our brother, Ricardo Trevor Alvarez, but to celebrate his life here on earth. His family does not want you to be sad, but rather to rejoice, for he has gone home to be with our Father in heaven. Let us bow our heads in prayer . . ."

Desiree found it hard to pay attention once the pastor began the service. She pondered over her options and how to deal with Derrik moving forward. If she decided to keep the baby and it belonged to him, did that mean he would overlook what she'd done with Troy? Would he believe she was finally over him? Then she thought of the baby being Troy's and dreaded the idea of telling him. What was his wife doing there? Why was she there recording their friend's funeral? She was so lost in her thoughts that she didn't realize it was time to view Rico's body until Brielle nudged her.

As they approached the casket, the women held on to each other's hands tightly. Desiree allowed the tears to fall as she said goodbye to her friend. When they walked past the family, Desiree tried to hide her look of shock when she saw Jamal and the woman from Troy's party in the front row. Jamal made sure to keep his attention on Angela instead of making eye contact with them. Brielle noticed when a cameraman moved in closer as they walked by. She shot Mia a glare, and Mia returned a smug grin.

Once they reached their pews, Desiree leaned over and whispered. "What the hell is that about?"

Brielle started to respond, but something else caught their attention.

A distinguished-looking gentleman approached the casket and planted a kiss on Rico's forehead. Another man shocked everyone with how much he cried over Rico while laying his head on his chest. "You did not deserve this. Not like this . . . no, not like this!" he cried out.

Desiree stared at Brielle in bewilderment. Before she could say anything, another man started crying out his name.

"Oh dear God, not you. Our dear, sweet Rico! Just look at you!"

"Oh, lawd!" a second one shouted.

Then a third man yelled, "Why Lord, whyyy!"

It took several of the ushers to get them away from the casket. Desiree couldn't help but join Brielle in chuckling at the tasteless spectacle the men were making of themselves.

Brielle whispered, "I'm sorry, but I've seen too many men and women crying over this pretty boy in here today."

Jamal knew they would come and show out. He watched as countless men and women cried over his former lover. When it was their turn to say goodbye, the guilt weighed heavy on his shoulders. He was the reason Rico was lying there.

He approached the casket with Angela holding on to him tightly. Jamal tried to swallow the lump rising in his throat, but it remained there. His feet didn't move. Rico was barely recognizable. The embalmer had done her best to make him look like the handsome man he once was, but the swelling had distorted his face, and his skin was dull and darkened from the lack of blood flow. That cold shell was all that was left of his friend. Jamal stared for what seemed like an eternity.

In between her sobs, Angela began to wail, "Oh Dios, no! Oh God, no! I'm so sorry, Tré! I'm so sorry! Please don't leave me! Please, don't leave me!"

Desiree and Brielle exchanged confused expressions, unsure what to think. It wasn't clear to either of them why the woman clinging to Jamal's arm was so upset.

They watched as Rico's mother raised her hands to the sky and cried, "¿Por qué a mi bebé? No Ricardo! Oh Dios, no a mi bebé. No es mi bebé precioso!"

Jamal held on to Angela's waist as she reached out to the casket. He pulled her into his arms, trying to console her as much as he could.

The pain in her eyes tore into his soul as she cried, "Nooooo, Jamal! Oh, mi Dios, por favor! Not my brother!"

Desiree gasped and whispered, "His sister!"

Brielle opened her mouth then quickly closed it, shaking her head.

Jamal and a young man, presumably another family member, guided the hysterical women back to their seats. Desiree watched as Jamal consoled her until she calmed down. It was unbelievable that he was sleeping with Rico's sister. Then seeing Troy's wife with her cameramen swarm around while she appeared to care but still record the whole thing, was appalling. Desiree had seen enough and was ready to go. Once the pastor closed the service, they tried to move with a big crowd heading out the doors, but a woman grabbed Brielle's arm, pulling her to the side.

"Brielle Stephens?"

"Leah, is that you?"

"Yes, it is." She and Brielle shared a friendly hug. "Too crazy running into you here. You knew Rico too?"

She nodded, "Yeah, Rico was my boy."

"Let me guess—you tried to holla."

"Girl! You know I did, but umm, looks like he was batting for both sides. We were just saying that, right, Desi?"

Desiree shot Brielle a look of annoyance. Brielle didn't catch on.

"Leah, where are my manners? This is Desiree Edwards, my very best girlfriend, my sister from another mister. Desi, this is a classmate and soror of mine, Leah Goldman. Wait, you didn't get married, did you?"

"Girl, no. You see where all the good men of Atlanta are going. I need to take my black ass elsewhere. But what have you been up to? I heard you got a popping event planning business. We need to talk."

Desiree grew impatient listening to Brielle and Leah's chatter. She was ready to get out of there. Just then, a bunch of people started heading to the exit. Someone grabbed her hand and pulled her through the crowd, guiding her towards a hallway away from everyone. Her hat obstructed the view in front of her, but she knew the smooth, manicured hand that held a tight grip on hers. *Derrik.*

He pulled Desiree into the middle of the corridor, gently pushed her against one of the doors, and tossed the hat. He placed his hands against the wall on either side of her, cutting off a route for escape. "It's time to stop avoiding me."

His hot breath tickled her nose. Fresh and minty as always, it mixed with the scent of his Giorgio Armani cologne. Her eyes traveled from the deep crevice in the center of his chin up to his full lips. She fought the urge to kiss them. She truly missed him. When their eyes met, she saw something unfamiliar: anger. They'd never been upset with each other. The vacancy in his dark brown eyes sent a shiver up her back. The increased pounding of her heart filled her eardrums. She closed her eyes.

"Desiree?"

She opened her eyes slowly and pleaded, "Derrik, could we do this later? This is Rico's funeral."

He leaned in closer, cheek to cheek, his lips pressed against her ear. His voice was low, almost raspy. "I respect our boy and all, but this shit is hard as hell, baby girl. You expect me to be in the same room with you and not say anything?"

"No," she managed to reply in a breathless whisper.

Being so close to him made her tingle, igniting every neuron in her body. Desiree could feel the heat from her core rising. Derrik moved his face to meet her at eye level, their noses and lips almost touching. "You're embarrassed this happened. I know. And I'm pretty sure you're worried about what's going to happen now. I get that too. We're going to talk about it. Not later, but right now."

The time had come to face what she'd done, and she felt unprepared. She was over the embarrassment, but she worried that there was no way to fix any of it. She rubbed her bare arm anxiously, and her eyes went to the floor.

Derrik cupped her chin and lifted it, forcing her to make eye contact with him. "I need to know how it happened."

Out of nowhere, Brielle squeezed herself between them. Derrik took a couple of steps back as Brielle picked up Desiree's hat and pointed it in his direction. "Dammit, Derrik! I can't believe you pulled this shit here of all places. Today ain't the day. Why couldn't you respect the fact that we're burying a damn good friend of ours? You two can deal with this mess later."

His eyes were on Desiree when he responded, "I've paid my respects. We all have. Desi's avoided me for almost two weeks. Not anymore, Bri. I know she came here with you, but she's leaving with me."

Brielle didn't show it, but she was happy hearing that. She nodded at Derrik and handed Desiree the hat. "Call me later, diva."

"Okay, diva."

He waited for Brielle to leave before guiding Desiree down the opposite end of the corridor and out the back door that led to the parking lot for the pastor and other church staff. Hodges stood waiting next to a black Bentley Bentayga with tinted windows and Forgiato rims. By the time they reached him, he'd opened the back door. Derrik helped Desiree inside and scooted in beside her, leaving no space between them. His gaze was fixed on hers. His expression was nearly terrifying. He'd been thinking about her reason for backsliding with Troy since that day in her living room. Could it be about revenge, like Troy said? Derrik didn't want to believe that, but he would have his answer soon.

"Where to, Boss?" Hodges asked over his shoulder after starting the ignition.

"Her house." His gaze was fixed on her hazel orbs.

Desiree's throat felt tight. She wasn't sure what to say or if she should say anything at all. It didn't matter. She didn't know where to begin. Her mind was a jumbled mess. Derrik finally averted his eyes and turned to look straight ahead. He relaxed against the buttery, red leather seats and tilted his head back. His thoughts were scattered, just like Desiree's.

Technically, his house was closer, and he would have liked to have taken Desire there, but he couldn't. Khloe's new venture kept her holed up in his guest suite. When she wasn't working on stuff for that, she spent her free time working on his dick. He'd lied, telling her he had to go handle some business out of state. But for the past few days, he'd been staying in a suite up at the Whitley, just down the street from his office. Derrik hated lying, but he couldn't think straight with Khloe around. He'd distanced himself to clear his head.

Desiree shifted in the seat, yanking him out of his mind and back into the SUV with her. The cool air from the vents blew Gucci Guilty right into his nostrils. Derrik lifted his head. When he glanced at her, she avoided his eyes. He gave her a once-over. Still beautiful and sexy as ever. The hem of the black dress stopped right at her thighs. Derrik's eyes followed the length of her curvy bowlegs all the way down to her Christian Louboutin stilettos. Her toenails were painted apple red. As his gaze swept up, he noticed the tiny bumps forming on her arms.

He caressed the arm closest to him. "Are you cold?"

Her entire body tingled from that touch. More bumps appeared. Desiree rubbed where his fingers were seconds before. "No."

"Are you sure? I can turn it down if you'd like."

"Yes, I'm sure and no, it feels fine."

"The air is blowing right on us, and you have goosebumps, Desi. It must be chilly in here."

"It's not from the air."

He studied her for a moment. "This happened from me looking at and touching you?"

Derrik's mere presence affected her senses and caused her body to react. Desiree swallowed and nodded.

He didn't say anything else after that. Instead, he turned and stared in front of them. He slid his hand from his lap to her thigh and squeezed hard. A short gasp escaped Desiree's lips. Her gaze followed the muscular tattooed arm down to his smooth hand, now wedged between her thighs. His caressed the inner part. The more he squeezed and rubbed, the more intense the thrumming inside her pussy became. She shifted again, and a puddle of lust filled her panties. Derrik didn't move his hand. He kept it there for the remainder of the ride.

It wasn't long before Hodges parked in front of her house. Desiree released a quiet sigh of relief. She couldn't take the torture anymore. She was on the borderline of delirium from being so close to him, inhaling the cedar musk scent of his cologne, and feeling his hand inches from her now drenched pussy. She'd secretly hoped they would hit a bump. Maybe his hand would've slipped and rubbed against her aching clit. Hodges opened the door. Derrik got out and offered his hand. Desiree took her time sliding across the leather seats, saying a silent prayer that she wasn't leaving a trail of lust. He helped her out of the SUV, and she peeked back. Nothing.

By the time they reached the front door, uneasiness crept in. Derrik stood no more than an inch behind her. If she took even half of a step back, her ass would've been on his crotch. She fumbled the keys and ended up dropping them. She watched as he bent forward to retrieve them. Desiree licked her lips when Derrik leaned in front of her to unlock the door. She inhaled deeply, enamored with his natural odor mixed with the cologne. He walked in and handed her the keys. She placed her bag and keys on the sofa table. Desiree turned to face him. It was then that she saw how sexy he looked in his casual attire. He was dressed in a white collared shirt, rolled up sleeves with a few of buttons left unfastened, revealing part of the cross and wings tattooed on his chest. His black, tailored slacks were fitted to him in all the right places. She smiled, noticing he also rocked a pair of red bottoms. Their outfits appeared to be well-coordinated, although it wasn't planned. When her eyes met his she saw the cold, vacant look again. She looked down, pretending to pick at her nails.

"Are you ready to talk?"

She remembered her panties. "Could you give me a minute. I need to use the bathroom."

Derrik's eyes narrowed, and Desiree realized right away why he gave her that look. She reassured him she was only going to the bathroom and would be right back. He chose to sit on the side of the plush sectional facing the direction of the staircase. Derrik checked his phone and saw the missed voice and FaceTime calls from Khloe. She'd also texted, asking if he'd made it back in town for the funeral. He responded quickly and slipped the phone in his pocket before Desiree reappeared. She sat in the corner of the couch facing him. Derrik moved to the edge, rested his elbows on his thighs, and clasped his hands together. He stayed in that position, staring at her for more than a minute.

She couldn't take the silence anymore. "Derrik, please say something."

"What do you want me to say, Desi?"

"Something, anything. This silence is excruciating."

"Heh, so you don't like the silent treatment either?"

Desiree frowned. "No, I don't. I thought we were going to talk. Are we? Or are you going to sit over there and shoot daggers at me?"

He leaned back and let out a sardonic laugh. "Funny how you're ready now, but only because I ambushed you. Were you ever going to call me? Or were you going to call Troy again?"

Her face reddened in embarrassment. She wasn't ready for that. "Yes, I was going to call you, and no, I'm never calling him again. I've blocked his number."

"When did you block it? After I found out you were fucking him too?"

Desiree flinched, but she kept her voice steady. "No, he didn't deserve to have access to me anymore. Derrik, I know I was wrong, and I'm so sorry. I didn't mean to cross the line, I—"

"Stop." His voice was low. "Tell me how the fuck you allowed that to happen? Was this some stunt to get back at him? I thought *we* were starting something. You played me."

Her eyes went to the floor.

"Look at me, Desi."

Her stomach twisted in knots. She'd never heard him sound angry. Her voice trembled when she spoke. "No, I didn't do it to get back at him. I swear it was never my intent to sleep with him. And, Derrik, I wasn't playing you. You have to know that."

He didn't say a word as he glared at her. Tears welled in her eyes. She took a deep breath and continued. "Running into you was the best thing that ever happened to me. Like it was meant to happen . . . destined. But when Troy showed up, everything got complicated." She paused and took another deep breath. "He told me how he'd changed, that he never meant to hurt me, and that he didn't love Mia the way he loved me. I believed him. I got confused and wasn't sure if I was making the right decision about us."

"And fucking him was a better decision?"

"No, and I'm not making any excuses for what I did, but we both know how things ended with Troy and me. I guess part of me wasn't over him. I fell for it because he was my first love and—"

"This doesn't make me feel better. At all. I thought it would, but I'm more pissed now that I'm talking to you."

Desiree's voice quivered, "Derrik, I—"

"The fuck was you thinking, Desi? I don't understand women doing this shit. Always running back to the nigga that hurt you. He wasn't even checking for you! Wasn't thinking about you! He didn't want you until he saw you!"

"I realize that now." Tears of shame slid down her cheeks.

Derrik frowned, unsure of how to continue. Her tears didn't sway him. He turned his head in disgust. The wall he had to repair was in his view. His jaw tightened. He squeezed his fists, and a vein bulged in his neck. "He put his fucking hands on you, Desi! Why would you want to go back to that? Did you like that shit or something?"

"No!" she whimpered.

"You thought—no, *believed* he changed though. Pfft, you really didn't know him. And this ain't on no snitching shit either 'cause the streets knew about it, but he was fucking Mia when y'all were together. That nigga loves her. You saw how fast he put a ring on it. Trust that if you did go back to him thinking y'all were going to be together, it wouldn't have lasted. He would've gone right back to her like he always does."

His words hit Desiree like bullets. Her mouth dropped open. Brielle always said Troy screwed anything that wasn't nailed down. She never wanted to believe he cheated while they were together.

"What you don't get is, yeah, he would've been pissed about us. So, what! He would've gotten over it. Hell, we still might've fought. Again, he would've gotten over it. But you had to fuck him for ol' time's sake, right? He threw that shit in my face, Desi. Fuck! I gave you my heart, and you stomped on it."

"I-I don't know what else to say, Derrik, except I'm sorry. I didn't mean to betray you, I swear. I know he doesn't love me. And I don't love him like I love you. I'm so so sorry."

He stood up and gave her a dirty look. "Sorry? That's it, and everything is supposed to be good? It doesn't work like that. You and me? Nah, I can't do this."

She hopped up. "Derrik, please! Don't do this."

"I didn't do this to us, Desi. You did. Fucked him, knowing I would find out. And I didn't forget how you hauled ass like some runaway slave. You didn't call me and try to fix this sooner. But you called that nigga. For what! Why? That shit is fucking with me more than anything else. Nah, you don't get to play with my heart, Desi. No woman does. I'm done. I've got to get out of here."

"Noooo! Pleeease!" she sobbed as desperate tears ran down her cheeks. "I'm sorry, so sorry. I love you. I swear I do, Derrik. I want you and only you!"

At that point, he felt nothing but contempt for her. There was nothing else to say. He headed towards the door. Desiree latched on to his forearm, trying to pull him back. He fought everything inside not to shove her away. Derrik closed his eyes and inhaled deeply. He opened his eyes, and his gaze went to her hand. "Let go."

"Please, Derrik don't go." Desiree pleaded, but Derrik wouldn't even look at her.

He looked towards the door and repeated his request through clenched teeth. "Let me go."

She released her grip on his arm. Feeling helpless, she watched him walk out the door and slam it closed. Overwhelmed by her aching heart, Desiree collapsed to the floor. She pulled her knees into the fetal position and bawled.

CHAPTER
13

Derrik kept his head low as he and Hodges walked through the family room. He barely acknowledged Khloe and her assistant as he made his way over to the bar. He poured a shot for himself and his bodyguard. "To Rico, one of the good guys. Gone too soon, right?" Derrik raised his glass.

Hodges held his glass up. "Yeah, far too soon."

They tapped the bar before throwing the shots back. Derrik refilled the empty glasses. They gulped those down. He started to pour again, and Hodges held his hand up. He motioned for Khloe's assistant.

"Boss, if you don't need me. I wanted to take her out for a little while."

Derrik refilled his glass and swallowed the contents before responding. "Nah, I'm good. You go ahead. If I decide to leave, I'll get one of the other guys to drive me. Thanks again, Hodg'. I appreciate you, man. Y'all have a good night."

"Aight, Boss. Remember what I said. See you later."

Khloe waited until they left the room before she walked over to Derrik. "Derrik, are you going to be okay?"

"Yeah, I'll be fine," he mumbled. He poured another glass and knocked it back.

"I've never seen you like this. Who was this guy Rico that passed away?"

Derrik didn't respond. His mind was elsewhere. He'd hoped talking to Desiree would resolve things, but that didn't happen. Perhaps he'd been in it alone the whole time, and Desiree wasn't feeling him the way she claimed. Derrik realized his foolish mistake of believing the time they spent together was enough to erase anything she might have felt towards Troy. Hearing her try to explain herself only made it worse. Out of anger he'd yelled, which he hadn't intended to do. But he couldn't help it. He'd never felt the kind of pain that swept through him. His heart ached. He could barely look at her. He couldn't think of anything else to do except cut ties. She'd cried so hard, worse than that day Troy dumped her. He'd almost caved in and retracted his words. Derrik had to leave. By the time he climbed in the back of the truck, his dam broke. Hodges had sat motionless for at least ten minutes while he sobbed.

"Man, Hodg' I ain't never cried over no fucking woman!" Derrik sniffled.

Hodges nodded in silence.

"She's not going to have me out here looking like a simp though. And I'm not competing with a nigga that wasn't even worth her time or energy. She knew I could show her the love she deserved, but she still went back to that abusive motherfucker. No, I'm done."

More tears came as Derrik thought about the years he spent pining over Desiree. She was probably damaged goods. He'd been a fool thinking she would be open to receive a love like his after Troy. It hurt like hell knowing she'd contacted Troy instead of him. He realized then that she would never truly be his. When the tears stopped and he calmed his nerves, Derrik told Hodges he was ready to go home. Hodges didn't move.

"Did you hear me, Hodg'? We can swing by the suite to get my stuff and go home."

The big man turned in his seat. His bodyguard, who spoke few words, stared him down and gave Derrik an earful once more.

"Boss, I've been rocking with you for almost a decade. There've been a lot of women over the years. But there's something special between you and Desi. It was there long before y'all even linked up. Okay she fucked up. Sometimes we do impulsive shit in the heat of the moment. My mama said ain't none of us humans perfect. We don't give each other enough grace when we make mistakes. Mama also said when it comes to love we can't control when it happens or where it might lead us. The heart, after all, is a compass. It just knows what it wants to feel and how to get there. It wants what it wants, and there ain't nothing you can do 'bout it. Yeah, you love her, Boss and there ain't nothing or nobody that's gonna change that. Not even this. And you ain't no simp for loving her the way you do. I ain't saying you should forgive and forget what's happened. But before you make a final decision, take the time you need to process all of this. All of it. Then let your heart guide you, and see if you're really done."

"Aww, my beloved I'm so sorry about your loss." Khloe's soft voice interrupted his thoughts about Desiree's betrayal. She came from behind and wrapped her arms around his waist, pressing her face against his back.

He pulled away, but she reached for his arm and pleaded. "I want to be here for you, my beloved. Can't you see I'm trying to console you?"

He couldn't tell her the real reason behind his silent behavior moments earlier. Nor could he explain why he wanted to distance himself. He was wrong to reject Khloe when her intention was to provide comfort. Derrik relaxed his shoulders. "Thanks, Klo. I'm sorry. This was unexpected, and all of us, you know, his friends are having a hard time digesting what's happened. I'll be fine. I need to take a shower. Maybe I'll grab something to eat and lie down."

"Well, dinner's been taken care of." Khloe told him she'd made dinner while they were out. She would get a plate ready, so he could eat after he showered.

A few minutes later, he was in his bedroom getting undressed. His thoughts went back to his dilemma with Desiree. Nothing would change the fact she'd slept with both of them and went back to Troy behind his back. Maybe Troy was right, and Desiree wasn't over him. Maybe Desiree was using him as a rebound, just like Brielle said she did with her husband, Jamal. Derrik stomped towards the bathroom. Several minutes later, he emerged from the shower feeling somewhat refreshed. He wrapped the towel around his waist and went into the bedroom. The faint scent of Khloe's cooking filled the room. He decided he would take her up on the offer of dinner. He went over to the dresser to grab a pair of sweats. He felt the towel being yanked off.

He turned around. "Khloe, what the fu—"

She took a handful of Derrik's package, squeezing and pulling. Khloe massaged the length of his shaft. She stroked from the base to the head producing the clear, sticky liquid from his pee hole. He looked down at his muscle swelling in her hands.

If he wanted to sulk about his woes, he couldn't. Desiree didn't think about him when she decided to backslide with Troy. Derrik's subconscious conjured up Troy's words again. *She don't want you! You see she came back!*

Khloe's soft voice interrupted his internal battle. "Oooh, look at what I did."

His voice was low and husky, "What are you going to do with all of that?"

She dropped to her knees, lifted the semi-hard muscle, and swiped her tongue across his balls. She ran her tongue along the length of his shaft and squeezed his balls as she licked the precum from the tip. She opened her mouth and allowed Derrik to guide it into her hot mouth. She bobbed her head, taking in as much of his thick muscle as she could, but she kept gagging on it.

It popped into his mind that Desiree wouldn't have had any problems getting all of his dick in her mouth. He pushed the thoughts of her to the side as he glanced down at Khloe sucking and slurping. She did a damn good job getting his dick to stand at attention. He helped her up to her feet and turned her around. Khloe spread her legs and bent forward gripping her ankles. Derrik rubbed the tip of his engorged head at her entrance. Leaning in more and rotating his hips, he attempted to loosen her, but she wasn't lubricated enough. "Come here."

He guided her over to the bed. She scooted up to the middle and opened her thighs. Derrik's lips aligned with her vertical lips. He used his thumb and forefinger to open them. His mouth covered the protruding button. He suctioned the nub in, alternating between sucking, nibbling, and licking. Khloe held his head and grinded on his face.

"Yes, that's it, my beloved. Eat this pussy!"

He sucked and licked her clit as if it were a lollipop. His slick tongue went back and forth, swirling around the swollen nub. Khloe reached down and spread her pussy lips wider. He slid his tongue inside. He flicked up, down, and around, darting in and out of her pussy. He went back to sucking her clit. With his palm up, he thrust his two middle fingers inside. She clenched the sheets and shuddered. Derrik sucked and finger fucked her until she begged for it.

"Fuck me, Derrik!"

He came up on his knees and wedged himself between her thighs. He used his dick to split the juicy folds, coating himself in her wetness. He pushed into the warmth of her body. Khloe wrapped her arms around his neck, lifting her hips to match his rhythmic strokes.

"This is some good pussy," Derrik mumbled as he squeezed her breasts, sucking her nipples.

Khloe echoed his praises, "This is some good dick!"

Derrik glided in and out. Her vaginal muscles clenched down on his shaft as if she were giving it a tight hug. She arched her back as he brought her to an orgasm. He switched positions, laying on his back and pulling Khloe on top of him. She straddled his thighs. Derrik held her ass, bringing her down slowly. He let her control the pace for a few. She worked her hips, gyrating back and forth, riding him slow and steady. He thrusted up and Khloe let out a yelp. She lifted up and came down, meeting his upward thrust. She cried out each time Derrik met her halfway. He smirked knowing it was too much. He flipped them over again, putting Khloe on her knees. She pressed her face into the pillows as he spread her ass cheeks. He sucked his thumb saturating it with saliva. He withdrew it from his mouth and pushed it in her anus as he slid his dick into her pussy. Slowly he worked his thumb and dick in both holes at the same time. Khloe's body trembled with intense pleasure. He removed his thumb and slapped her ass as he fucked her hard.

"Ooooh shit!"

"That's it. Throw that ass back, girl."

Khloe made her ass cheeks clap when she moved forward and backward on his dick. Derrik watched as the cream trickled down her thighs. The juicy sounds sent him overboard. He felt her walls constrict around his dick again.

"Shit!" Derrik grunted. He pulled out and exploded, coating her ass of his hot seed. They collapsed onto the bed with Derrik's body covering hers. A few minutes later, he rolled off Khloe onto his back and laid there staring at the ceiling.

She was an insatiable lover. Hodges was right; he enjoyed being with her, and he did care deeply for her. However, it wasn't enough for him to forget everything he'd begun to build with Desiree. Khloe's fingertips traced the tattoos across his chest. When she lifted her head and looked into his eyes, it was as if she could read his mind.

"Derrik, how come you never give us a real try?"

"I knew this was coming. There's always an angle with you. Is that why you're really here? Am I also one of these so-called business ventures?"

She half nodded. "I'd be lying if I said it hadn't crossed my mind, knowing I'd be coming this way. Yeah, why not try and lock this down?"

"Klo, we know where this always ends up. Why try to go down this road again? We don't have to fix what's not broken. We're good."

"What is it, Derrik? What would it take for this to work where it's you and me? Is it because I'm too old now? Don't you think I'm beautiful anymore? Or is it because I can't have babies for you?"

He gazed down at her. He pushed the hair to the side that covered her eye. "You're more than just beautiful to me, Khloe. Why would you ask that of all things?"

She shrugged bashfully.

"Age isn't a factor either. You're the model for black don't crack. Shit, you could put a 20-year-old to shame. And I understood why you couldn't have kids. I knew it back then, and I've always been cool with it."

"Then what is it?"

He lied. "I don't know, maybe it's been timing. I've been so wrapped up in growing BlakBeatz all these years, a relationship and kids have been the furthest things from my mind." Derrik knew focusing on his business was not the reason he was hesitant to start a relationship with Khloe. For a couple of years, they tried but it didn't solidify into anything. Initially, it was both of their busy schedules preventing them from being together the way he wanted. He wasn't returning to Boston, and she wasn't relocating to Atlanta. He hated long distance relationships, so it worked for them to hook up when they could. Then he met Desiree. His undying love for her kept him from trying anything further with Khloe. There were times he thought about the day he would have to cut their ties. He knew it wouldn't be easy.

She snuggled closer. "I think you should give us a try. What if I moved here?"

"You wouldn't like it down here."

"This area is absolutely gorgeous. Besides, I'm growing tired of the cold winters up there."

"You'd never leave Boston, Klo."

She lifted her head and spoke with certainty, "Say the word, and I swear I will."

CHAPTER
14

Mia ended the call and reclined in her chair. A smile crept onto her face. She'd done the right thing.

She was intrigued when she noticed her husband's best friend, Derrik, show up at Tré's funeral. She became suspicious when she saw him grab a mysterious woman and escort her to the back of the church. He appeared angry as he led her away from the funeral attendees. When Derrik and the woman stopped in the middle of the hall, they didn't notice that Mia and one of her cameramen had followed them and slipped into a side hallway nearby. As Derrik and the mystery woman began a heated exchange, Mia instructed her cameraman to keep recording.

"You know they're going to confiscate this video," Tanya pointed out.

"How? Weren't you listening? I never told them we recorded anything. And I know they weren't tracing my call because it was the anonymous tip line. I didn't have to give them my name. They have no clue who or where the info came from. At least they have a lead now."

Tanya sighed. Her client was on a mission to gain fame even if it wasn't associated with her husband. She couldn't believe Mia gave the police misleading information about Angela's brother. She didn't feel the footage captured had anything to do with his murder. Mia was insistent they could be the ones who helped crack the case. This had Tanya baffled.

Mia questioned. "What are you so worried about? I told you we might catch something. You never know how this might help with the investigation."

"I'm not worried. I don't think this will help them. Do you even know who that girl was with Derrik?"

"No, but it feels like I've seen her somewhere before. I thought it strange he would pull her off to the side. Then there's Brielle Stephens, the coordinator from Troy's party. She was back there too. That's what really got to me. It all seems suspect."

"That's what I don't understand, Mia. Is that what you got out of their whole exchange?"

"Yeah. He was pissed about something he found out she did. She was probably one of Tré's flings. Maybe she was the one who helped with his murder."

"No. It sounded like they had something else going on and it wasn't about Angela's brother."

Mia tapped her chin. "Only way to find out is if we take another look at it. But I'm pretty sure I gave the police a possible lead."

"No, you didn't. I bet it was a waste of footage," Tanya debated as she got up from the lounge chair on the other side of Mia's office. She retrieved the remote control from her desk, turned on the wall-mounted, fifty-inch flat screen, and played the video. "Right here, pay attention."

"Turn it up, so I can hear better." Mia ordered.

"Desiree?"

"Derrik, could we do this later? This is Rico's funeral."

"I respect our boy and all, but this shit is hard as hell, baby girl. You expect me to be in the same room with you and not say anything?"

"No."

"You're embarrassed this happened. I know. And I'm pretty sure you're worried about what's going to happen now. I get that too. So, we're going to talk about it. Not later, but right now. I need to know how it happened."

Tanya paused the recording. "See, that didn't sound like it had anything to do with Tré. It sounds like they've got something else going on." She rewound the video a few frames and pointed. "Do you see how he's looking at her? Wow, he's in love with her."

"Wait, go back a little bit. No. Rewind it some more."

Mia moved from behind her desk and made her way over to the television. She squinted and held up her hand. "Right there! Play it now." She inched closer to the screen and whispered, "*Desiree*." Then she scoffed, "You've got to be shitting me."

"What, Mia?"

"Unreal, but this just got better. Waste of footage, my ass. I told you being there we were going to get something. This might not be about Tré, but we've recorded something far more invaluable. Hell yeah, better than you can imagine," she said aloud but mainly to herself.

"Uhh, hello, am I missing something here? What do you see?"

Mia ignored her questions and asked frantically, "Where is the footage from my fight with Troy? Do you still have it? Did you give it to JaJuana yet?"

"Why?"

"Do you have the damn video, Tanya?" Mia snapped.

Tanya frowned. "No, we had to give it up. JaJuana already handed it over to Mark."

"Fuck!"

"Mia, why do you want it?"

She didn't bother responding. Her mind was on the woman on the screen. There was something familiar about her. Mia's brows knitted as she considered how crucial it would be to validate what she already knew in her heart.

"Did you keep the SD card?" Tanya asked, pulling Mia out of her mental reverie.

She whipped her head around to look at Tanya. A smug grin spread across her face as her dark obsidian eyes seemed to twinkle. "I have to show you something."

When Troy purchased their home, they'd converted the guest bedroom downstairs into an office for Mia. She'd always wanted to start a high-end interior design firm, so having her own workspace was must. The floor-to-ceiling windows provided natural light, and the walls were painted green and yellow, creating a tranquil and inspiring atmosphere. She'd ensured specific office necessities were present in her upscale workspace, including a sizable executive desk, an expensive, opulent office chair, a lounge area with plush couches, and a wall bookcase stocked with design publications. Mia stepped into the walk-in closet which was large

111

enough to be a separate room. Tanya watched as she rummaged through a storage cabinet. Mia returned moments later with a card reader. It took a few more minutes to get her MacBook connected and set up to project.

"You've got me wondering what all of this is about."

"The producers wanted me to have an interesting storyline, right?" Mia responded smugly. "I'm definitely going to add a different flavor to the show. Hand me the remote." A few minutes in, Mia flinched as she saw the sped-up moments from the night of Troy's assault.

Tanya knew that no matter how tough she came across, Mia was vulnerable when it came to Troy. She loved her husband, and this ordeal had done more damage than she was willing to admit. "I'm sorry you had to go through that, Mia."

She hadn't told Tanya that Troy had come by the house. Nor did she mention his constant harassing calls and texts. He was doing everything to get her to bend. He'd shown up on three separate occasions, but she didn't open the door. She requested to have their gate code changed so he wouldn't pop up anymore. Mia responded with a dismissive wave, "I'm fine. Just pay attention, okay?"

"Okay," Tanya said quietly, turning her attention back to the television.

A few frames later, she slowed the speed of the video to the part she wanted her agent to watch. Her suspicions had been validated. The woman in her bed and the one who was with Derrik at the funeral were the same person.

Tanya didn't miss the look of hurt in Mia's eyes. She opened her mouth in shock but didn't say anything. She tugged on a few of her auburn curls as she let it sink in what she'd just seen. "Mia, goodness, I'm so sorry." *I know you said you're fine, but this? Hell no, I know you're not. I wouldn't be. That's trifling. How could he do you like this?"*

"Tanya, I'm not happy about what happened to me. I didn't deserve any of this, which is why I said he had to pay. They think I'm done with him. I'm just getting started."

"What are you planning to do with all of this?"

Mia returned to her desk and sat down. She leaned back, twiddling her thumbs as she thought about the magnitude of the information she was sitting on. She sat up. Suddenly, a smile formed across her face.

"What's that smirk for?"

"Do you still have your connection with that talk show producer?"

Tanya's brows furrowed. "What are you thinking about doing, Mia?"

"You don't answer a question with a question, Tanya. Do you still have your connection or not?"

Tanya reluctantly caved and gave her the contact's number. Mia was determined to share this information about Troy. It concerned Tanya that both Mia and her attorney, JaJuana, would be in a lot of trouble. Mia had signed documents stating that she wouldn't reveal any details of what happened in that video, let alone show it. Tanya decided to remind her.

"Who said anything about me showing this? Furthermore, that stipulation is strictly for the attack. They don't know what else we've stumbled across." Mia added with a smirk, "I'm sure there's someone who wants to break this juicy scandal about Troy."

"You're really going to do this?" Tanya's tone was full of disapproval.

Mia released a heavy sigh. "Why do you always question me? For god's sake, Tanya. You're supposed to give me everything I need to be successful. Yet, you always worry." She mocked her agent, "*You're really going to do this?* Bitch, yes, I am."

"What exactly are you planning to do? Let me know, so at least I can get our publicist to prepare an amazing press release."

Mia laughed maniacally as she spun around and around in her chair. "More than you can imagine, and it's just the beginning."

The doorbell rang. Mia picked up her phone and checked the front door camera. She was almost certain it wasn't Troy, but she had to make sure. He'd already conned one gate attendant into letting him in. She smiled, recognizing her visitor. She went to answer the door and returned moments later with her brother, MJ.

Mia bore a striking resemblance to her Korean mother, so she and MJ didn't share the same features. His Bajan mother gave him his tanned olive skin with golden undertones. However, Mia saw a younger version of their father in MJ. He was tall and handsome like the senior Wynters. His face was a carbon copy of their father's, down to the thick eyebrows, light brown eyes, broad nose, thick lips, and

113

five o'clock beard. Unlike their father, who wore his hair short and faded, MJ wore his curly hair longer and faded.

She remembered when Maxwell Sterling Wynters, Jr. came into her life. The bold and precocious seven-year-old boy stole her heart the moment he walked through her parents' front door. She couldn't contain her excitement. She practically smothered him with hugs when their dad introduced them to each other. She'd always wanted a younger sibling, and it didn't matter to her that they didn't share the same mother. MJ didn't seem to mind either, and the two hit it off right away. Even though he was four years Mia's junior, the two were inseparable. He'd entered their lives and seamlessly integrated into their family dynamic.

Mia had wanted to know why they hadn't learned of him sooner. Maxwell eventually revealed that MJ's mother had fled the country and returned to Barbados after learning she was pregnant. She'd lied and claimed MJ's father was someone else. Maxwell didn't believe her and conducted his own investigation. Once he saw the two-year-old MJ, there wasn't any doubt of his paternity. For almost five years, Mia and her mother, Mai, had no idea that her father had visited Barbados multiple times to see MJ. His mother reappeared after a failed marriage, broke and wanting money. She tried to blackmail Maxwell Sr., threatening to publicize their affair if he didn't pay up. But Maxwell wasn't going to be bullied into anything by anybody. Mia and MJ had no idea how it happened, but MJ's mother consented to let him live with his father and left quietly.

Given the circumstances surrounding her brother's birth, Mia imagined it would be difficult for her mother. If Mai was opposed to it, she never showed it. If anything, she couldn't help herself either. She couldn't get enough of the sweet boy, and she adored him just as much as Mia did. After all, he was Maxwell's son and protégé.

"MJ, this is Tanya Ryan, my agent I told you about. Tanya this is my little brother, Maxwell Wynters, Jr., or MJ as we call him."

Tanya jumped up from the chaise lounge and pushed the stray curls out of her face. Her eyes quickly scanned MJ, noting everything attractive about him, from the top of his curly head down to what she knew had to be a size twelve shoe. The short-sleeved polo shirt fit snug against his bulky chest and revealed the Omega brand on his right bicep. Everything about his custom-tailored slacks served to highlight the package between his bowed legs. As she smiled up at the handsome man who appeared to fill the entire room, Tanya could feel the heat rising in her face. His cologne drifted right into her nostrils as he extended his hand, arousing all of her senses.

He grasped her small hand with his big, soft hand. Tanya's brain almost short circuited when he caressed her palm. "Uh . . . hey . . . Max—MJ, I mean. It's . . . uhh, yeah, nice to meet you."

MJ nodded at her and smiled. Then he spoke in a deep, sexy voice, "There's nothing little about me anymore, sis. My sister tends to forget that sometimes. But likewise, it's a pleasure to meet you, Tanya." He released her hand with a wink.

"Uh huh," Tanya mumbled as she backed away from him. His eyes didn't leave hers. She was happy she made it back over to the chaise. She needed to sit before her knees gave out. No, she needed to quench her throat that felt dry all of a sudden. Tanya picked up her cup and gulped the water down. *Damn her brother is fine!*

Mia was oblivious to their exchange as she stepped behind her desk and turned off the television. "Anyway, *little brother*, you got here just in time."

MJ lifted his brows. "I got here in time for what?"

She motioned to the chair on the opposite side of her desk. "Come sit. There's much to fill you in on. I need you."

He sighed and lowered his long body into the cushy accent chair. "When don't you ever need me, sis?"

Mia had initially asked him to stop by to go over the documents they'd received from Troy's agent. Rather than entering politics like their father, MJ had decided to practice law. After finishing with a J.D./M.S. degree in Sports Administration, MJ had a job lined up working for the reputable sports and entertainment law firm, Coleman & Reynolds, LLP, thanks to their father's connections. Within the past year, he'd transitioned into a role as a professional athlete representative, becoming one of the youngest attorneys at the law firm to represent top-paid athletes in the NBA and NFL. Mia wanted to up the ante after what they uncovered from the two recordings moments before, and she needed MJ's advice on how to strike Troy where it hurt.

Once Mia finished explaining everything, she watched as her brother processed it. Another major difference between her father and brother was their personalities. Their father was a powerful figure, instilling fear in anyone who dared question him on anything. But MJ was kind natured and would never want to cause anyone too much harm. Mia knew involving him in her drama was asking a lot of him, but she needed to be sure she could get away with her plans to expose Troy without jeopardizing what she'd already attained.

MJ rubbed his chin. "I don't know about this, Mia."

"Yes, you do. That's why I need your help."

"Uh huh, well Dad's still upset about this whole ordeal, and so am I. Why didn't you tell us Troy was doing that to you?"

She sighed. "You know how daddy is. And it was none of your business."

"But now you need me to be in your business to help you."

"Come on, MJ. I was handling it. Look at how I came up."

He chastised her for showing the video. She was lucky Troy hadn't been arrested. MJ explained that Troy's conduct could still be brought up for investigation. If the Conduct Committee found his behavior out of line with the NFL's "No Nonsense" policy, Troy could face a fine, suspension, or be released from the sport altogether. With Troy no longer in the NFL, Mighty Burger and Power-Aid would be entitled to cancel those endorsement deals and get their money back. As his wife, Mia would have her accounts seized and potentially lose everything.

"Did you or your lawyer even think this through? I'm surprised she went along with that."

Mia glanced at Tanya. Her agent was trying to keep her expression neutral, but Mia could see she was getting a kick out of MJ's lecturing her. Tanya had attempted to say the same thing, but Mia didn't want to hear it.

Her shoulders drooped. "No, I didn't."

"Obviously."

She whined, "MJ what am I supposed to do then? Troy shouldn't be able to get away with this."

"No, he shouldn't, but you don't want him to go to jail either because you want the money, right? Going after him for anything else is pointless, sis. You got the money, the house, the cars, and trucks, right? What is exposing him for a cheat going to do for you?"

Mia didn't know what to say except to humiliate him for what he'd done to her, and she knew her brother would object. It didn't sit well with her to have so much information at her fingertips. MJ didn't have to agree with her, and she didn't need his help. She would do what she needed to bring Troy to his knees.

CHAPTER

15

Jamal finished entering the notes in the system from his last patient. He logged off the work computer and made his way to the front office to say goodnight to his staff. After the office manager left, he locked the door to the suite and went back to his office. He wasn't on call this week at the hospital, but he wished he was. He wasn't ready to go home. Jamal knew it would be another night of tolerating Angela's depressing mood, and he didn't feel like dealing with it. That was selfish considering he was the reason for her present mental state. And even though he should've felt sadness and remorse over the loss of his friend, he didn't. He truly felt it wasn't his fault. Rico shouldn't have forced his hand. There was no bringing him back; Jamal simply wanted to move on.

The week before Rico's funeral, Jamal spent time scouting new sites for companionship. Rico had told him about the dating sites, but Jamal never thought of putting himself out there. He didn't have to. Rico fulfilled his freaky desires. But with Rico gone, Jamal needed a replacement, especially now that Angela was emotionally and physically unavailable. Once his dual profiles were active, he instantly connected with a few people on the site Link Up. Women were reaching out to him, but they weren't open to casual hookups. Then he started chatting with this guy. Jamal liked his profile and how well it was put together. He was intrigued by his confident attitude and wanted to know more about Christian Hilcrest, Senior Buyer for Gucci.

119

Christian Hilcrest was thirty-two years old, an only child, a native of Georgia, and lived in Sandy Springs. Christian was the only man he'd been interested in chatting with for the past couple of weeks. Jamal was enjoying getting to know him, and he decided today he'd take a chance and suggest a meetup. He logged in to his personal laptop and opened a browser that took him back to the site. A minute later he received an alert for a new message.

Hey are you there, Jamie? - **Christian**

Jamal chose to use an alias. He wanted to keep his identity anonymous since he wasn't sure if he'd go through with meeting someone online.

Hey, yes, I am. - **Jamie**

Where did you go earlier? You're always dropping off in the middle of our conversations. - **Christian**

You know I'm a doctor. Sometimes my appointments run close together. I apologize for not letting you know when I need to step away. - **Jamie**

It's cool. I know how it is being busy with work. I just got back from a fashion show in New York. - **Christian**

That sounds like a lot of fun. -**Jamie**

It is, but very chaotic. So, what do you like to do for fun? - **Christian**

I play golf. - **Jamie**

Ooh, golf, I've always wanted to learn how to play. - **Christian**

I could teach you if you're serious about it. - **Jamie**

I'd like that. - **Christian**

What's up? I'd like to meet you and soon. - **Jamie**

Well, I'm free this afternoon. - **Christian**

So am I. - **Jamie**

Any suggestions of where we could meet? - **Christian**

Jamal gave the name and address of a bar Rico had told him about. They'd never gone together. He knew if he'd agreed to go, Rico would've taken it as a sign that they were more than just hanging out.

Yes, I've heard of this spot. It's been on my list to check out. I'll be at the bar in red bottoms. Trust me, none of the men there would rock them like I do. See you soon! - **Christian**

Before Jamal could object or change his mind, Christian logged off. "Did he mean red bottoms as in the heels or shoes?" he asked aloud. He began to picture the men at Rico's funeral. Jamal wondered if Christian was living in the lifestyle shamelessly. Would he show up dressed over the top? Would he be as flashy as some of the men at the funeral were? Jamal was taking a big risk meeting this guy, but he was intrigued, curious. To avoid bringing any embarrassment to himself, he wouldn't show his face if the guy came dressed like a woman. He'd be sure to stake out the place before.

He needed to check in with Angela first. Jamal decided he would go with his usual lie of having a late shift at the hospital. He called Angela. When she responded, her tone was sluggish, and her words were slurred. If she wasn't sleeping, she was drinking all afternoon. She must've taken the anxiety medication.

"Listen, I'm going to stop by before I go to the hospital. I want to check on you."

"No, no, you go ahead. For real. I'll be fine."

Jamal hesitated, but he didn't want to miss the opportunity to continue with his plans either. He convinced himself she would be fine. He was worrying for nothing.

"Okay, sweetheart, get some rest. I'll see you later this evening."

"Mmm-hmm, okay."

"I love you, sweetheart."

"Yep, you too. Bye."

Angela was choosing to cope with her brother's death by drinking. Jamal had intended to enlist some help so that she could manage better. However, his focus had been elsewhere, especially since he'd started chatting with Christian. His current plans didn't include her. Just then his phone alerted for an incoming text. He looked down and smiled.

Hey, I'm on my way to the bar. Let me know when you're here. See you soon! - Christian

He gathered his things and made his way out the door. He'd have to deal with Angela later. It took him over an hour to maneuver through rush-hour traffic. As soon as he pulled into the parking lot, his thoughts went into overdrive. *What am I doing here? What if someone sees me? I need to get out of here.*

He picked up his phone and considered sending a text to say something came up at the hospital, but the picture Christian sent earlier popped up. His honey skin tone, those soft brown eyes, and that infectious smile stared back at him. Jamal pushed aside his conflicting thoughts. He got out of the car and made his way across the street.

He walked in casually and carefully scanned the room. It shocked him to be in a space filled with other handsome black men. There was an assortment to choose from: light to dark skin shades, short or tall, and slim to well-built. No wonder the women in Atlanta were upset about the number of unavailable men in the city. He knew there happened to be a number of them sitting in this particular club hooking up with one another. He focused his attention on the bar. Almost immediately, he recognized the well-dressed stranger. Just as he'd said in their chat, he wore red bottoms! Jamal was relieved to see they were the men's designer shoes. He walked over and stood next to him. He didn't speak. Instead, Jamal got the attention of the bartender.

"I'll have a Jack straight up. Thanks."

"That's the kind of drink you have when you know it's going to be a long night."

Jamal turned his head. His eyes locked on to the soft brown eyes of the strikingly handsome man. Christian's thin, jet-black mustache was trimmed around a set of full lips. He revealed a perfect Colgate smile. The button of his blazer opened right at his midsection. By his solid build, he could tell his new friend was a gym buff too. Perhaps he would join him as Rico did. Jamal gawked at the opening of his shirt that exposed a perfectly tanned, smooth, and chiseled chest.

"Damn, you make it quite obvious you like what you see."

"Huh? Oh, I'm sorry I wasn't, you know uhh—"

"It's okay, boo. I get this all the time. I'm used to it. The boys make me feel like it's, you know, cleavage." Then Christian bit into his bottom lip.

Did he just call me boo? Cleavage? Jamal couldn't do anything but stare. He rubbed a hand across his waves and licked his lips. Speechless, he was relieved when the bartender returned with his drink. Jamal didn't waste time turning the glass up. Before the bartender could walk away, he ordered another.

"Well damn, was it that kind of day?"

"Yeah, yeah, it was."

Christian was attractive and exuded a sex appeal he'd never felt from a man. He was more handsome in person than in his picture. But it wasn't just his looks. Unlike over the phone, being able to watch his lips move and hear his voice was captivating. Jamal found himself feeling something unfamiliar.

"Well, you can tell me all about it."

No, Jamal couldn't. He'd never felt this way before. This attraction was far stronger than anything he'd felt for Rico, let alone any other man.

"Or do you need to have that other drink first?"

Jamal sputtered, "Uhh . . . umm yes, I think I'm going to need it."

"Damn, what kind of patients do you deal with?"

Jamal decided to calm his nerves and break the ice by sharing a recent experience with a female patient who'd made a pass at him. When he finished, he realized it was dumb to mention anything about a woman. Before he could apologize, Christian responded.

"Well, I haven't been into women my entire life, so I can't relate at all. Although they push up all the time, I can't ever be so bothered by the kitty. It does absolutely nothing for my dick."

Jamal nodded. "Right."

"Now, a man like you? Yeah, you'll have me standing at attention with no problems." Christian touched his arm.

Jamal purposely flexed his bicep, "Really?"

"Yeah, Jamie. You're one fine-ass man."

Jamal found himself blushing. There was something about the way Christian spoke and said his alias. He licked his lips and took the last swallow from his glass. "Let's get out of here and grab something to eat. I'm starving."

"I'm following your lead," Christian said, flirting.

Jamal enjoyed his dinner with Christian. The conversation flowed easily between them, and it amazed Jamal how poised and well-spoken Christian was. He traveled abroad, spoke French fluently, and owned a couple of rental properties in Florida. Although his mannerisms could be flamboyant at times, they were never too over-the-top. Everything about Christian intrigued Jamal and made him want to know more. When their server came to the table with the bill, Jamal took care of everything and asked Christian if he was ready to call it a night.

"That's your call, Jamie. However, I think it's rather convenient that we're in a hotel. Now, I realize coming here might have been part of your plan all along, eh?"

Jamal decided he didn't want their evening to end. With a smile, he flirted, "I thought we could have a nightcap."

"Again, I'll follow your lead."

The two men exited the restaurant and walked over to the hotel lobby. Christian excused himself and went to the restroom while Jamal took care of their reservation at the front desk. When he returned, Jamal told him they were good to go, and they headed toward the elevators. When a younger couple entered along with them, Jamal and Christian continued their conversation as if the other couple weren't there. Jamal was surprised to note that he didn't feel embarrassed or awkward knowing a heterosexual couple was in their presence. Christian's laid-back attitude helped put him at ease. The moment the young couple exited onto their floor, Christian moved in closer.

Jamal stared at him for a moment and then did something he'd never done with Rico. He leaned forward and tilted his head. He felt Christian's lips brush up against his lightly. Jamal opened his mouth. Their tongues touched. He heard Christian moan. He felt their dicks touching. Something ignited in his stomach. It was a different feeling, and it wasn't the alcohol making him feel giddy. Moments later, a tone from the elevator alerted them they'd arrived at their floor. He gave Jamal's bottom lip a light peck before stepping back.

The doors of the elevator opened. Without saying anything, Jamal walked out, and Christian followed. He unlocked the door to the king suite. It had huge windows overlooking the Atlanta skyline. Once Christian entered, he closed the door. Jamal came up from behind and turned Christian around. They stared at one another for a moment.

Jamal almost never took control when he was with Rico. Only once did Jamal take the lead in having sex with Rico, and that was only after he'd drunk himself into oblivion first. He'd always needed Rico to get things started between them. Maybe it was to deny the fact he was fucking his boy and enjoyed it. He relished the moments of their secret affair, but there was no passion in it. This time, he was standing in the middle of a hotel room nowhere near obliterated and completely turned on.

It hit him.

Holy shit! Maybe . . . yes, that's it! He didn't want to put a label on it. Yet, Jamal knew this was something different than he experienced before with Rico. He still wanted to be with women, but his genuine attraction to Christian made him realize he must be bisexual.

"Are you okay, Jamie?"

"Yes, I'm better than ever before," he proclaimed.

Jamal admired him for a moment. Christian stood a few inches shorter, which made it sexy to have the smaller man looking up at him. Jamal unbuttoned Christian's blazer, helped him out of it, and threw it over the chair. Christian slowly unbuttoned the rest of his shirt and let it fall to the floor. Jamal's dick throbbed. He started rubbing Christian's smooth, bare chest and pinching his nipples.

"Oooh," Christian moaned.

Christian was fit with a smooth chest. He didn't have six-pack abs, but his belly was completely flat. Jamal moved his hands around to Christian's perfectly round, firm ass.

"Wow, somebody's been working on his squats."

Both men laughed. Jamal began undressing. He was proud of his muscular body. The hours he'd put in at the gym had earned him firm muscles and ripped abs. He left his boxers on to allow Christian to uncover the package bulging underneath.

"Damn, Jamie!" Christian exclaimed as he fell to his knees. He peeled off Jamal's boxers like a wrapper to a chocolate candy bar. He didn't waste time going to work on his new toy with no hands. Christian tried to take in every inch until his tonsils met the head of Jamal's dick. He gagged.

Jamal grabbed Christian's face and began grinding, making him gag more. Each time he pulled out more spit dribbled down his chin. He looked down at this handsome man now giving him the best head he'd ever received. "Fuuuuuck!" Jamal hissed.

Jamal couldn't take any more of the suction on his engorged rod. He pulled Christian from the floor and moved them over to the bed. He began loosening Christian's belt.

"Wait, we have to use protection, Jamie."

"Of course, do you have condoms? If not, I have them."

"I have some."

Christian pulled them from his pants as well as a couple of individual packets of lubricant. While Jamal put the condom on, Christian finished undressing and moved to the middle of the bed. Then Jamal observed as Christian opened his legs, lifted his nuts, and squirted the liquid between his cheeks. He motioned for Jamal to come to him, and looking at the sexy man lying sprawled out in front of him, he didn't hesitate to do as he was instructed. It was as if some strange animal magnetism were drawing him to Christian. Lust burned in his brain, and he could think of nothing else as his dick pulsed. Jamal crawled on the bed and positioned himself between Christian's thighs. Christian slid his hands under his ass cheeks and spread them open. Jamal took his time easing into the tight, puckered hole.

"Mmm, yes, Jamie, that's it."

After pushing in and pulling out, his girth stretched Christian, and the barrier of skin loosened. Finally, he was deep inside. Jamal groaned and pulled out a little, then drove back in. Christian moved his hands to hold on to Jamal's strong forearms, taking the long, deep strokes Jamal began delivering.

"Don't stop, Jamie! Ooooh, please, don't stop!"

He looked down and saw that Christian had begun masturbating. He held the base of his dick, slowly stroking up and down. Jamal looked into his eyes and Christian gazed back, taking him to another sexual high. He growled, "That's it, Jamie. Fuck me! Fuck me harder!"

Jamal loved him calling out his new alias. He thrusted and stroked and continued plying into Christian's ass. Jamal went faster as he watched Christian stroke in rhythm.

"I'm about to come, Jamie! Yes! Keep fucking me! Yes!"

Jamal felt the hot, tingling sensation in his loins as he watched the white, creamy fluid shoot from Christian's dick. He went deeper and harder. "Fuck!" Jamal shouted.

Christian shouted in response, "Don't stop! Yes! Yes!"

Jamal continued grinding until there was nothing left. He collapsed next to Christian completely drained. Jamal pulled him into his arms and cradled him close. He'd never done anything like that with Rico. Yet, it felt natural, and Christian didn't pull away. Instead, he cuddled underneath the larger man until he was fast asleep.

When Jamal opened his eyes, there were rays of sunlight illuminating the room. He looked down and noticed Christian was still snuggled underneath him. He thought it was cute he was still lying there. A few minutes passed before Jamal eased out of bed and went into the bathroom. After quickly washing himself off, he came into the room and started dressing. Just as he was putting on his shirt, his phone began ringing. "Shit!"

Christian was startled out of his sleep. "What happened? What is it, Jamie?"

Jamal looked at the name on the phone. "I'm sorry, but I have to get to the hospital. You're more than welcome to stay until checkout. I'll call you later, okay?" Jamal didn't give Christian a chance to oppose or ask questions. He kissed him on the forehead and bolted out the door.

CHAPTER
16

"I don't get it, Bri. Why would they think we had something to do with Rico's murder?"

The detectives handling Rico's case had paid Brielle a visit. They questioned her about Desiree and Derrik's confrontation after Rico's funeral, revealing only that their information came by way of an anonymous tip line, and they were following up on all leads. Brielle explained to the detectives that their anonymous source had done some very poor ear hustling; they had nothing to do with their friend's death. The detectives still wanted to speak with Desiree.

"Just call them, okay?"

"All right. I'll call them later."

There was silence on the phone until Brielle asked about Derrik. At Brielle's urging, Desiree had tried to contact him. She'd reached out at least twice a day, letting him know she missed him and still loved him. She asked for forgiveness and a chance to at least talk to him. It had been a week, and Desiree still hadn't heard from him.

Desiree fought back the tears. "I'm going to leave it alone, Bri. He's not going to respond. He said he was done."

"No, you will fight for your man, Desi!" Brielle protested.

Her voice cracked and was almost a whisper. "But he's not my man."

Brielle did her best to comfort her friend. She explained it would take time for a man like Derrik to come around. Desiree needed to be more patient.

"I guess you're right. Listen I have to go. It's been a little crazy in here. Wait, I almost forgot. Could you come with me to my doctor's appointment?"

"Hell yeah!" Brielle's claps could be heard through the receiver.

Desiree pulled the phone away from her ear. "Ouch."

"My bad, you know I'm excited."

She couldn't hide her sadness. "Yeah, I'm trying to be excited too, but it's hard under the circumstances."

"Desi, don't do this to yourself."

"I'm not. Look, I have to go before I start bawling all over again. Talk to you later, diva." She hung up, took a deep breath, and dialed her assistant's extension. Her eyes rolled the moment she heard the familiar sounds of gum popping. "Tiana, do you have a minute?"

"Sure thing, boss. What do you need?"

"I need to make some changes to my schedule. I have a doctor's appointment, so I'll need my Wednesday afternoon clear. I'm also planning to head back out to LA, probably the middle of next week. We'll need to get my itinerary ready."

"Okay, no problem, I'll take care of it."

"Before we do all of the scheduling for this, could you schedule a meeting with Carolyn this afternoon? Try to get me in right after lunch if possible."

"You must not have checked your emails. I thought that you knew Mr. Moretti was meeting with you today. He's taken up your afternoon. I'm sorry. I should've called to confirm."

Desiree frowned. She wondered why he hadn't called or sent a text. "No, I had no idea. I'm looking over my emails now."

Tiana continued, "He and two people from his team should be arriving at the office shortly. I've already booked the conference room on the other side of the floor."

"Looks like I've got my hands full today."

Tiana popped her gum and snorted, "Hmph, I wouldn't mind having my hands full with that one."

"Seriously?"

"Sorry, I can't help it when we get a fine specimen like him on deck. And good lawd, he's one fine vanilla brotha."

"Really, Tiana?"

She whispered. "I'm just saying. Everybody getting down with the swirl now, so why not?"

"I hope you realize that man has a girlfriend."

"Uhhh, correction, he used to. Not anymore, from what the girls in the Cali office told me. Boss lady, he's free game. It's time for me to shoot my shot!"

"Tiana!"

Her assistant popped her gum again and continued fawning over Aaron. "Boss lady, he ain't your average white guy. He's like what, six-feet-four maybe five, give or take. That's a tree I'd like to climb. And you can tell he lives in the gym. Those biceps, triceps, and quads be bulging through his suits like the Incredible Hulk. And let's not forget about those pretty brown eyes with them long lashes. Oooh, I just love his dimples, and how can I forget about that man bun? Wooo lawd! Mr. Moretti is a helluva catch. So yeah, I'd holla."

Desiree decided it was time to rein her assistant in. "Tiana, this is a place of business. I'd appreciate it if you kept it professional."

"Sure thing. Sorry, you're right. I got a little carried away."

She couldn't blame her assistant and held back the chuckle. "I do understand, though."

"I'll buzz you once they arrive," Tiana said.

"Okay, thanks."

When she hung up, Desiree dialed into her manager's office. After a couple of rings, her assistant conferenced them on the line. Carolyn apologized for not checking in since Rico's death. It'd been busy without her around. Desiree jumped right to the reason for her call. She wanted to know if Carolyn was aware that Aaron Moretti would be there. Carolyn explained that one of her previous clients, Pryce Holdings, had requested Aaron to be their legal representation for this acquisition and merger.

131

"I thought they were waiting until the fourth quarter or spring next year. I hadn't heard anything until now."

"Yes, neither had I. Either way, it looks great for our projections coming in for the rest of the year. Keep me posted and let me know how everything works out," Carolyn requested.

"Okay, I'll catch up with you later."

Once Carolyn ended their call, Desiree grabbed her cell and leaned back in her chair. "The nerve of this man," she said aloud as she keyed in a text.

Talk about not letting someone know when you're coming to town. Why didn't you tell me you were going to be here for this acquisition? - Desiree

A few minutes passed without a response from him. Tiana called before she could send another message.

"Mr. Moretti and his team are on their way up. I'm going to get them set up in the conference room. You can head down when you're ready."

"Okay, great. Thanks."

Desiree carefully went through the email and printed the documents she needed before making her way to the conference room. She took a deep breath before lightly tapping on the door. After opening it, she saw and greeted Aaron, a young man, and a woman sitting on one side of the large table.

"It's good to see you again, Aaron."

He nodded. "Likewise, Desiree."

She went to the side of the table where he was seated. Aaron introduced his team then gave Desiree the greenlight to begin the presentation. Desiree was meticulous about her work and took a couple of hours to lay out Charlton's strategy. They worked through lunch and all the way into the evening to lay out plans for a smooth acquisition that their client would be happy with.

"That was a lot, but personally, I think you're right. Pryce will be very pleased after everything is finalized," Aaron declared. He addressed his colleagues across from them. "Are you able to pull together what's needed for our sections?"

Both nodded in agreement. There was a knock on the door. Desiree called out for the person to enter, and Tiana poked her head in.

"Hey, boss lady, Carolyn needs you in this other meeting. I'm sorry, but she said it's rather urgent."

"Would you all excuse me for just a moment? I'll be right back."

Aaron nodded. "Sure, of course. We'll wrap up things here in the meantime."

Several minutes later, when Desiree returned to the conference room, she saw that it was empty. She started to head out when Aaron grabbed her and whirled her around. In one swift move, he closed the door and locked it. He pressed her back against the door and devoured her lips. His kiss was fervent as he explored her mouth. He moved a hand down to the single button in front of her blazer and unhooked it. He traced the bra outline underneath the silk blouse before cupping her supple breasts. He squeezed gently. Desiree's moan was muffled in their kiss.

Aaron pulled away and stared into Desiree's eyes for a few seconds. He leaned in. His breath tickled her ear as he whispered, "I couldn't wait for you to get back. I wanted to—no, I *needed* to see you. So no, I wasn't going to call or send a text. This was an intentional surprise visit."

She felt his hands beneath her blouse. He lifted her bra and released the brown mounds. He pinched her nipples until both were poking out.

She grabbed his forearm. "Stop! You can't do that here."

He pushed her breasts back underneath the material and adjusted her bra before buttoning her blazer. He nodded towards the door. "You're right. Let's go. I've made dinner reservations."

She looked down at her clothes in amazement. It was as if he'd never touched her. He motioned for her to move. She stepped aside. He smiled, revealing those dimples as he unlocked the door. Desiree took a deep breath and blew it out slowly as she followed him out of the conference room. They stopped by her office to pick up her things. On their way out, Desiree went to her assistant's desk and advised her of their plans.

"Okay, boss lady." Tiana switched her attention to the handsome man hovering over her desk. "Bye, Mr. Moretti. It was *really* good seeing *you* again."

He returned a full smile, exposing the deep dimples in his cheeks. He laid it on extra thick and winked. "You too, Tiana. Thank you for your help, as always. Until next time."

As he walked away, Desiree caught Tiana fanning herself. She shook her head. Her assistant shrugged her shoulders.

Tiana giggled like a schoolgirl as she picked up the phone. "Hello, you've reached Desiree Edwards's office. How may I help you? I'm sorry, she's left for the day. May I take a message?"

Desiree followed Aaron to the elevators. It was no surprise he garnered attention wherever he went. He was a big, attractive man. His height made him tower over most people in a crowd, and his broad shoulders, bulging biceps, and muscular quads were visible in the trendy business attire he wore. Tiana was right about him being in the gym a lot. However, unbeknownst to her assistant, Desiree had already climbed him like a tree. She smiled to herself. As soon as the elevator doors closed, she chastised him for openly flirting with her assistant.

"Hmm, jealous, are we?"

"I think not," Desiree said, shaking her head. "But you need to stop getting the girls riled up. You do the same thing in the Cali office."

Aaron snickered, showing his dimples. "I have no idea what you're talking about."

"Whatever."

Once they reached the lobby, Aaron shared the address of the restaurant so Desiree could meet him there. Half an hour later, they were seated in a booth at a swanky spot in the Virginia Highlands.

Desiree pointed her index finger playfully. "Nobody ever comes out here. How did you find out about this restaurant?"

"I have my sources."

"I must say, you have good sources. This is one of Atlanta's best-kept secrets."

"Good thing I'm good at keeping secrets then. This will be another one of ours."

Desiree wasn't so sure she could agree with that. She and Derrik had dined at this very restaurant just last month. Her thoughts shifted to him. He'd finally responded to her while she was in the meeting with Aaron's team. She'd hoped they could speak again and move past this, but he was preparing to head out of town until next week. Desiree still hadn't made up her mind whether to tell him about the baby, but she at least wanted to see him. She was missing him. A server approached the table, snatching her from her thoughts. Before she could say anything, Aaron ordered a bottle of pinot. She frowned.

"Are you in the mood for merlot instead?" he asked.

Desiree knew she probably shouldn't in her condition, but she needed to unwind. She convinced herself that one drink wouldn't hurt. "It would be more appropriate to go with what I'm ordering for dinner."

"As the lady suggests."

Their server nodded and left to get the drinks. Aaron made small talk while they waited.

"What do you think about this Pryce acquisition? Was it really necessary for Samuel to proceed with things now?"

"From my brief conversation with Carolyn, it appears they had to. It's all part of their strategy in the marketplace. Samuel is in it to take it all. He plans to be the largest holdings company in the northeast. A lot of people are in on this deal."

"True, I'm not surprised. Hey, I forgot to ask. How are you holding up as far as your friend? You know, since his memorial service?"

"I'm okay, but that service was . . . let's just say it was . . . rather entertaining." Desiree filled him in on the amusing tidbits from Rico's funeral.

"You've got to be kidding me?"

"No, I'm not. Who knew he was swinging the bat for both teams?"

Just then, their server came back with the bottle. He poured their glasses and took their entrée orders. When he walked away, Aaron smiled and held up his glass.

"I know this was last minute, but I'm happy you agreed to join me. Cheers to this evening."

"Thank you for the invite." The sound of their clinking glasses echoed.

A few hours and two bottles later, Desiree finished off another glass. She'd lost count of how much she'd drunk, but she couldn't ignore she was starting to feel the effects. "Aaron, we need to call it a night."

"Yes, I agree." He took care of their bill. As they waited in the vestibule for their cars, he ran the drill to ensure she could make the drive home.

"Thank you, but I'm fine, Aaron. My house isn't that far from here. If anything, you have a longer ride than I do. As a matter of fact, this is me pulling up."

He walked her out but didn't allow the valet to do his job. Aaron walked over to the driver side. He handed the valet attendant a generous tip and shooed him away. "Thanks, man, I got this. Yeah, yeah, here you go." He held Desiree's car door open. They stood facing one another. She didn't say anything as he stared. For a moment, there was awkward silence until she spoke.

"Okay, I'm going to get out of here. I have another crazy morning, and I need to get some rest. You have a good night. I'll let you know when I get home." Desiree stood on her tiptoes and attempted to kiss him on the cheek.

"You can't be serious. Since when do you give me kisses on the cheek? I don't think so." He pulled her into a tight embrace.

Desiree tried to pry herself free. "Aaron!"

"No, come here."

"You're squeezing me too tight!"

He planted a soft kiss on her neck and made a trail up to her lips. "This is how *we* say good night." Aaron held nothing back. They shared a lengthy brazen kiss that left her breathless. Desiree felt her legs getting weak. She leaned into him to keep steady. They were so lost in their heated exchange that neither noticed the valet had returned. He cleared his throat. Aaron groaned as he released her lips and took a step back. Desiree continued hanging onto his arm as she gathered herself. She needed to get out of there. Her pussy wasn't just throbbing; it had started to ache.

"Umm, sorry, I didn't mean to interrupt. I have your car, sir."

Aaron chuckled. "No worries, but can you blame me?"

The valet smiled nervously.

"I'm going. I'll call you. Good night, Aaron." Desiree hastily jumped into her car, not wanting to encourage him. It was dangerous to be around him and under the influence. She shifted her Mercedes in gear to begin the short trek home. A few minutes into the drive, Desiree realized just how much wine she had consumed. She knew Brielle was up and would help talk her through the rest of her drive home. Desiree hoped she wasn't with Justin. Brielle answered after a couple of rings.

"Hey, diva, what's going on?"

"Nothing much except I just finished having dinner with Aaron."

"Aaron? Are you back in LA? He put you on a private jet or something?"

"No, girl. How about he's here, in Atlanta! One of our clients hired him for another acquisition. He cornered me in the conference room and was feeling all up on me, and then he stopped in the middle of it to take me to dinner. We were leaving a few minutes ago and he tongued me down in valet. I had to haul ass."

"Ahh shit, he was trying to get some tonight. Considering what's going on with Derrik now, would you let him hit it?"

"No, because I still love Derrik, and don't forget I'm pregnant."

"Desi, you know you can still fuck when you're pregnant. I heard it's really good then. Your hormones should have your ass horny."

"I am! My pussy is aching right now."

"Hold up. I thought he was annoying. Desi, have you been drinking?"

"Well, he is . . . and even though I know I probably shouldn't have, yes. Maybe I did have a few too many glasses over dinner. I didn't want to drive alone. That's why I called you."

"And there we have it, folks."

"Shut up."

Brielle teased, "Nope, let me guess, you were seeing his aura, too. Did he look like he was stepping out of a *GQ* magazine in a hazy glow?"

"God, I can't stand you."

"You can't stand me because you know I'm not lying. A little alcohol in your system, and all bets are off. You never make good decisions under the influence."

"Not true."

"Who are you married to?"

"That's not fair, Bri."

"I'm not lying though, am I?"

Desiree couldn't argue with Brielle about how she'd seen Jamal that night. But in her defense, Jamal courted her in the right way and won her heart effortlessly. Her initial feelings for him didn't have anything to do with alcohol. At that moment, she was pulling into her driveway. She opened the garage door, and her eyes went to the boxes sitting where Jamal's car would have been parked.

"Ugh, I'm pulling into this garage, and it's hit me. I'm sick of looking at this man's shit. I need to hurry up and finish packing this stuff, so he can come get it. Maybe you should come help."

"Say no more. Let's get his shit up outta there!"

Desiree laughed, "Okay, how about this weekend? Wait, do you have anything planned with Justin? Any events?"

"Nope, nothing and even so, I'll come through to help my girl."

Desiree thanked Brielle for ensuring she made it home safely. She ended the call, closed the garage door, and collected her laptop case and purse from the back seat. She walked into the kitchen, dropped her bags on the island, and kicked off her heels. She pulled the pins from her messy bun. A toss with one shake, and her thick, honey-blonde tresses fell past her shoulders. The moment she came out of her blazer, the doorbell rang.

She clutched her chest and released a sharp breath. Who would come to her house unannounced at this hour? It immediately occurred to her that Troy might. She quietly crept to the front of the house and moved to the window on one side of the living room. She held her breath, inched the curtain back, and lifted one of the blinds. "Damn," she muttered.

From that angle, she couldn't make out the figure standing at the door. She noticed a black Suburban with tinted windows sitting in front of the house, but she didn't recognize it. The doorbell chimed again. Perhaps if she didn't answer, they would go away. Then she heard his voice.

"Desiree, I'm sorry to show up unannounced like this, but—"

It was him! She bolted to the door and yanked it open.

CHAPTER
17

Surprise was etched on her face, but she didn't invite him in. She couldn't find the words to offer the invitation. They were lost as he gazed into her eyes. He tilted his head towards the house. Desiree nodded and stepped to the side. As he moved past her, he glanced down, wearing a blank expression on his face. Once he was inside, she closed the door and fell in step behind him. He was walking through the living room when she finally spoke up.

"Umm, I thought you were leaving town." Her breath was caught in her throat when Derrik abruptly turned around. She trembled with both desire and fear. He held her with his eyes. His masculine energy dominated her. He looked good as fuck. He wore the hell out of the gray *retraC* sweatsuit that complemented his hard, muscled body. The cedar musk scent of his cologne floated into her nostrils, overpowering her senses. He smelled amazing, almost as intoxicating as the wine she'd drunk earlier.

Derrik's voice was low. "I couldn't leave town without seeing you, baby girl."

Her heart fluttered. She loved hearing his endearment for her. She hadn't heard it in weeks. Suddenly, she became guilt ridden as her brain reminded her of what she'd done to them. Her eyes went to the floor. She lowered her head in shame. "Derrik, I—"

"Shhh, no talking. Not tonight." He lifted her chin. "I needed to see you, be with you." He paused. Pure need and desire were in his eyes when he whispered, "Inside of you."

He gave her body a sweeping gaze and moistened his lips. He took another step forward, eliminating the space between them. He was close enough to kiss. She felt his hands massaging and caressing her breasts. He moved down to her ass. He squeezed gently as he grinded their pelvises together. The ache between her thighs grew more and more insistent.

She parted her lips allowing a moan to escape as he covered her mouth. His kiss was possessive, greedy for more. Desiree wrapped her arms around his neck and immersed herself in his kiss, rubbing his head and neck. He skillfully unbuttoned her blouse and released the hooks of her bra. Derrik withdrew from her lips and helped her remove both pieces of clothing. He stepped back to admire her partially nude body. He unzipped her skirt. It fell and pooled around her ankles. The sound of material ripping followed. He tossed the tattered thongs to the side.

He lifted her from the floor and moved to the front of the stairs. He climbed a few steps, carefully placed her on the landing, and knelt in the center of the staircase. Desiree opened her thighs wider. He spread the plump folds, exposing hot, wet, pink flesh. Derrik dipped his head and licked her throbbing nub. While lifting her hips, she ran her hands over his bald head. He sped up the flicking motion of his tongue, licking up and down. Her thighs shook as he suctioned her clit into his lips and sucked so hard that her thighs trembled.

"I've missed you, Derrik . . . that feels so good. Please, don't stop." Desiree moaned. She pushed his head closer. He welcomed the help and slid his tongue inside, slurping up the juices she leaked. She moved her hips to the rhythm of his gifted tongue. Derrik inserted his index and middle fingers inside and rotated them upward. Desiree couldn't catch her breath. Her walls tightened around his fingers the moment he hit her G-spot.

"Do you want to come again?"

She hissed, "Yes, pleeease!"

Derrik squeezed her breasts and pinched her nipples alternately, while licking her clit and fingering her. He sucked harder, working his fingers in and out until she lost control. A bone-tingling sensation ripped through her, and she came in waves. Desiree's thighs clinched tightly around his head as she shuddered. Derrik had to pry them open to free his neck. He brought his face up to meet hers. Juices dripped from his chin. He pushed his fingers in deeper.

Desiree opened her mouth, and he silenced her moan with his mouth. Their tongues did the tango as she savored the sweet flavor of her pussy. She was sure she tasted the red wine from dinner. She continued to grind her hips on his fingers as their kiss deepened. She writhed against him until her body went taut. She screamed in release, "Fuck!" Desiree erupted like a volcano when Derrik withdrew his fingers. The next time the housekeepers came, she'd have to ask for a thorough cleaning of the staircase.

"See what you do to me."

She peeked down at the tent erected in his sweatpants. Desiree licked her lips and nodded seductively. Derrik got up. He stepped out of his Jordans, hurriedly pulled his sweatshirt over his head, and along with his boxers, pushed the pants down. He stepped out of them and grabbed his engorged, thick rod. She reached out for it, but he swatted her hand away and shook his head. He motioned for her to open her thighs wider. She did and watched as Derrik knelt on the step beneath her.

He stared in her eyes while rubbing the tip of his manhood against her clit. She moaned, releasing a waterfall. While covering her lips with his own, he pressed his thick, rigid shaft into the tight, silky heat between her thighs. Desiree's moan was muffled in his kiss. Derrik slipped his hands under her thighs and tightened his grip on her butt as he went deeper. She embraced every inch of it. His manhood filled her up. He worked his hips from left to right, expanding the tight space.

"Oooh, Derrrrik," rolled off her tongue. Her pussy released more fluids with each thrust. Desiree's insides were heating up. Her stomach muscles constricted. He paused when he felt her walls clamp down his dick. He lifted his head and fixed his gaze on her.

"Fuck, Desi. I'm not trying to come yet."

"But, Derrik," she whispered.

"Yes?"

"I want to come again."

141

He pulled out and repositioned himself on the lower stairs with his feet planted on the floor. He held his hand out for Desiree to hold as she came down a couple of stairs. She planted her feet on each side of his thighs and squatted, straddling him. He slowly slid into her. She gasped at how he filled her up, better and more fully than any other. He held onto her waist and worked his hips, thrusting up, grinding, and pumping. She threw head back.

Desiree cried out, "Mmm, yes! That's it! Yessss!" She squeezed down, trapping him inside. He gritted his teeth, fighting against his own release. Derrik's hips jackhammered upward, thrusting into her wetness. The sensation crept into his lower abdomen. When the climax came, it came for both of them. Her body was on fire as pleasure rippled through her. He continued grinding against her pelvis, bursting into Desiree and filling her with his seed.

They stared at one another. Derrik's fingers traced the softness of her bottom lip. He replaced them with his lips. Their kiss was hard, soft, then hard again. Desiree thought if this was 'I miss you' sex, it was the best she'd ever had. She truly missed being with him and told him again.

"I've missed you too," he said and planted another kiss on her lips.

"I know you said no talking, but—"

"And I meant that, unless you're talking dirty to me." He kissed her nose. "We've only got an hour before I have to leave. So, for the next hour, I'm going to be balls deep inside of you, baby girl." Derrik lifted them up effortlessly. Desiree held onto his neck and crossed her ankles around his waist as he began to make his way up the stairs.

As promised, an hour later they lay curled together, her pussy deliciously sore from their intense lovemaking. He was propped up on the pillows, watching her come down from their sexual high. She enjoyed and savored the nearness of him. Desiree nestled into his body just as the alarm on his smart watch went off. Derrik groaned. He didn't want to, but knew he had to leave. He reluctantly lifted Desiree from his arm and turned off the alarm.

He got up from the bed slowly. Desiree asked if they had time to shower. He didn't but opted for a quick wash up. While he took care of that, she slipped into a short, red satin robe and went downstairs to grab his clothes. She sat on the bed and watched quietly as he dressed. They always talked. This awkward silence between them was unfamiliar to her.

"Derrik?"

After pulling the hoodie over his head, he gave her a serious look. He placed his foot into one of the sneakers while shaking his head. "No, Desi, we're not doing this right now. Not after what we just shared and certainly not before I have to leave. We can talk when I get back."

Once he put the other sneaker on, he held his hand out and motioned for her. She got up from the bed, placed her hand in his and they went downstairs. By the time they reached the bottom of the staircase, his phone rang. "That's probably Hodges letting me know it's time to go. Hang on."

Derrik pulled his phone out. He hastily let go of her hand in order to transfer the call to voicemail. He put the phone away and turned to face her. He didn't say anything as his eyes met hers. Instead, he wrapped his arms around her waist and bent forward. His kiss was tender, and his embrace was firm, as it always was.

He released her and kissed her forehead. She walked him to the door. He hadn't made it to the truck when his phone rang again. Desiree watched as Derrik answered the call, climbed into the back of the SUV, and pulled off.

She hadn't missed his reaction when he realized it wasn't Hodges who'd called. And even though his phone had a privacy screen, from that angle, the name on the display didn't escape Desiree's eyes. A burning question was now on her mind: unless he had an upcoming project with the Kardashians . . . *Who the fuck is Khloe?*

CHAPTER
18

Troy gulped down the remaining ginger ale. He inhaled deeply and let out a belch as he exhaled. That seemed to calm his stomach, which was what he needed. The release of the bodily noise was loud enough to disturb Mark. He looked up from his iPad and stared at Troy with raised a brow.

"Man, Mark you know this helps."

"There's no need to be nervous," he said reassuringly.

"We haven't been on SportsCentral since my rookie year. That was an easy interview. This won't be. They're out to embarrass me, I know."

"Relax, Troy. Everything's going to be okay. If they ask anything we didn't agree to discuss, just respond the way I told you. Don't dare try to answer anything we didn't go over, understand?"

Troy nodded. Mark reassured him he was in capable hands. He'd also recruited a seasoned and well-known public relations firm to help him project a more positive image of Troy to the public. They'd be in charge of arranging and coordinating his media appearances in the months leading up to the season's start. He needed all the positive press he could get, considering the damage Mia had done.

A woman wearing a headset and a t-shirt with the show's logo on it approached them. She carried a notebook in her hand. "Mark Wilson?"

"Yes, I am, and you are?"

"I'm Tiffany. Nice to meet you and Troy. I'm really excited you guys are here. I'll be assisting the stagehands in getting Troy set up here shortly."

"Okay, great," Mark said.

She pointed. "Troy, the gentleman to the right over there will be assisting you with cues and the teleprompter."

He looked at Mark, puzzled. "Teleprompter?"

Tiffany responded, "I'm sorry . . . umm, I guess they didn't tell you. There will be a few times in the show where we'll need you to follow along with the hosts in certain dialogue. It's basically fillers for conversation to keep the flow of the show going. Is that cool?"

Mark held up his hand. "May I take a look at what he's expected to say?"

"Yes, of course. Hang on. Let me grab it from my planner. Ahh yes, okay, here you go. We should be getting underway as soon as the hosts are hooked up."

Mark scanned the show's scheduled itinerary. Nothing looked out of place. He nodded at Troy. "It's all good. Nothing for you to be concerned about. Like she said, follow along."

Tiffany smiled and nodded. "Troy, if you would come with me, please."

Mark followed, trailing a few feet behind them. Tiffany talked to Troy after she instructed the staff to get him prepped. "I have to tell you I'm really excited to be working with you today, Troy. My husband is one of your biggest fans. He's happy that you're coming back this year."

Troy beamed. "Please tell your husband thanks for the support. I appreciate it.

"I sure will."

As they hooked up his microphone, he asked, "Do you have something I could autograph for him?"

She almost let out a scream but kept her cool. "Would you—you'd really do that for him?"

"Of course I would for one of my biggest fans."

Tiffany squealed. "Okay, I'll be right back while these guys finish setting you up."

Moments later, she returned with a miniature football and a Sharpie. Troy signed it and handed it back. He spoke with confidence. "Tell your husband we're taking it all the way this year."

"Thank you so much, Troy. And keep your head up. No matter what, you've got people who support you."

He'd seen the downshift in his fandom and support in the last several weeks. He looked at Mark, who gave him a nod of approval. He gave Tiffany a friendly smile. "Thanks. I needed to hear that."

It took a few minutes of getting the audio equipment in place and working before the bright lights on the set were shining on Troy. He looked over at Mark who seemed to be cool and relaxed. Seeing that his emotions were in check seemed to ease the tension Troy had started to feel coursing through his body. When Tiffany walked away, Troy motioned for him. Mark came over to the desk.

"What's up? You good?"

Troy shrugged. "I'm still a little nervous, I guess. I feel unprepared. I know you told me how to respond, but you know how they do."

"Yes, it's possible they will ask you about what happened. Remind them this is an interview about you and your return to a game we all love. Stick to answering questions about your plans for this season. Anything outside of that, I'll handle. If I have to shut the taping down, I have no problem doing it. Now what I need you to do is chill."

Troy nodded quietly and straightened his back. He shifted in his seat and rested his elbows on the desk. Mark stood there watching as Troy twisted about once more, attempting to iron out the imaginary wrinkles on his shirt.

Mark leaned in. "Relax, Troy. I've got everything handled. You're going to do fine."

"Nah uh! Hell no! What is he doing here?"

Troy and Mark turned. Even without seeing her face, Troy knew exactly who that voice belonged to.

Mia stepped into the studio in a form-fitting, white mini dress and a pair of gold Giuseppe stiletto sandals, her luxurious, jet-black tresses hanging loose. She exuded nothing less than goddess vibes. She moved with the style and grace of a model as she made her way toward Troy and Mark. His gaze traveled up and down with each step, taking in her swaying hips, shapely thighs, and long legs. In terms of natural curves, his wife's figure was unrivaled. Troy did everything not to let his mouth drop open. He shifted in his chair and pressed his hand against his bulging crotch.

"Who's over this set?" she demanded from a small, brown-skinned woman in her early twenties. "Go get Tanya. Somebody needs to have answers. I didn't come here to deal with this."

The girl rushed out of the studio, and Tiffany and another producer made their way over to Mia. Mark could hear them attempting to reason with her, but it was useless.

"I don't care! This was supposed to be my studio for the morning. Don't worry, Tanya will be here shortly. Either you or your boss has some explaining to do."

Troy began to stand, but Mark stopped him with a raised hand. "No, you stay put."

Mark noted that Mia had entered the studio with cameramen following close behind. It was a hunch, but he was certain the cameras were already recording everything.

Troy frowned but remained seated. He had no idea what his wife was up to. He'd done everything he could to rectify the situation. Normally, they would've made up and moved on by now. But despite his attempts to reach out, Mia continued to ignore him. She'd changed the passcodes on the house and the entry gate too. Troy was frustrated that she kept this nonsense up and refused to speak to him. He caught her staring at him. She quickly averted her eyes when their gazes clashed. He smirked, remembering she had the same look on her face that night he stopped by the house and they had sex in his office. He noticed her hair wasn't up in a bun. It hung loose the way she knew he loved it. She'd said they were done, but Troy knew they weren't. He could feel she still cared for him, wanted him.

Mia lowered her eyes and fiddled with her phone as if she were sending texts. Her husband, as expected, was dressed to impress and looking finer than ever. She hadn't planned for her heartstrings to pull and her pussy to purr at the sight of him. Her plan couldn't be derailed by her lustful desires for him. She didn't want to send him any mixed signals, after all. She wasn't there to make amends. Mia wanted Troy to know this time she meant business.

A few minutes passed before Tanya came into the studio. Her face became flushed when she looked around and recognized what was happening. Mark moved closer to where Tiffany, Mia, and Tanya were standing.

Tanya extended her hands. "Mia what are you doing in here?"

"What do you mean what am I doing in here?" she snapped. "I'm here for our taping, as you instructed."

"Goodness, Mia, this isn't Studio Nine. This is Studio Ten." Tanya then spoke to her young assistant, "Perhaps there was some miscommunication, but we're not taping on this set."

Mia sneered and adjusted the tone of her voice. "You know what, it's all good, Tanya."

Mark noticed Mia signaling the camera crew. He moved back to the desk and whispered to Troy, "Don't say a word. Please let me handle this."

"You're a trifling son of a bitch!" Mia spat from behind Mark as she started to approach the desk.

Troy's eyes widened, but he didn't respond. Mark immediately took a few steps to keep the distance between them and gestured for Mia to stop.

"Not here, Mia. You don't have to handle it like this."

She retorted, "Handle it like what, Mark? I haven't done anything to be handled."

"You're ready to go off on Troy, and he hasn't done anything. We also know you shouldn't be here." He looked at Mia's agent. "Tanya, is that your name? You're her agent, right? How did this even happen? Did you know we would be here? I know she has her cameramen recording. Are you two out of your mind?"

Tanya responded coolly, "Yes, I'm Mia's agent. You've asked a lot of questions. Perhaps we all can sit down, and they can discuss things amicably."

"Are you serious? Absolutely not! What are you up to here? Where's JaJuana?"

Mia responded, "She's not up to anything. JaJuana is busy handling other affairs of mine. Now, I was supposed to be taping in this studio today."

"I think we all heard the inability of your staff to relay important information. This was not the set to do your video shoot. It was Studio Nine, correct, Tanya?" Mark quipped. "It's quite obvious you're baiting your husband for a reaction, Mia. You're making a spectacle of yourself, and all for what? This reality show? Ruining your marriage for ratings? Your husband doesn't want that. No thanks, Mia. Now we're heading to the back until you leave, so we can avoid this unnecessary, yet

149

obviously staged confrontation." He spoke to Tiffany, "Do me a favor and make sure your people do not allow her back there."

"Yes, of course, my apologies. And trust me, I didn't know anything about this," Tiffany pleaded.

Mark reassured her that he wasn't accusing her or blaming her for anything. Troy finally stood up and walked toward Mark and the others. His eyes found Mia's, searching for a reason for her anger and the bizarre behavior. There was no love in her eyes as she glared back at him.

"Yeah, why don't y'all just leave? And don't you worry about the reality show. You need to be concerned about your precious wide receiver. They won't think you're so great when they find out how you really are," Mia taunted.

The muscle in Troy's jaw twitched. She was going too far. Why was she so hell bent on destroying his career? He realized why Mark told him to stay seated and remain quiet. The show's hosts and crew members were watching him intently. Troy had the feeling everyone expected him to explode or lose control. Mark began walking and cleared a path between the cameras and the other side of the stage. Troy followed without making eye contact with anyone.

Mark stopped and turned around. "Tanya, I suggest you have JaJuana give me a call as soon as possible so we can discuss this scene being omitted from the reality show. I do not recall my client ever agreeing to make guest appearances. Also, do not schedule anything with Mia when you know Troy will be present. It's better for everyone involved if they are not in the same room."

"Yes, of course," Tanya responded quickly.

Mia rolled her eyes at Troy as they exited the studio. "You make me sick!" she shouted at his back.

"Don't turn around, Troy. Just keep walking. She knows the cameras are rolling. Hell, I bet she was the one that set this entire thing up. Everyone in here looks caught off guard and embarrassed. You did a great job staying quiet."

Without slowing his pace, Troy responded through gritted teeth, "Yeah, but I'm sure I would've done an even better job in helping her shut the fuck up."

CHAPTER
19

"Did you call the detectives?"

"No, I forgot. I've been so busy at work with this new project. I'll call them after my appointment."

"I know your ass is happy Derrik showed up and put that make-up dick on you."

She'd told Brielle about Derrik's surprise visit but omitted the part about the phone call he got before leaving. It wouldn't have bothered her as much if the mystery woman, Khloe, hadn't called so late at night. And the way he quickly sent her call to voicemail was so obvious. Desiree didn't expect things to go back to normal right away, but their interactions since that night had been short and sporadic. She didn't want to overthink things and allow insecurity to set in, but it all seemed suspicious.

"So, when do you plan on telling him?"

"Telling him what?"

Brielle glanced at her before looking back at the road. "Since you're acting slow, let me rephrase the question. When are you going to tell Derrik about his baby?"

"Bri, we don't know if this is *his* baby." Desiree paused then spoke slowly. "And I've decided I'm not."

"What do you mean you're not?"

Desiree turned her face towards the window and mumbled, "I can't do this, Bri. On top of not knowing who this child's father is. I'm not entirely ready to be a mother."

Brielle realized what Desiree meant. "Hell no! I know you're not talking about doing what I think you are. Desiree Michele Edwards, you selfish bitch! I'm sorry you're not ready to be a mother, but, diva, that is not the solution."

"You don't know what it's like, Bri. You're not in my shoes, so don't you dare judge me on what I want to do with my body."

"I'm not judging you, and I don't have to be in your shoes to know what to do in this situation, Desi. That baby didn't ask to be created. I'm disappointed that you would even think *that* is an option. *We* don't do shit like that. *We* handle our business like grown women. What the hell's the matter with you?"

Desiree realized they weren't going to agree on the matter, but she remained firm. She threw up her hands, "This is my decision, Bri. I don't expect you to understand. Do you know how embarrassing this is?"

"Get the fuck over yourself, Desi! You made this mess for yourself. I told you that you were playing with fire, fucking with Troy's stupid ass."

Desiree tried to reason with her, "I've thought about all my options. I don't want to think of going through a pregnancy and giving my child up for adoption."

"I can't believe you're saying this. We all make mistakes and can learn from them. No matter what, that child would have love from you. And I know that if it's Derrik's baby, whether you're together or not, he'll support both of you."

Desiree closed her eyes as she thought about that day in the restaurant when she and Derrik described their children. She wanted a child, but not when she wasn't sure who its father was.

She opened her eyes. "That's just it. *If* isn't something I want to gamble with. I can't imagine how much it would hurt Derrik all over again if this baby is Troy's—a baby that would be a reminder of my betrayal." She paused for a moment and shuddered remembering everything Derrik said after the funeral. "No, I can't do this, Bri. I just can't."

"Of all the things you could do, this would be the one thing I cannot and will not support you on. I'm sorry, but I won't stand by your side. The truth hurts, and you need a reality check. Fucking without a condom brings consequences, and you're not some dumb-ass hood rat who doesn't know any better. You've been selfish about a lot of things, but this takes the cake."

"I understand, Bri."

Brielle's forehead creased. She couldn't believe Desiree was considering terminating. She could never even think of that if she had the chance to bring a life into the world. They remained silent for the rest of the ride. When they arrived at the medical park, Brielle followed Desiree into the building and to the obstetrician's suite. While Desiree checked in at the front desk, Brielle found a couple of empty chairs for them in the semi-full waiting room. When Desiree made her way back to the waiting area, Brielle was on the phone with Justin.

Derrik should've been there instead of Brielle. But Desiree needed to know for sure that the baby was Derrik's. Perhaps he would be more forgiving knowing that it wasn't his best friend's.

"Mrs. Edwards? Mrs. Edwards?"

"Desi?"

She snapped out of her thoughts when Brielle lightly tapped her shoulder. "Huh? I'm sorry, what?"

Desiree saw the nurse holding a folder with her name on it. "Dr. Logan will see you now."

"Uhh, my friend is going to come with me since my husband couldn't make it."

"That's fine. Y'all can come back with me."

They followed the nurse through the door that led them down the hall filled with examination rooms. After Desiree provided a urine sample, the nurse took her vitals, weight, and additional blood samples. Then she escorted them to an exam room and instructed Desiree to remove her clothing and put on a gown.

"Dr. Logan will be in with you shortly."

"Okay, thank you."

Once the nurse closed the door, Brielle sat down in one of the empty chairs across the room from the exam table. She didn't bother talking to Desiree. She was busy on her phone, probably texting Justin.

A few minutes later they heard a knock at the door. Desiree answered, "You can come in, Dr. Logan."

A short, fair-skinned woman walked in. She had long, gray locs and appeared to be in her early fifties. "Why hello, Mrs. Edwards!" she bellowed out in a bubbly tone.

"Hi, Dr. Logan! How are you doing?"

"I'm doing well, thank you for asking. How are *we* doing?" she asked pointing at Desiree's mid-section.

Desiree couldn't help blushing. "Pretty good. I haven't had any morning sickness, thank goodness."

"Consider yourself to be one of the lucky ones." Dr. Logan looked back at Brielle and smiled, acknowledging her. She turned back to Desiree. "Where is Dr. Edwards? I thought he'd be here to join us for the first visit. I know how much he wanted this baby too."

Desiree smiled nervously. "He couldn't be here."

Brielle stood and extended her hand. "Dr. Logan, I'm Brielle Stephens, the baby's godmother. It's a pleasure to meet you."

"Likewise." Dr. Logan said. They exchanged a quick handshake before Brielle sat back down.

"All right then, let's get started. Let's get you to lie down," Dr. Logan instructed as she went over to the sink and washed her hands before getting everything prepped for the exam. She pulled the stirrups from the table and instructed Desiree to place her feet in them. She slid the gloves on and began asking Desiree a few medical questions. Once she completed the pelvic exam, they discussed her family history and the results of the tests she'd taken a few weeks before. Dr. Logan then grabbed the ultrasound gel from the table.

"We get to hear the baby's heartbeat today?" Desiree asked.

"Yes, and this is going to be a little cold at first," Dr. Logan said right before she squeezed the bottle.

Desiree nodded and gasped as the cold gel made contact against her flat belly.

As she moved the Doppler over Desiree's abdomen, Dr. Logan spoke. "I can tell you this much Mrs. Edwards, with the date you gave for your last menstrual cycle, you're a little over nine weeks pregnant."

Desiree peered over at Brielle and repeated, "Nine weeks?"

"Yes, so we should be able to get a strong heartbeat," Dr. Logan replied. Right then the sound of rapid galloping filled the room. "Well, will you look at that? He or she heard me and wanted to let you know they're okay, mommy."

"Wow," Desiree whispered. Tears streaked down the side of her face as she listened to her baby's heartbeat for the first time.

Fascinated by it all, Brielle had questions. "It's going so fast. Is that normal? When will she get to see him or her on an ultrasound?"

"Yes, that's very normal, Brielle," Dr. Logan confirmed. She went on to explain the speed of the baby's heartbeat as well as the other developments they could expect as the weeks progressed. Desiree's next appointment would include an ultrasound. "You'll get to see your jellybean then."

Desiree grinned. "Okay, thank you so much, Dr. Logan. We'll see you then."

As soon as Dr. Logan closed the door, Brielle quizzed her friend, "So, who's this baby's daddy?"

CHAPTER
20

"Thank you inviting me to join you for golf."

"You're welcome. I needed to get out and relieve some stress anyway," Jamal said, smiling.

"I've wanted to learn how to play the game for a while now. I had a friend who played, but he wasn't trying to show me. He said it would take too long to teach me."

"Don't worry, it's not that difficult. Once you get the hang of the swing, you'll be fine. Come on, let's go."

Jamal got Christian through the eighteen holes within three-and-a-half hours. Christian had caught on quickly after the first hour, and that made the rest of the afternoon with him move along smoothly and effortlessly.

"Wow, either you're a natural, or that was beginner's luck," Jamal said, chuckling as he put his bag and the rest of his things in the trunk.

"Hey, I'm an easy study you can say. I pick up things pretty fast for the most part. I didn't tell you this, but I was valedictorian at my high school. I graduated from Tuskegee with summa cum laude behind my business degree. I also graduated with honors when I received my master's in marketing from Columbia," he said in a snooty, yet mocking tone.

Jamal chuckled. "Well, excuse me. I'm just a surgeon with his own practice."

"Ha! This is true. I almost forgot about that. I'm sure you're probably smart too." They started laughing but were interrupted by another man stepping up to them.

"Hey, Jamal what's going on, man?"

"Hey, Horace! What's up?" The two men exchanged a quick handshake and short hug. Another man joined the circle and also gave Jamal a handshake.

Horace spoke first, "Hey look, I'm sorry. I've been meaning to call. We heard about Rico. How are you doing?"

Jamal forced a smile and shrugged. "I'm all right considering."

"Yeah, understandable."

"Oh, let me introduce y'all to another friend of mine," Jamal said.

Christian extended his hand. "What's up? How y'all doing?"

"This is Christian Hilcrest. He hasn't played the game but learned quickly today thanks to me, I believe. Chris, this is Horace and Tim. They're friends of mine I met on this very course a few years ago."

Christian kept his expression neutral.

Horace grabbed his hand first. "What's up, Chris?" He laughed, "Don't worry, Jamal here didn't know what the hell he was doing when he started."

After shaking Christian's hand, Tim chuckled, "Yeah, remember how he swore he was Tiger Woods?"

The three men laughed, and Jamal bragged, "Whatever, man, but I got as good as him though."

"You're right. Your golf game is on point now. Can't nobody really mess with you," Horace said.

An awkward silence surrounded them for a brief moment.

"Uhh, Jamal I'm really sorry that happened to Rico. Any word on if they found out anything?" Tim asked.

Jamal could feel Christian's gaze on him as he explained he hadn't heard anything. He hadn't considered the possibility they might run into anyone who knew him and Rico.

"You know what? Maybe we can hang out for drinks. I know your schedule's crazy but hit us up."

"I sure will. Thanks, Horace. All right, Tim, thanks man! See y'all later!"

Jamal gave each man another handshake and hug before they exchanged handshakes with Christian.

"Yes, it was nice to meet you guys as well."

When they walked away, Jamal closed his trunk. He smiled at Christian. "All right, let's go."

Christian stayed quiet for most of the ride. He answered when Jamal asked questions, but he didn't engage much more than that. Jamal knew he had some explaining to do. As they approached the gate Christian finally spoke.

He rotated his neck. "First of all, my name is Christian, not Chris."

"Yeah, my bad. I've said it more than a few times. I didn't think you minded."

Christian glared at him before squinting his eyes. "Why did they call you Jamal, and who was Rico?"

Jamal ran a hand over his waves and exhaled. "Jamal is my name to those who know me outside of this lifestyle. Rico was a friend of mine who passed away unexpectedly last month. He used to play golf with me and sometimes with those guys."

Christian scoffed, "I see. *Outside of this lifestyle.* So they don't know you're gay?"

"I uhh . . . I'm . . . well . . ." Jamal glanced over at Christian.

Christian cocked his head to the side, pursed his lips, and folded his arms across his chest.

Jamal swallowed and confessed quietly, "No."

"Was he your lover?"

"Who?"

"The guy Rico."

He'd never given much thought to it. Rico had wanted more, but Jamal had never thought for a moment that they'd ever be more than casual partners. He wasn't attracted to his friend in that way. He had sex with Rico on the side for fun. Since he'd been open with Christian about everything else, Jamal came clean with his new lover.

"No, I mean yes. I suppose you could say that he was. I didn't expect anything to happen between us. It was supposed to be a fling. He kept pushing me to come out of the closet, but he welcomed this lifestyle more than I ever could. I was still with my wife at the time. I-I-I didn't know what I wanted, and I wasn't ready. It's complicated, okay?"

"Wow, so I guess I'm just something you're trying to figure out too then?"

Jamal frowned. The idea of being with a man for more than a fling hadn't cross his mind. But now he felt things for Christian that had him rethinking what he truly wanted. "No, no it's not like that. I can't explain it. With you it's different. I really like you, Chris—I mean Christian. What we have. I like this, and when I'm with you, I'm not afraid of it. Okay, so I'm not *out* out, but you're helping me with all of this."

Christian laughed and responded in a sarcastic tone, "You're not *out* out. There it is. Look, I'm done with the helping-brothers-come-out-of-the-closet phase, Jamie, Jamal, or whatever your name is. I've been down that road. Either you know what you want, or you're doing what society says. It's as simple as that."

Jamal shifted the gear into park. He turned to face Christian. "I know what I want. You asked me about Rico, and I told you."

"You just said you're not out of the closet. And you lied to me! Your name isn't even Jamie." Christian folded his arms across chest again and turned towards the window.

It tugged at Jamal's heartstrings. He shouldn't feel like this. He wasn't supposed to behave this way. But he couldn't ignore the magnetic energy between them. Jamal grabbed Christian's chin and guided him to look in his direction.

"Christian, please. I'm so serious when I tell you there's something about you. I can't put my finger on it but . . ." he paused and swallowed, "I'm starting to have these feelings, and they're pretty strong—more than I thought I could feel towards a man. That much I'm sure of."

Christian leaned forward, and Jamal met him the rest of the way. They stared at each other for a second before Jamal pressed his lips against Christian's. In that moment, it felt as though he kissed away all fear and shame. Jamal tilted his head and opened his mouth, sliding his tongue inside. They embraced each other as their kiss ignited a lustful fire.

Jamal slowly pulled away but only inches from Christian's face. He looked directly into Christian's eyes as he whispered, "I'm sorry I lied to you. I had no idea I would be falling for you."

"Come on, let's go. You're gonna make it up to me—right now."

As they emerged from the car, Christian came around to the driver's side and grabbed Jamal's hand. Jamal didn't pull away. Instead, he looked down at Christian lovingly as another couple walked by. The man shook his head in disgust and turned away. Jamal ignored him as he allowed Christian to lead them through the complex to his condo.

The moment Christian closed the door, Jamal pinned him against the wall and began kissing him even more passionately than he'd done in the car. It was as if Christian were a drug he couldn't get enough of. Christian pulled away long enough to remove Jamal's shirt and unbutton his pants. Jamal stepped out of his pants and Christian grabbed his boxers and pulled them down, releasing the thick, stiff rod already at its full length. He went down on his knees and licked up the salty precum oozing from the engorged tip. He gazed up at Jamal and winked as he opened his mouth and made his entire dick disappear.

Jamal threw his head back. "Shit!" he exclaimed, feeling Christian's tonsils.

Christian held on to the base of Jamal's dick and continued working it in and out of his mouth. He squeezed, pulled, and jerked as he sucked. The thick, dark muscle glistened from the saliva he intentionally left on it after each head bob. Jamal grabbed his throat and began fucking his face harder. The saliva increased and dribbled down Christian's chin. In his mind, no matter how good Rico thought his head game was, Christian's was the best Jamal ever had by far.

He slowed down in an effort not to release too soon. He eased out of Christian's mouth, leaving an oozing trail dangling from his lips. As he rubbed the tip across his lips Christian stuck his tongue out licking at it. Then Jamal helped him up from the floor and began removing his shirt and pants. He admired Christian's body. The sun's rays that seeped through the blinds seemed to bounce off his smooth, honey-toned skin. Jamal pulled Christian's boxers down, revealing his manhood. It didn't have length and wasn't as thick as his, but it was just as beautiful in tone. For the first time in his life, he felt a desire to touch a dick other than his own. Some of Christian's precum was oozing at the tip and Jamal gently rubbed his thumb across it.

"Hmm," Christian moaned.

"You like that?" Jamal whispered.

161

"Yes, more please."

Jamal slowly began giving Christian a hand job while tongue kissing him. They both moaned with pleasure as their lust deepened. Christian slowly pulled away from their lover's embrace, grabbed Jamal's hand, and led him into his bedroom. He stopped in front of the California king bed, sat down, and scooted to the middle, never taking his eyes off Jamal. Jamal crawled on after him right in between his legs, spreading his thighs. Once again, he grabbed Christian's dick and began stroking it as he played with his asshole with the tip of his dick. In one swift motion, Christian reached over and grabbed the KY jelly from his nightstand and handed it to Jamal. A couple of squirts on his head and in Christian's crack were all that he needed. He let go of Christian's dick and opened his thighs wider exposing the tight hole. Without thinking of protection, Jamal eased his thick head inside, then penetrated deeper and deeper until the base of his balls touched Christian's ass.

He shrieked, "Owww!"

"You wanted me to make it up to you, right?"

"Yes!" Christian cried out.

Jamal pushed Christian's thighs back and began delivering deeper strokes while he stroked his dick.

"I wanna see you come, Chris. Come for me!"

Christian started massaging and stroking his dick as Jamal pounded at his ass harder and faster. "Yes, Jamie! Fuck me! Yes!"

Enjoying the fact Christian still chose to call him Jamie, he went harder. "Yeah, that's right! What's my motherfucking name?"

"Jamie! Jamie!"

"Say my name!"

"Jamie!"

Jamal smacked the side of Christian's ass, making him shriek loudly.

"Oh shit! I'm about to come, Jamie!"

"Yes! That's it! That's it!" he shouted.

Jamal drove deeper as the creamy fluid shot all over Christian's chest. Jamal watched as he stroked the last bit out, and at that moment, he felt his balls tighten in response. Jamal began bucking harder, making Christian cry out more.

"Yes, Jamie! Fuck me!"

Jamal clasped his hips, pulling him into his final thrust. Then he fell forward after he released everything inside of Christian. He didn't think about the sticky remnants from his lover as he lay on top of him and rolled them over to the side. As he'd done in the hotel, Jamal cuddled Christian in his arms, falling fast asleep from their brazen act.

CHAPTER
21

"I'm glad you were able to come with me today," Mia said to Angela as she merged onto the highway. It had been a week since she last saw her friend. She'd checked in, and Angela told her that she wished she could live with her new normal, but each day felt harder than the day before. Mia figured having a girl's day out would do Angela some good.

"Of course. You know it's no problem. Besides, I needed to get out of the house."

"Did he come home last night?"

Angela shook her head as she turned her attention to the passing traffic. "No, he sent a text saying he would stay up at the hospital to give us some space. Maybe he's right. I've been lying around the house depressed about Tré's death. I haven't quite been myself lately."

"Yeah, about that, you haven't been drinking this morning, have you?"

Angela started fiddling with her bracelet. "No, but I'm wishing I'd had a glass before we left."

"Angela?"

"You know, just to take the edge off. I'm feeling a little anxious."

"What's up with that? I know you've always had a hard time handling challenges thrown at you. But I've never seen you like this. I'm worried about you, girl."

Angela shared that she'd been on prescription medications since her brother's death to help with the anxiety and depression. Some days she was okay. Other times it was unbearable. She wasn't sure when the dark cloud looming over her head was going to move. "I'm sure I'll be fine eventually. Jamal's right. I just need time to accept all of this."

After Mia parked the truck, she turned to face her friend. "It's not good that you're doing all this drinking, Angela. Especially while you're taking these meds."

"Come on, Mia you're starting to sound like Jamal. I haven't been drinking as much as you think, and when I do drink with the meds, it's only to get sleep."

Mia gave her a stern look.

"I promise you it's nothing to worry about," Angela maintained.

"What exactly did you say to him that he didn't want to come home and felt that y'all needed space?"

She lied, "I can't really remember, but I know he's getting tired of this."

"Tired of what? You're going through the grief of losing your brother unexpectedly and tragically. No, you shouldn't be drinking like this, but he should've stayed his ass right there to help you through your pain."

"He's been helping me, Mia."

"Hmph, I think it's strange. Haven't I told you don't put anything past a man? Is he really done with his wife? Is he really going to the hospital? How do you know he hasn't gone back to her?"

"He hasn't, that's how I know," she answered with pride and confidence.

Mia rolled her eyes and started to say something, but Angela defended Jamal before she could speak. She told Mia that Jamal had moved most of his things in and rented a storage space. His wife was supposed to call him to pick up the rest of things when she was out of town again. They were even talking about looking for a bigger house and keeping the condo as an investment property.

"I still say he should be there to console you."

"He is. He even calls and texts to check on me throughout the day. It's me. I've been blowing him off. It was no different the night before." She paused and confessed, "Okay, here's the truth. He came home and questioned me about drinking and taking the meds. I got nasty. I mean I was really rude, Mia."

"You're grieving, so you're lashing out."

Angela ran a hand through her long, curly hair before wrapping one curl around her finger as she sighed. "Yeah, well he tried to talk to me about possibly going to see one of his friends. I figured he was talking about a shrink, and no, Mia, I'm not going to see one, so you can forget about it too."

"I didn't say anything."

"Anyway, I yelled and cussed at him after he said I needed to sober up. I told him to leave. I even acted like they were calling him at the hospital, 'Paging Dr. Edwards.' Then I told him to go see about his patients. They're the ones that really need him—I don't."

"Damn, Angela that was cold. Maybe he's right about the drinking and popping pills."

She hung her head in shame. "Yeah, but it keeps me less anxious. I don't mean to lash out at him. I know he's only trying to help. It's just so hard. It's always on my mind."

Mia rubbed her friend's hand as she spoke gently, "I'm so sorry you're going through this. Have the police said anything else?"

"They have nothing, which is making this even harder to deal with. My brother didn't deserve this. I don't want his murderer to think we're letting up."

"No, and we won't let up. Tré's murderer will be brought to justice. Believe that, okay?"

"Yes, that's what Jamal says, and I know. Thank you, Mia. I really appreciate it." Angela quickly looked away as tears began to pool in her eyes. "We're here, right?"

Mia exhaled, "Yeah, we are, aren't we?"

"Well, let's get this visit over with and then you're off to do your first taping with the ladies from the show. I know you're excited about that."

"Yeah, I'm looking forward to it," she said as she unlocked their doors. After she stepped out, Mia took a moment to pull herself together as she looked at the medical building. Her stomach did a somersault.

"Are you okay?"

"It just hit me again why we're even here." Angela was grieving, but Mia had been dealing with her own loss. It had been several weeks since her miscarriage, and she still fought with feelings of guilt for having provoked Troy that night. Mia grieved the loss of her baby, but Angela reassured her it was best she didn't have any reminders of Troy lingering in her life, let alone a permanent link to him.

"You're right. Just saying though—it would've been nice to have a little crumb snatcher," she said chuckling.

"It'll happen eventually, but with the right man, just like you always tell me."

Mia smiled at her girl, and they began heading towards the building. Once Mia checked in at the nurse's station, she joined Angela in the waiting area. They were chatting about plans for her non-profit organization when Mia overheard a conversation on the other side of the wall.

"Shhh, wait a second."

"What?"

Mia held up her finger. She tiptoed towards the entryway that led to the nurse's station and pressed her shoulder against the wall. She peeked behind it then quickly pulled her head back so she wouldn't be seen. She continued to eavesdrop on the conversation until it was over, and two women emerged from behind the wall and walked past the waiting area. Mia waited until she heard the door close before peeking out again. She came from behind the wall and went to the entrance of the suite.

Angela came up behind her. "What's going on, Mia?"

"Nothing, but I need to speak to someone at the front desk."

"What's wrong?"

She looked out the window as Mia headed towards the nurses' station. Angela wasn't sure what she'd seen that appeared to upset her.

"Go ahead and sit down. I'll be there in a minute."

Angela frowned but went back to the waiting area as instructed.

Mia tapped on the glass window at the front desk. A young girl with blonde weave slid the glass window open. "Yes, Mrs. Harris, may I help you?"

"Uhh, yes, maybe you can. You see I . . . well, I think that might have been my sister that was just in here. I don't know but, I . . . it looked like her a-a-and . . ." Mia paused then turned her back as if she were looking at the entrance of the suite. When she turned back around, tears were streaming down her cheeks. "Look, I didn't want it to be weird okay. My dad wasn't faithful to my mom, and well, you know, I uhh—"

"Oh goodness, Mrs. Harris, here you go." She handed her a couple of tissues.

Mia dabbed her eyes as more tears fell. She sniffled, "No, no I'm sorry. I know I probably should've said something. But I couldn't get the words out. I saw her, and I just froze. That was Desiree, wasn't it?"

The young girl couldn't mask her shocked expression. She opened her mouth, but quickly clamped her lips shut.

Mia continued sniveling, "You know, I hate that my mom kept me from my dad after he cheated on her. I've been trying to locate him and Desiree for years."

She noticed the young girl was the only personnel up front. She leaned into the window as she pleaded, "I wouldn't dare ask you to do anything that would jeopardize your job, but please. I just want to talk to her."

The receptionist held up her hand. "Mrs. Harris, I don't think—"

Mia dismissed her and laid it on thick. "You've got to believe me. I would do anything to get back all those years we lost, but I can't. If it were you in my shoes, you'd want to do the same thing. This is my only chance. Do you think you can help me with that?"

Not wanting to give the young girl a chance to object, Mia pressured her relentlessly. "I can pay you," Mia leaned in and whispered. "Let's say a year's salary . . . doubled. And you know I can. No one would ever know. It would just be between us. So can you do that for me?"

The receptionist leaned back in her chair and stared back at Mia blankly. A few minutes later Mia returned to the waiting area where Angela was thumbing through a magazine. When she saw her friend, she quickly put it down and stood up.

"Hey, what was that all about? Who did you see out there?"

"Oh, it was nothing. I thought it was somebody I knew, but it wasn't her," she said dismissively.

Angela frowned and started to say something, but at that moment the nurse called Mia to come back. After Mia left with the nurse, Angela pulled out her cell. She dialed Jamal's number and got his voicemail. She left a short message apologizing for her behavior and asking that he come home so they could talk. Then she started watching the television, but her thoughts went to Mia's strange behavior moments earlier, and she wondered what her friend was up to. Suddenly, her heart started racing and her hands became clammy. "No, not now," she whispered to herself.

She quickly left the waiting area, made her way to the restroom, and stepped into the last stall. Although she tried counting silently and breathing slowly, she couldn't calm her nerves. She left the stall and went over to the sink. She ran cold water in her hands and splashed her face. When that didn't help, she rummaged through her bag, grabbing the prescription bottles. She quickly popped the pills and went back into the stall to sit. After a few minutes, she seemed to relax. Once the pace of her heart returned to normal, she walked out and almost bumped right into Mia. "Hey!"

"Hey!" Mia said. Then she leaned forward, looking at Angela closely. "Are you okay? Were you crying?"

"Oh, uhh no, no, not at all. I just needed to splash my face a little. I felt hot for some odd reason."

Mia leaned in closer to get a better look. "Are you sure?"

"Yes, I'm fine."

Mia beamed. "Everything was fine with me too. Let's get out of here. I've got to catch up with Tanya before this taping."

CHAPTER
22

"Hey, y'all! Heeeeeey! What's happening?"

Sounds of clapping filled the room. A tall, brown-skinned woman with a big, sandy-colored afro sashayed across the floor of the studio dressed in a multicolored form fitting dress and platform red bottoms. The bright lights behind the video cameras illuminated the stage as she made her way over to the oversized armchairs in the center of the studio.

"Welcome to another episode of *Baller Bizness* with yours truly, LaLa," she said waving to a studio audience.

"Annnnd Sisko!"

As the audience erupted into more cheering and applause, LaLa turned her attention to the man making his way over to her from the other side of the stage. He was short and stylishly dressed in a navy Tom Ford suit and brown shoes.

LaLa laughed heartily and joined the crowd in clapping. "Yes, my co-host, Sisko, is back in the building y'all!"

The pair playfully embraced and shared French cheek kisses before taking up seats opposite each other. Lala grabbed one of the coffee cups from the table between them and took a sip before speaking.

"Hmm, yes indeed! Welcome back, Sisko. You know we missed you last week."

Sisko's southern twang was thick. "Oh, my goodness, you know I missed you too! But I'm back, and baby, do I have some juicy stuff to tell y'all."

"Ooh weeee, y'all, he knows how to kick in the do' waving all the juicy info!"

"Yes, oh my goodness, and you won't guess which baller's business we'll be exposing today."

LaLa gasped and held up her hand. "Hold up, is it somebody I know? Did we ever?"

Sisko popped his lips. "Oh, my goodness, why do you always think it's somebody you done—"

"Hey, I gotta check. Hmph, you know these ballers be out here acting like they got amnesia come Monday morning when the Henny's out their system. But anyway, since it's not anybody I need to worry about, what's up? Which baller's business are we up in this week?"

Sisko cleared his throat and popped his lips again. "Okay so, it's somebody you know and are pretty close to."

"Who?"

"I have some juicy info on your boy Troy Harris."

"Wait a minute, I know it's not my friend that got exposed by his wife last month for putting hands on her. Nah uh, not my friend, the Falcons' star wide receiver, Troy?"

He nodded and popped his lips, "Ahh huh, yep, the one and only."

"Mmm, shut yo' mouth."

"Nope, I got too much juicy stuff to tell y'all about him."

LaLa shrieked, "Haaa, okay then! So, are they still expecting him to come back this season? 'Cause he's been out for a minute. They definitely need him back out there."

"I'm assuming yes. I haven't heard anything about him being released or traded. He's been out there practicing with the team the last couple of weeks. They've had him doing interviews and promos. However, I don't know how he's gonna be able to focus on the game with all of this drama brewing around him."

"Please, he's been in the news before. To be honest, it's no surprise we're hearing all this noise about him now, especially since he's about to play again. It's all a publicity stunt," LaLa said dismissively.

Sisko nodded in agreement. "Oooh remember a few years ago when he was accused of domestic abuse?"

"Those were charges brought up by a former girlfriend, correct?" LaLa asked.

"Yeah, and they were dropped."

"You know, that was probably another cover up by the league for one of its favorite players."

"Well, this time around, it ain't something they can just cover up. His wife showed that video of him attacking her, and from what I heard it was uuuggg-ly," Sisko stressed the word.

"We're talking about an alleged video that has gone unseen by the public. Troy's agent says the allegation of domestic abuse is a rumor at best," LaLa said, sarcasm thick.

"There were a lot of people at that party, LaLa, and they were on the blogs the next day saying they saw it for themselves. I'm mad we missed it."

"Me too. It would help if we had this alleged video."

"You know *Baller Bizness* attempted to get an exclusive about it from Mia's camp, but we were unable to reach them."

LaLa pursed her lips and shook her head, "Remember I said it looked like they were covering something up."

"Hmm, she *is* the senator's daughter. I know he ain't trying to have all this drama around the Wynters family. I just think all of this is interesting considering the scoop I have on Troy now," Sisko hesitated and started fanning himself. "It was way more than I should've seen girl."

LaLa smirked. "What's the scoop, Sisko?"

He leaned in and popped his lips, "Now you know there's always been rumors of him cheating on his wife, right? Looks like Mia has all the proof she needs that those rumors were true. Troy can't lie about this being photoshopped, that's for certain."

"Whaaaaat?"

"Yes, girl. And I tried to reach out to Troy and his publicist about it. You know, to hear it directly from the horse's mouth."

LaLa leaned in. "Right, right so what happened?"

"We've been camping out everywhere, and we finally caught up to Troy when he was leaving the gym. Let's just say he was not happy about us ambushing him."

"Would you be? Hmph, this guy is trying to get back to the game he loves after being out for the last year and a half. And here comes all of this drama threatening to keep him off the field."

Sisko rotated his neck and popped his lips. "Ion know, but let's roll that beautiful baller footage."

Music began to play as the stage lighting dimmed until the room was dark. Then the flat screen televisions around the studio powered on, and the video began to play.

"Troy! Hey, what's up, big guy?" Sisko placed a microphone in front of his face.

"I don't believe this sh—talk to my PR rep, man," he mumbled.

"We've already tried that, but no one has returned our calls."

"Not my problem," Troy retorted.

"I know it's not, but you can speak for yourself, can't you?"

Troy tried to maneuver around Sisko, but Sisko kept in stride with him. "So are your lawyers trying to keep that video of you abusing your wife from coming out?"

"Go ahead, yo. Why are you even talking to me? 'Cause I ain't saying nothing."

"Tell us, Troy, how do you feel about your wife putting out the video footage of you abusing her?"

"I didn't—" Troy paused and spoke through clenched teeth, "Yo, man, talk to my rep or my agent."

"You didn't get arrested. Does this mean y'all are getting back together?"

Troy turned to walk away, but Sisko followed, shouting at his back, "Hold on! Wait a minute, Troy! What I really wanted to ask was if you knew about this other video. I think you should know it's of you having sex with another woman."

Troy spun around. "What did you just say?"

"Whoa, don't kill the messenger. I'm just letting you know somebody is ready to expose you and a woman that's clearly not your wife. I came here to get the story directly from you. You know we can do an exclusive."

"Man get the fuc—go ahead, yo. I'm done talking to you."

"Wow, you look surprised."

"Get out my face with the cameras for real."

"Who is the other woman, Troy?"

"I told you get that *bleep* camera outta my face!"

"Troy don't touch the camera! Oh, shh—"

There were sounds of a scuffle before the screen went black. The studio lights began to rise again and illuminate the stage as gasps and mumbling rose from the audience.

"Yeah, well, I guess he didn't know," Sisko said shaking his head. "And clearly, he didn't appreciate hearing about it from us."

LaLa put a hand on her chest, "Did he really swing on you?"

"Hell no! That would've been a whole 'nother show. He slapped the camera out of my guy's hand and walked off. I don't know why he acted like that. It doesn't change the fact that we still have the video. Now it's too hot for TV, but it's been on our site since last night. Last I heard, it had close to a million views."

"Well, while we were watching your footage, the producers handed me this," LaLa said as she held up a piece of paper.

"What's that?"

"Troy's camp has issued another cease-and-desist order to all blogs and news outlets to prevent either of the videos from being shown. Whatever was published previously has already been taken down from the sites. They've threatened to sue if any of this footage gets out."

Sisko shook his head. "I'm sure there's more to be revealed about this story." He looked at the camera in front of them. "And we'll be here to give you all the juicy 411."

LaLa nodded. "Stay tuned, folks. We'll be right back after a word from our sponsors."

CHAPTER
23

Desiree rubbed her stomach. A smile formed across her face as she thought about the baby she carried. The decision to terminate her pregnancy wasn't as easy as when she'd first considered it. She'd heard her baby's heartbeat. The date her doctor gave was too close for her to be completely sure, but she felt the baby was Derrik's. She told Brielle the only thing she could do was pray the baby belonged to him.

Her phone rang. "Hey Bri, I was just about to call you."

"Uh huh. Well, you didn't, so I take it you haven't heard about your boy."

Desiree walked over to the desk and sat down. She swallowed hard. "Who, Bri?"

"Troy, girl. It was on *Baller Bizness* a little while ago. I was checking the gossip columns. Desi, this shit is crazy."

"What happened?"

"Hold up, let me ask you. Do you know if Troy recorded y'all doing it?"

"What? Hell no! At least I don't think so. Why on earth would you ask me that?"

"Girl, somebody leaked a video of Troy having sex with another woman."

"But why would you think it's me, Bri?" Desiree asked angrily.

"Did you conveniently forget his wife recorded him beating on her ass? And uh, didn't you sleep with him in their house?"

Desiree didn't respond. Her heart started pounding.

"Nothing to say, right? There's no telling if she had cameras installed all over that house to catch him in the act. And from the looks of it, she got some footage of his stupid ass cheating too. I didn't see it, but people have been sharing some screenshots. The quality is choppy, but Desi, that woman sure as hell looks a lot like your ass."

Words failed her. She remained silent trying to process Brielle's announcement.

"Uh hello? Are you there? Desi?"

"Yeah, I'm here. I don't know what to say."

"Girl, what is there to say? But I do think you need to be ready to deal with some shit if your identity is exposed. That chick Mia is ruthless. Your ass will be on that reality show right along with Troy. But unlike him, you don't have an agent or a publicist who can keep your image clean. Why don't you call one of your brothers?"

"I can't involve them or anybody else in my family," Desiree argued.

"Well, you need to find somebody to help protect your image and reputation."

"I can't believe this, Bri."

"Believe what? How you created all this drama for yourself? I told you to leave Troy's punk ass alone. He's never been good to or for you."

Desiree attempted to defend herself. "We don't even know if it's me. You said the picture quality was choppy, right? And who knows who else Troy's been sleeping with? You've always said he screws anything not nailed to the ground."

"Okay, that man and his wife are Atlanta's biggest side show act right now. Would you like to join the circus with these clowns? Desi, I'm pretty sure that's you. Now go find somebody who will keep your ass from ending up in *The Shade Room*."

Desiree knew she couldn't argue with what Brielle said. There was a chance the woman in the video was her. She began thinking about Brielle's suggestion to protect her image. There were a couple of entertainment attorneys Aaron knew personally. "Okay, I know who I need to call. Let me go, Bri."

"Good, call me later. I'll be listening and watching to see if anything else comes up. Love you, diva."

"Thanks. Love you too, diva. Bye."

CHAPTER 23

Desiree grabbed her laptop and began searching for the articles. Almost immediately, the search came back with the popular blog sites' headlines: "Troy Harris Caught Cheating - Sex Video Leaked!" and "Atlanta's Star Wide Receiver, Troy Harris - Sex Video, Click to Watch." Reluctantly, Desiree clicked on the link to the Atlanta-based show, *Baller Bizness*, but she noticed the link to the recording was no longer valid. She breathed a sigh of relief and continued reading.

According to the article, Troy was caught on tape having an affair with an unknown woman. At the time the show aired, the woman's identity was unknown. They speculated that Troy's recent split from his wife was likely due to the physical abuse, and now the woman from the sex video attempting to extort money from him. Desiree decided she'd read enough and closed the browsers. She didn't waste another minute in calling Aaron. Without revealing too much about the situation, she asked for his connections. He was able to give her a couple of names to start with.

"Is everything okay, Desiree?"

"Yeah, I'm fine. I really appreciate your help. Although I work with a lot of people, I know you have more connections than I do. I couldn't think of anyone else."

"Right, well, one of them should be able to help. If not, let me know, and maybe I can help." For a moment there was an awkward silence on the line. Before Desiree could end the call, Aaron spoke up, "I am glad you called, Desiree. I wanted to ask you something."

"Sure, what's up?"

"That night after dinner, was everything good between you and Jamal?"

Desiree frowned. She didn't understand why he was concerned about her husband. "Aaron, why are you asking about us? I thought we already discussed this. I had too much wine to drink, but just like in LA, we shouldn't have kissed."

"You're right. I guess, you'll let me know if you need anything else."

"Yeah, I will. Thanks again. Talk to you later. Bye."

Desiree thought for a moment about Aaron's question. It was a mistake to let him kiss her in LA and at the restaurant. Like she'd told Brielle before, there was something about the man that unnerved her. She was adamant about not leading him on. She wished she didn't have to bother him about anything. After taking a deep breath, she pressed the button to call Derrik.

"Hey."

"Hey, yourself," he said.

Desiree picked up on the various voices in the background. She could hear women's laughter. A feeling of jealousy rose in the pit of her stomach. She did her best to push the thoughts to the side and laughed nervously, "I figured you were probably busy in the studio. I didn't think you'd answer."

"What's up, Desi?"

She heard the curt tone in his voice. Perhaps he'd seen the video. The pace of her heart sped up.

"I'm sorry, did I catch you at a bad time?"

"Yeah, as a matter of fact you did. I just got settled here in Miami, and we're trying to get ready for this awards show. You need something?"

"No, I, umm, well yeah. I was hoping we could talk about—"

"What did I tell you? We're not doing this over the phone."

"Okay, I . . . well, I want to make sure I have a chance to talk . . . to explain things," she appealed.

She heard him take in a deep breath and exhale. It sucked to hear him sounding so annoyed, but she had to accept it, especially after what she'd done.

"I'm going to be down here for a couple of days. We'll talk when I get back."

"Okay, then. I guess if you get time later, text me or you can call. I'll answer. And, Derrik, I love you."

"I'll holla at you later." He ended the call.

Desiree stared at her phone. She noticed that once again, his tone was off. He didn't call her "baby girl" once. He didn't respond with "I love you" either.

Suddenly, her mind began racing. *Was that girl Khloe with him?*

CHAPTER

24

Troy hopped out of his Range Rover in a hurry. He made it to the sidewalk in seconds and headed towards the building across the street in long strides. Mark could hardly keep up.

"Wait a minute, Troy, where are we? You haven't told me everything about this meeting." Mark gripped Troy's shoulder to slow him down to a stop. "Will you hold up for a minute? I agreed to do this because you said this involved your foundation to help the kids. With all that's going on we certainly don't want any surprises. Now who are you meeting with? What do you plan on talking about?"

Troy pointed towards the door. "I forget the girl's name. She said I needed to be here by noon. We better go. They probably already started."

Mark didn't protest and allowed Troy to lead the way into the building. His phone rang as they walked in. While Mark was on his call, Troy spoke to the man at the concierge desk, who pointed in the direction of a hallway off to the right.

"He said the conference rooms are that way."

Mark nodded and followed Troy down the long hallway until they reached the last set of double doors on the left. By the time Mark read the placard listing the event's information and its attendees, it was too late. Troy opened the doors and bolted in. There was a woman on a stage speaking behind a podium.

"Ladies, I want to thank you all for taking time of out of your busy schedules to join me in this endeavor by a beautiful soul. When I met her, I was intrigued and inspired not only by her

story but what she wanted to do for other women like her. We are here today to forge a network of women across this country and one day worldwide . . ."

Troy scanned the room until he found her in the front row. Mark grabbed his arm, but he yanked away from his grip. Troy made his way to the right side of the room and leaned over whispering in her ear, "I need to talk to you, now!"

Mia turned her head and greeted him with a sneer. Without breaking eye contact she got up. Troy straightened his back. She acknowledged Mark with a threatening glare. Shaking her head, she leaned over and whispered to the woman sitting next to her. Then Mia looked back at Troy and motioned for him to follow her. As they walked out, they heard whispers behind them:

"Was that him?"

"Yes, I think that was."

"No, it couldn't be."

"The nerve of him coming up in here. I hope he's not going to put his hands on her."

"Somebody should go out there with her."

Mark picked up his pace to ensure he stayed between the two of them as Mia guided them out into the hall. When they were in the hallway and several feet down from the conference room, she spun around on the both of them.

"You two have some fucking nerve showing up here."

"Give me the video or I'm fucking you up!"

Mark gasped. "Troy!"

Mia rotated her neck. "Oh, you ain't fucking nobody up! You thought you could come down here and bully me. That might have worked before but nah uh, I have too much on you now, and I will completely ruin what's left of your precious little career and worthless reputation. I dare you to touch me, Troy."

Mark opened his mouth, but Troy leaned in and spat, "Stop with the fucking games. Give it to me."

She laughed evilly and continued with even more confidence, "Your career is steadily going down the drain, yet you're worried about some amateur sex video of you and your lil' ho. Ha! We've done better, Troy."

Troy frowned, and Mark could see that her taunting was fueling his rage. He forced Troy to take a few steps back to put some distance between him and Mia.

Then Mark looked back at her and spoke in a low but stern tone. "Mia, I hope you're not the one behind this other video coming out."

"How can I control what these gossip sites get a hold of?"

"Man, why are we letting her get away with this?" Troy asked desperately.

"Letting me get away with what? I haven't done anything, yet," Mia replied with a smug grin.

Troy shot daggers at her. "I know you did this! Stop playing fucking games, Mia!" he bellowed.

"Troy, lower your voice," Mark pleaded.

"Games? This isn't a game, you trifling son of bitch! You should be more careful about who you fuck with!"

Troy's fists were tightly clenched, but Mia did not flinch. She stared back at him, her chest heaving. "Wait, why are y'all even here? I thought we were supposed to stay away from each other," she said finally, addressing Mark.

"Mia, I had no idea he was coming here. I want to apologize for that."

"Nah uh, apology not accepted, especially coming from a man who would work for and defend a client who repeatedly beat on his wife over stupid, petty shit."

Mark stared blankly at her. When he opened his mouth to respond, Mia cut him off. "I've always had Troy's back. I supported and encouraged him when everyone else out here gave up on him, including Troy himself. Did you know that last time while I was lying up in a hospital bed getting treated for another one of his attacks, I lost a baby I didn't even know I was carrying? How about fuck him and your apology."

Troy's face transformed. His rage dissipated instantly as a wave of remorse flooded over him.

Mia continued her rant. "You didn't think I'd ever find out about your side bitch, did you? I'm so glad I did, and now everything has come out. Let's see how long everybody keeps cheering for your sorry ass."

Troy dragged his hands down his face. "Mia, you—you were pregnant? Why didn't you tell me?"

"I just said I didn't know! Even if I knew and told you, do you think that would've stopped your evil ass!" she shouted.

He nodded vigorously and his voice was full of regret. "Yes, it would've. A baby? My—our baby? Mia, I know how much you wanted one. I wouldn't have touched you, I swear. I'm really sorry."

"You really are a sorry-ass motherfucker! But you're not feeling sorry over me losing our baby or for bringing that bitch into our house. Fuck you!" she spat.

Mark tried to calm things between them. "Troy, Mia, please. This is not how we should handle things."

Mia turned on him and snapped, "How should we go about this, hmm? Tell me, Mark Wilson, sports agent of the decade. You know how to swoop in and save the day with some lies so he looks good for the public, right?"

Mark pleaded, "Please, Mia, this can be handled in a different way."

Troy tuned out their exchange. He rubbed his forehead as the memory of that night came back to him. In his rage he'd beaten their baby from her body. He couldn't believe he'd taken the life of his child. Without saying another word, he began walking away.

"Hold up! Where the fuck are *you* going, asshole?" Mia yelled after him. "You came down here all big and bad, poppin' shit. Don't leave now. I was just about to let you in on the little secret I found out from your sorry ass cheating." She shouted at his back, "Did you know that Desiree is pregnant?"

Troy stopped dead in his tracks.

"Ahh, yeah. I'm sure that got your attention."

He turned around and looked into Mia's cold eyes. "What did you just say?"

"I know that was her in our house, you lying-ass bastard! Ohhh, but I wonder if Derrik knows. I saw them at my people's funeral, and they were awfully chummy. Tsk. Tsk. Tsk. If she was fucking you and your best friend, I wonder which one of you is this baby's daddy?" Mia paused and rubbed her hands together. "This is going to be sooo good. I'm pretty sure the media is going to have a field day with this one." She chuckled as she looked at Mark. "You better get your press releases ready." Mia folded her arms across her chest, a look of satisfaction on her face. She'd done everything she set out to do. Troy turned and walked away.

The conference room doors flew open. The event's coordinator, Tanya, the cameramen and a few of the guests came out and headed in Mia's direction. Mark jogged to catch up to Troy. He grabbed his arm, pulling him to move faster as people began filling up the area. They could hear Mia's voice down the hall as they walked away.

"Yeah, you heard me! I know about your side chick, Desiree, getting pregnant. If it's not Derrik Carter's baby, she'd better be careful. You'll probably beat it out of her too!"

By the time they got outside, Troy was flustered, and his breathing was erratic. Mark led him away from the building and guided him to a nearby bench. Troy sat down and covered his face with his hands, choking as tears streamed down his face.

Mark stood over him. "What the fuck was that, Troy?"

He shook his head.

"First of all, don't you ever lie to me again! Second, what the hell were you thinking showing up here of all places? Did you come down here to be a part of this reality show nonsense?"

Troy removed his hands from his face and appealed, "No, of course not! I just wanted her to, you know, stop with all this. I figured I could talk to her. I didn't even know she was pregnant. I swear I wouldn't have touched her. I know I wouldn't have."

He ignored Troy's claim of being innocent in the matter. He was busy assessing the damage of everything that had just transpired. Mark wasn't sure who had seen or heard their exchange, but the fact that his client showed up to a public event for an explosive confrontation with his wife was enough drama for the gossip columns to drag him for days.

"Troy, I'm sorry buddy, but you can't bring that baby back. We've got something bigger to deal with right now. The fact that you showed up here is one thing I have to clear up, but did you hear what she said about Derrik and Desiree being pregnant?"

He nodded.

Mark continued to probe. "Is she the woman on the video?"

Troy thought about the only woman he would be so bold to bring into his home. "Yeah."

CHAPTER
25

"Did you bring the rest of the boxes?"

"Yeah, I picked them up on my way home yesterday. Here, take these bags. I grabbed us some chips, dip, fruit, and wine for me, of course."

Desiree placed the grocery bags on the granite-top island and peeked inside. "I see you weren't playing."

Brielle started singing the popular chorus from Erykah Badu's "Tyrone." When Desiree completed the rest of the verse, the ladies burst out laughing.

"That's right, girl! Let's get his shit outta here!" Brielle cheered as she carried some boxes into the kitchen.

Desiree finished pulling the items from the bags and began setting up the trays for their snacks. Brielle took a wine glass from the cabinet. After everything was ready, they headed to the living room.

"For real, I can't wait until my lawyer tells me he's been served and we have a court date."

"Speaking of lawyers, did you call one about the video?"

Desiree told her she had indeed retained a lawyer—a female attorney who listened to her concerns and put her mind at ease. The lawyer reassured Desiree that she would do some research on all parties involved, but for now, her identity was safe, and she had nothing to worry about.

"Good, I'm happy you did that. And what about Derrik?"

187

"No, nothing else from him since we spoke the other day. Do you think he knows about the video?"

"I don't know. Maybe. It's the biggest gossip going on right now. And then your boy went to one of Mia's events and showed his ass. Derrik's been traveling, and he had this awards show, right? Matter of fact, it's coming on in a few. Let's watch it. We can pack later."

Desiree handed Brielle the remote. "I can't seem to let go of this feeling he's going to say it's not his baby. What if he doesn't want to be a part of this pregnancy because of what I did?"

"You're worrying for nothing. Derrik will be ecstatic to know he's going to be a father. You said it yourself. Y'all were already talking about it before that asshole popped up."

"Exactly. That was *before* he popped up. Bri, Derrik was rude and short with me. That's not like him."

"Desi, y'all had bomb ass 'I miss you' sex, as you put it, but did you really think this man was going to make it easy for you after you got caught and blew him off for weeks? I wouldn't make it easy for you either. I'd let that ass marinate for a few more days. Maybe weeks depending on my mood."

"Bri, you're not helping."

"I know I'm not. You lied to me too. I want you to feel this. Next time you'll be smarter than to play with this kinda fire. Stop acting like one still ain't enough for you. Derrik's a good man."

"Yeah, I know."

"But I told your ass that years ago. They might've been boys, but he knew Troy was messing around on you. I don't think he ever gave two shits about that fool and his feelings. He's been waiting for the chance to snatch your ass up."

"You act like Derrik didn't have a lot of girls too, Bri."

"Yes, I'm sure he's had his fair share of women, but he was single. Troy wasn't. Let's not forget Derrik's never been serious about anyone except you."

Desiree burrowed herself into the corner of the loveseat and pulled her knees to her chest. "I didn't like how that felt, you know, when I called him, and he was so short with me."

"I'm sure it didn't feel good. But I hope you know his feelings are bruised far more than yours."

Desiree sighed. "I just want to talk to him and get this out in the open."

"And you will when he gets back. Oooh wait, it's coming on. Girl, you know I need to see my future baby daddy, C-Breezy."

"Oh god, you with this man again. You need to get with his people and try to put something together."

"Don't worry about all that. I'm already on it. I'm waiting on his people to contact my people."

Desiree gave her a look of disbelief. "Hold up. What's up with Justin, *Peaches*?"

"You ain't funny, heffa. We're still going strong. He comes over almost every day to either cook or fuck or cook and fuck. I'm seriously considering getting out the game for this one. That man has me—"

Brielle stopped mid-sentence. She looked over to see Desiree scooting to the edge of her seat, eyes glued to the TV screen.

"Turn it up," Desiree said. "I want to hear what he's saying."

Derrik was giving an interview on the red carpet. Desiree could not stop staring at the beautiful woman on his arm. She took note of their playful and overly familiar exchanges as photographers snapped photos. They were giggling like teenagers. Desiree's blood began to boil.

"Who is that?"

"I don't know, probably one of his artists or a groupie. What I do know is she's killing it in that dress. She's petite and about my height. Do you see those stilettos? I wonder where she got 'em from. I want a pair!"

Desiree cut her eyes.

"What? Come on, you've got to give it to the woman. She's absolutely gorgeous and stunning in that dress."

Desiree looked at best friend and sucked her teeth. "Whatever, she's okay."

"No, she's really beautiful, Desi."

"I said she's okay!" she snapped back.

The women stared at each other. Desiree turned her attention back to the television when she heard the interviewer ask if they were a couple. Derrik

189

introduced her as a good friend and business associate that agreed to accompany him for the evening.

"Now it makes sense," Desiree mumbled.

"What?"

"I told you how rude he was."

"You can't think she means anything. You heard him say she's a business associate."

"Bri, how can you sit there acting like you didn't see the chemistry between them? And you didn't hear how he sounded on the phone."

"Desi, you need to relax. I'm telling you the man was giving you a taste of your own medicine. You decided to come around, but he wasn't about to drop everything he had going on. It's nothing, so cut it out."

"No, Bri, it's something and exactly the reason I'm not going through with this. I don't know what I was thinking. This won't work."

"Going through with what? What won't work?"

Desiree got up from the couch and went over to the mini bar on the other side of the living room. She pulled out the bottle of rum.

"What in the hell are you doing? You better put that bottle down."

Desiree stared back at her with defiance as she grabbed a glass. Brielle jumped up and made it over to her friend in seconds. Brielle snatched the bottle from Desiree's grip, returned it to the cabinet, and stood in front of the door.

"Have you lost your fucking mind?"

"Did you forget? I've already been drinking, Bri. And I can keep drinking. Soon enough, this won't be an issue."

"Desi, stop it."

"No, why should I carry this baby if it's his, and he's already moved on to the next woman? Bri, I messed up, but I'm not begging him to be with me."

"Who in the hell said you had to? And he hasn't moved on. Stop thinking the worst. That woman is nobody."

Desiree threw her hands up. "No, Bri, you stop it! You can't tell me that was nothing. You and I both know Derrik doesn't deal with his groupies on that level. They would never walk the red carpet with him. We've seen *all* the women he's had on his arm, especially that last one, Marley—the actress with the big ol' booty. Nah, there's something up with this one."

"Why are you doing this to yourself, Desi?"

"I'm not doing this. It's obvious that Derrik would rather be with her instead of giving me a chance. You know how it is with men like him and Troy."

"Desi—"

"No, I messed up, okay? I get it. I messed up!" Desiree opened up and told Brielle about the call Derrik received as he was leaving her house that night, his reaction, and the mystery woman named Khloe. Everything had felt off since then, and this had to be the reason why. She went back over to the loveseat and plopped down. She pulled her knees to her chest and wrapped her arms around her legs as the tears started to fall.

Brielle sat next to Desiree and pulled her close as she sobbed. No, she couldn't ignore the chemistry she'd witnessed between Derrik and his companion. She hoped she was wrong.

CHAPTER

26

"Hey, Derrik over here! Yes, over here!"

He smiled and exchanged a quick hug with the woman. "Hey LaLa, what's up? I didn't know you were going to be here."

"I have exclusives to do on a few of our Atlanta natives. And I've been meaning to call. We have to talk about your boy."

"Oh no, we don't."

"Come on, Derrik, you know him better than anybody. I need to get the whole story behind this video."

"Hell no, girl. You're not about to use me to drag him any more than you already have. Why don't you just call him?"

"I tried, but he isn't returning my calls. Y'all know how this works. It's my job to dish out all the juicy business on y'all ballers."

Derrik shook his head.

"Anyway, who's the lovely lady? Is she our new love interest?" She didn't give him a chance to respond. LaLa moved over to examine the beautiful woman. She looked back at Derrik, nodded, then returned her attention to the woman and laid it on thick. "Heeey, girrrl! How you doing? I must say it's good to see somebody finally settle this playa down."

He hadn't intended on bringing Khloe. She invited herself to come when Hodges brought her assistant. She practically begged to tag along to see what she'd invested in years ago. He made sure to clear it up for the nosey gossip show host.

"Ahem, for the record, I'm not a playa. This is Khloe Dillon of Dillon Ventures. We're business associates. That's it and that's all. Got it?"

LaLa frowned at him.

He cocked his head to the side and gave her a stern look. "LaLa?"

"Okay, okay, I got it. Business associates."

"Good. Now, Khloe, this is LaLa. She's a good friend of mine and one half of the dynamic duo from the popular show *Baller Bizness*. She's also a blogger for a gossip column, so watch what you say."

"Shut up, Derrik. Don't mind him. I don't put out anything you don't want me to put out. Anyway, I love your dress. Those sandals are bomb-dot-com. Girl, you are killing it!"

"Thank you," Khloe responded, beaming.

"Wait a minute, you kinda look familiar. Have we met somewhere before?"

"I don't think so. I've never been to any of Derrik's events."

LaLa tapped her chin. "I can't put my finger on it at the moment. It'll come to me eventually."

"You've probably seen me featured in a few business magazines such as *Forbes* or *Black Enterprise*." Khloe replied almost in a snooty tone, holding her head high.

"That's probably where it was." LaLa eyed him and smirked. "You're really stepping out with the hotties this year, Derrik. First, it was Sienna, then Marley—"

"Okay, LaLa we have to get inside. Thank you. Have a good night."

"You know you owe me an exclusive interview when we're back home. I want to hear from you!"

Derrik threw up the peace sign as he and Khloe walked away. "Sorry about that. Like a lot of these vultures, it's her job to report the gossip in the entertainment world."

"Was she being phony? How does my outfit really look? Was she just saying that only to write something else? I'm not sure how it goes with fashion at these events. Looking at the rest of the women, I almost feel underdressed."

Derrik looked down at her and smiled. "Relax. I highly doubt she was being phony. You look stunning, Khloe. Your dress and those sandals . . . yeah, bomb-dot-com, girl."

She blushed. Her bronzed skin tone glowed flawlessly against the Vera Wang gold, strapless dress that hugged every inch of her curvaceous body. Jimmy Choo stiletto sandals showed off her shapely calves. It was no wonder Khloe had captured the attention of several photographers: not only did she look stunning, but she was on the arm of the most sought-after bachelor in the entertainment industry.

Derrik knew the gossip columns were going to speculate about them attending the event together. LaLa was right. As an eligible bachelor, he'd been on the dating scene quite a bit. Last year he'd dated an international model. After her, there was the professional dancer, Sienna, and then the actress, Marley. He'd almost gotten serious about her. She was like Desiree in many ways, and for a while Derrik felt as though he'd found a woman who could make him forget about the love he'd carried for Desiree all these years. But he had to end things when Marley's obsession with Khloe went too far. One night he'd forgotten to lock his phone. Marley went through his texts and saw some racy messages from Khloe. She saved her number and began harassing and threatening Khloe, who in turned taunted Marley. Khloe told her she wasn't going anywhere, and she would always have Derrik. Derrik downplayed his relationship with Khloe, but Marley couldn't let it go. They argued about it endlessly, and he got tired of trying to prove he wasn't cheating with Khloe. Marley let her insecurities about Khloe get the best of her.

His thoughts shifted to Desiree. It was clear she hadn't given up on them. She reached out daily letting him know she loved and wanted to be with him, and if not, she hoped they could still be friends. At first, he didn't listen to the messages or read the texts. When he finally did, Hodges's words hit him hard. There was something special between them. He missed being with her. It was the reason he'd decided to see her that night. He had a feeling she saw the call from Khloe. After an explosive session of lovemaking, he wasn't going to ruin it. In the days that followed, Khloe was nearby every time Desiree called. He hated blowing Desiree off, but he couldn't speak freely with Khloe around. He was also adamant about not discussing anything over the phone. He couldn't wait to get back. He was ready to make a decision.

"Are you okay, Derrik?" Khloe asked, interrupting his thoughts.

He couldn't tell her truth. "Yeah, it's just jitters kicking in. No matter how many times I come to these shows, I'm still nervous getting up on stage to present."

"I'm sure you'll do fine."

A photographer approached them and asked to take a couple of photos. "Thanks, Derrik. You guys look great together."

Khloe squeezed Derrik's arm. "You know we really do make a cute couple."

He responded with a smile and led her into a waiting area where other photographers bombarded them.

"Hey, Derrik! Are you ready for this evening? I heard BlakBeatz is going to walk away one of the evening's top recipients."

"I sure hope so!" he replied.

Another photographer stopped them for a few pictures. "Wow, you two make an awesome pair, Derrik."

Without responding he guided Khloe through another swarm of photographers. Then he leaned in whispering, "Sorry I didn't warn you about the paparazzi and media vultures. They're always looking for a story or photos like me leaning in to tell you this. It'll be on the blogs tomorrow that you're my new love interest."

Right then, a photographer snapped the two of them in the moment.

"I think that was our official couple alert pic," she whispered.

He burst out laughing. "At least you're being a good sport about it. Just don't let it go to your head, Klo."

As the lights from the cameras continued flashing, she tried to keep up with the requests to smile. In between the flashes she spoke up. "Derrik this is a lot. I wasn't ready for all this attention."

"Understood. Let's get out of here, away from the cameras. Come on, I'll introduce you to some of my artists." Derrik guided Khloe into a banquet room where artists, presenters, and other guests of the evening were popping bottles in celebration. He introduced her to so many people that she couldn't keep up with their names. They mingled until the show producers came in to let them know it was time to begin.

As the photographer predicted, BlakBeatz came out as the top recipient of awards that night. After the show, Derrik's entourage were in great spirits and decided to head out to the after parties to celebrate. Since he'd hung out with his artists the night before for pre-celebratory drinks, Derrik decided against going out again. He wanted to bask in the moment of his company's success, but away from the fans and paparazzi.

"You probably want to go and hang out with your assistant," Derrik said to Khloe. "Miami nightlife is where it's at. Far better than 'the A' in my opinion. This night scene hasn't been my thing for a while though. Been there done that. And we have to head out early, so I'm going back to the hotel."

"Would you mind if I chilled with you?" she asked softly.

He'd enjoyed her company throughout the evening and didn't mind spending the rest of the night with her. Several minutes later he was escorting her towards his presidential suite. When he opened the door to the massive space, Khloe dropped her mouth in awe. She'd been in executive suites, but nothing like this. The suite had separate sleeping and living quarters, both with fireplaces. Derrik showed her the master bedroom that led into a huge bathroom. There was a large soaking tub with a TV above it. She couldn't wait to try out the glass-enclosed rain shower. There was a wet bar, full-prep kitchen, and a furnished outdoor terrace with a gorgeous view of the city.

"Dayyyum, Derrik Carter, this is how we doing it? I guess being the CEO of BlakBeatz, you can afford something like this, huh?"

"Cut it out. You know good and goddamn well I can. My money's as long as—hold up, I'm sorry. It might be a little longer than yours now." He winked. Then he went over to the bar and poured each of them a drink.

"So, it's like that now? Well, lemme hold something before them hoes get it then."

Derrik laughed heartily. "You're crazy. Hell no, I'm definitely not letting none of them hold anything of mine. Here." He handed her a glass.

Khloe grabbed his hand when he lifted his glass to his mouth. "Wait, we have to toast, especially after tonight."

"You do the honors. I've done enough speeches for the night."

She cleared her throat. "Let's see. First off, congratulations! Thank you for allowing me to accompany you as your guest tonight. I had a wonderful time. Honestly, all these years I had no idea this was the other part of what you've worked so hard on. If anything, I can say I am very proud of you. At least my investment wasn't a total bust."

He chuckled and flipped her the middle finger.

"All jokes aside, Derrik. I knew back then you were someone special. Your ambition and enthusiasm for the business was infectious. You're an amazing, intelligent, and hard-working man that deserves everything your heart desires. I wish you nothing but continued success in all you do. Not just in your business endeavors, but in your personal life as well. Here's to many, many more years of success for BlakBeatz Entertainment. More importantly, cheers to you, my beloved." She lifted her glass.

He nodded. "Wow, thanks, Klo."

The sounds from their glasses clinking echoed throughout the room. Derrik moved the glass to his lips but paused for a moment to observe her. He thought about what she'd said. He truly couldn't have done it without her financial backing, guidance, and mentorship. Even if she had selfish motives, she'd taken a chance on a young man with a dream, not knowing if he would accomplish the goals he'd set. He could've taken her money and blown it. Khloe's investment hadn't been a bust. His company flourished due to his dedication. He genuinely appreciated everything she'd done for him over the years.

Derrik smiled before gulping the drink down. He poured another and finished it off within minutes. They moved to the couch with another round of drinks in hand. He attempted to listen as she kept going with praises on his accomplishments, but he was starting to feel the effects of all the alcohol he'd consumed throughout the evening. His mind went elsewhere as he watched Khloe's lips move. Instinctively, he licked his. Trying to stay focused was useless. His eyes roamed the length of her body. She lifted her glass to her mouth. Before she could take another sip, he took it from her.

"Hey what the—umm, where are you going with my drink? I wasn't finished," she pouted.

"Hush, you talk too much. Come here." He cupped her face between his large hands. His lips brushed lightly against hers. Khloe leaned into him. He moved one of his hands to the back of her neck, guiding her face closer. She tilted her head and opened her mouth, welcoming his tongue to explore hers. She tasted like vodka and cranberry. It was sweet on her tongue. His kiss was fervent as his hands explored her body. He massaged her plump breasts and groped her thick ass.

She began caressing his chest. She slipped a hand underneath his shirt. Her index finger and thumb found a nipple. She pinched gently rubbing it between her fingers. Derrik's moaning vibrated in their kiss. She repeated the same with the other nipple. She moved her hand down to his growing package. His hand covered hers. Khloe pulled away and stared into his eyes for a moment. She squeezed harder.

"Fuck," he groaned.

She moved in swiftly and locked lips with him again. Her taste was intoxicating and sent him further into a drunken haze. She rubbed her hands across his bald head. He gripped her ass tight and rocked her hips. She grinded against his crotch.

"Hmm," she moaned.

"You like how that feels don't you?"

"Yes!"

Derrik unzipped the back of her dress with ease. She helped by releasing the hooks of the halter bra. Her perky breasts popped out. He bobbed his head to get to her areolas. Once his mouth latched onto one, he started sucking like a newborn nursing. He alternated from one nipple to the other, giving each the same amount of attention. Khloe grabbed at his shirt. He helped her by pulling it over his head. She went for his belt buckle and loosened it. Derrik assisted her, getting the rest of his clothing off as she stood up, shimmied out of her dress, and eased her thongs off.

"Damn, you're sexy as fuck. Get over here." He pulled her onto the couch, and she snuggled underneath him. Her hair fell across her face, shielding her left eye. Derrik pushed it away. Khloe gave him a look that begged him for more. He kissed her again before making a trail of wet kisses down to her belly button. His fingers played at the entrance of her pussy, and she spread her legs wider to welcome them. He slipped two inside. His nose rested on her mound. He inhaled the scent of her pussy and couldn't resist it anymore. Derrik joined his fingers and began sucking on her clit.

"Yessss!" Khloe hissed.

He sucked and fingered her pussy until she dripped. He pulled away long enough to reposition himself above her and ease every inch of his thickness inside. Khloe held on to his forearms as he began his rhythmic strokes. She writhed against him and arched her back, lost in her climax. Derrik eased out of her and sat down on the couch.

"Come on. Ride this dick," he growled.

Khloe squatted over him, lowered herself, and guided his thick shaft inside. She placed her hands on his washboard abs to steady herself. She worked her hips, sliding up and down. Derrik thrusted his hips up and pistoned harder. She squealed. "Ow! Oooh shit! Fuck!"

A few thrusts in he stopped. "Damn, after all these years, you still can't take the dick in this position."

She grinded against his pelvis and bit into her bottom lip. "No, you have a big dick, my beloved."

He grinned and lifted her up, rolling her over into doggystyle. She poked her ass out. Derrik rubbed his dick back and forth across her clit before sliding inside. He pumped a few times, and her heated walls clinched him tight. The tingling sensation rose in his abdomen, but he wasn't ready to release. He slowed his pace, paused, and withdrew from the creamy heat. Khloe dropped lower, putting a dip in her back. She reached behind and spread her round ass cheeks apart welcoming him. He plunged into the warmth and delivered hard, rough strokes. The juices came flowing. The sloppy sounds of their lust sent him in a frenzy. Derrik pumped faster and harder. He clasped her hips and pulled her into his final thrust. "Fffffuck!"

Minutes later, he eased from her and collapsed on the couch. Khloe rolled from her position into his arms. Derrik planted a kiss on her forehead and relaxed into the cushions. He closed his eyes.

"Derrik?"

"Hmm, what's up?"

"I love you."

She'd respected their friends with benefits arrangement all these years. She'd never spoken those words to him. Yet, Derrik knew when things had changed. Several months ago, when he ended the relationship with Marley, Khloe made it known she wanted more. He knew after they'd spent the past couple of weeks together, she probably felt like they had a chance. She'd already hinted about relocating to Atlanta.

"Did you hear me?"

He opened his eyes, eased her out of his arms, and sat up straight. He rubbed his hand across his head a few times. "Yeah, I did . . . I umm . . . Klo, that's loaded." He glanced back at her. "You don't mean it like that way, right? Like *love*, love?"

"Yes, I did mean it that way because I love you. I've loved you for years. Don't you love me, Derrik?"

"Why are you asking this now? What do you want me to say?"

Khloe was rebuffed by his response. She got up from the couch and turned away as her voice cracked. "Nothing at all."

"Damn, you know I got a lot of love for you, Klo, but it might not be the way you want it."

"Excuse me. I need to go to the bathroom."

He mumbled, "Fuck." He knew he'd hurt her feelings. He leaned back, staring at the ceiling. For years they'd managed to keep their business and personal relationships separate. He knew he should've ended things between them a long time ago.

It wasn't her fault. She wasn't Desi.

CHAPTER
27

Troy paced the floor frantically, recalling the events that had unraveled everything in his world. He stopped and mumbled incoherently before starting to pace around the living room again.

"Troy, you need to calm down. This isn't helping."

"How do you expect me to do that?" he snapped. "If all this shit was happening to you, tell me what you would do, huh?"

Mark chose his words carefully. "First, I'd do my best to come to terms with what I couldn't change. What's been done cannot be undone. Secondly, I'd be grateful that in spite of all the drama, I still have my career that I can look forward to getting back to in the coming months. Finally, I would sit down and listen to my agent's suggestions. I'd trust that he wants the best for me and will do everything possible to fix the problem."

Troy stopped pacing, walked over to the couch, and sat down beside Mark.

"Look, "Mark continued," I'm sorry about what happened to Mia, and it's unfortunate you had to find out like that. But it's in the past now. You can't let this take you out of your element, Troy. You have to focus on moving forward."

Troy sighed deeply. "I know you're right. She's getting under my fucking skin doing all of this shit."

"You have to let it go. All of this about Mia, let it go. You didn't have to show up there for anything."

"I get it, Mark, it's just that—"

Just then, Mark's phone rang. "Hang on let me get this."

Mark answered the call, and his expression changed instantly. He got up abruptly and walked toward the middle of the room, keeping his back to Troy.

"Yes, I understand what you read, but that's not what happened. You can't believe everything people post on the internet. Your sources are wrong. I am not at liberty to release any information or conduct an interview until we've done our research to refute any false claims towards my client. Fine, thank you. Goodbye." He turned around to see Troy frowning.

"They're dragging me through the mud, right?"

"Troy—" His phone rang again. "Hello, this is Mark Wilson. Yes, I'm aware of what's going on. Yes, my client was in an altercation with his wife. No, that's not what happened, and you do not have any sources to back up that claim. No, we do not have a statement at this time. Yes, we will release one soon. Thank you. Goodbye."

"Who was that?"

Mark tried to reassure Troy everything was under control, but unfortunately, Troy's latest stunt had gained a lot of attention and threatened to deal another blow to his credibility in the public's eye. That second call was Sisko from *Baller Bizness*. They'd published a blog post that included photos of Troy and Mia's latest confrontation. One photo showed Troy pointing and yelling at Mia. Another displayed his fists balled up. Mark was furious, and Troy knew it.

Troy sighed heavily. "I was just trying to get her to stop with all this shit."

Mark yelled, "What the hell do you think I get paid to do? That's my job, not yours! What's the point of us doing all this work to keep your image clean just for you to ruin it? Now you're messing with *my* money, Troy!"

"I'm sorry, yo."

"How did you even know she was going to be there?"

He confessed, "One of the guys. He said his wife was going to support her cause."

"Great, this is just fucking great. Look, I'm not going to repeat myself. I don't care what you hear, stay home. You understand?"

"Yeah, Mark."

"I'm serious, Troy. Stay in the house!"

"I heard you, and I will, I promise. I don't wanna mess up my chances to play," he replied humbly.

"Good. I have to get to the office and meet with the PR team on the strategy for our next move. I'll call you later."

After Mark left, Troy grabbed his phone. He needed to know if Mia was telling the truth. He'd called and texted Desiree, but she hadn't responded. He tried calling her again, but the call wouldn't connect. He stared at the phone for a moment. His instinct was to call the only other person who could possibly confirm it.

"Eh yo, what's up, D? Is there something you wanna tell me?"

"No. Why, what's up?" Derrik asked.

He hesitated for a moment before blurting out, "Did you know that Desi's pregnant?"

"What? Hell no! Did she tell you this?"

"No, Mia did."

"Huh? How would she know?"

"I don't know, but somehow that bitch knows about us—me, you, and Desi. Trust me, she was the one that leaked that video of us fucking."

"Wait, what video and of who fucking?"

"Nigga, she recorded me and Desi fucking at the house!"

Derrik heaved a sigh of frustration. "So that's the video LaLa was talking about."

"Yeah, and when I see LaLa's ass, I'm fucking her up. She ain't have to do me like this. And Mia said she saw y'all hugged up at her people's funeral."

"Are you talking about Rico? She was there?"

"Man, I don't know nobody name Rico. But I guess that's who she was talking about. But that ain't the point. She's saying Desi's pregnant. How do I know if that baby is mine? Clearly, y'all was fucking longer."

Derrik argued, "Whoa, hold up, T. You just blew my mind. This is all news to me. Desi didn't say anything about this when I saw her last week."

"So you still fucking with her? Man, this shit is . . ." His voice trailed off.

"What?"

"Nothing except I was trying to get shit straight with us, but Mia's doing her damnedest to fuck my life up. All for this stupid fucking show. She's threatening to put it out there that Desi's the girl in the video and she's pregnant. But that's not scandalous enough for her. 'Cause she knows my best friend fucked her too, and he might be the daddy. You know she's gonna to do it. She's right, D. The media's gonna have a field day with this one!"

Mia bragged, "I wish the cameras were there for it. You should've seen his face when I told him I knew about the woman he cheated with."

"I had no idea he was there until one of the cameramen told me. I'm sure this will be the trending gossip for the rest of the week," Tanya said.

"More like the rest of the month. It's not my fault he chose to crash the event and a make a spectacle of himself. Did you check to see if anything's been posted about it?"

Tanya turned her laptop so that Mia could see the screen. The internet was lit up with the news of Troy and Mia's confrontation, and it didn't help that the event Troy crashed was a fundraiser to raise awareness about domestic abuse. Blog articles detailed Troy's bad behavior; the gossip pages posted various pictures of the altercation; Instagram and Black Twitter dragged Troy yet again and encouraged Mia to leave him once and for all. There were different versions of what happened, but the social media outlets all agreed that Troy was an abusive cheater.

"I guess we have *Baller Bizness* to thank for giving everyone the 411!"

"Did you send them that sex tape, Mia?"

"Remember your connection, the talk show producer?"

Tanya's eyes widened. "No, you didn't."

She snickered. "I did. She was eager to pay a nice sum of money for a copy. She probably sold it to *Baller Bizness* and the rest of them."

"You're so scandalous."

Mia grinned and rubbed her hands together. "I know. Now it's time for us to execute the next phase."

"Huh, next phase?"

"Yes, we're not done."

JaJuana walked in. "Oh, yes you are, Mia. I told you there would be repercussions if Troy's situation changed. He has to remain employed by the NFL in order for him to keep those endorsements. Did you somehow forget that in your efforts to discredit his character?"

Mia tilted her head to the side. "You think I give a fuck about his credibility right now?"

JaJuana peered over at Tanya who shrugged. A line etched between her brows as she appealed, "Mia we've come far enough. Let go of this vendetta you have against Troy. I don't know how *Baller Bizness* got hold of this other video, but it's not helping his situation. If Troy gets released, you both will lose everything. Is that what you want?"

Mia looked up at the ceiling and sighed. "You know something, JaJuana? I have no use for people who don't support me. I'm trying to secure what will be a lucrative future for the empire I'm building."

Tanya raised her eyebrow at the statement. JaJuana crossed her arms. "What are you getting at, Mia?"

Mia tossed her long, jet-black tresses and drew in a long breath before exhaling. She looked her lawyer in the eye and announced, "You're fired."

"What?"

Tanya's jaw dropped open.

"You heard me. I'd like to terminate my contract. Your services are no longer needed. I'll find representation from someone who'll find ways to help me instead of spending their time chastising me.

JaJuana scoffed, "I did help you. It's obvious I'm not the help you wanted. I had a feeling you would do something impulsive and irrational."

"This is neither impulsive nor irrational. My plans involve more than what you're willing to do as my legal counsel. I've paid you for the services you've provided thus far, but right here? Yeah, this is as far as I'm willing to go with you."

"That's fine, Mia. I hope you can find a lawyer that's equipped to deal with these kinds of shenanigans. This isn't the kind of business I prefer to handle anyway. And you haven't paid for all services rendered. I'll send you a final bill. Good day."

Without allowing her to say anything else, JaJuana pivoted and exited the conference room.

"I can't believe you just fired her. Why would you do that?" Tanya asked.

"Yeah, why would you do that, Mia?"

Mia's eyes widened at MJ standing in the doorway. "MJ? Wh-what are you doing here?"

He closed the door behind him. Instead of responding, he moved around the large conference table to sit at her right hand. He nodded and winked at Tanya sitting across from him. A flush crept up her face as she ran a hand through her curls and nodded back at him. She caught Mia giving her a dirty look. She averted her eyes back to the laptop. MJ rested his elbows on the table and turned to his sister.

"I'm here because dad and I see you're on a reckless path of destruction. Why did you fire your lawyer?"

"She wasn't doing her job, MJ. Lawyers like her are annoying. She was getting on my last damn nerve, challenging everything without listening to my side of things."

"Your side of things? Mia, what the hell is going on? Why is that video of Troy circulating? After I told you not to put it out, you did it anyway."

Mia lowered her eyes. "Did Daddy see it?"

"He heard about it. And you weren't returning his calls. That's the other reason I'm here."

"Are he and mommy back in town?"

"No, but when he does get back, he wants to see you. Be ready to explain how Troy's been abusing you and you haven't said a word. And he didn't like hearing it's none of his business."

She gave herself the facepalm knowing she would hear some choice words from their father. "You really told him I said that, MJ? Ugh!"

He shrugged. "Yep, I sure did. He said what you're doing is embarrassing, and he's not going to tolerate it much longer."

She leaned back in her chair and closed her eyes. Troy's words echoed in her head. He'd been right. Mia didn't want her father involved. It wasn't any of his business. She would handle it herself. She opened her eyes and spoke with her head held high. "I've got this, MJ."

"I beg to differ. From what I've assessed, you're about to ruin everything and lose what you've already gotten out of Troy."

"How so?"

"I heard what JaJuana said—that's her name, right?"

Mia nodded.

"All right let me ask you something. Was Troy showing up at that event and y'all arguing part of a publicity stunt?"

"No, that was on him. I had no idea Troy was even going to be there. Him and that grimy ass Mark couldn't wait until it was over. He demanded that I give him the video. Things got heated after that."

"Okay then, him being dragged online was your idea of justice?"

Mia tossed her hair and pretended to inspect her fingernails. "Somewhat."

"Big sis, that wasn't the right route to take. I'm with JaJuana. We don't know the implications that will come from the video and this confrontation. I can tell you right now, the Falcons management won't tolerate negative publicity. I don't think they'll impose a fine either. Troy could very well lose his job."

"Over a video and us arguing in public. Really?"

"Yes, really. The man has a lot of heat on him for somebody that's not even back on the turf yet. It's not a good look, sis."

"What am I supposed to do then?"

"Damage control. That's what we need to do at this point. I can talk to Mark to see how they're going to handle things." He looked at Tanya. "I suggest you and Tanya work on a statement to put out. I can look it over when you've drafted it."

Tanya perked up and nodded happily. "Okay."

"Wait a minute! Why do I have to put anything out? He was beating on me, MJ! I did what I could to help him deal with that busted-up knee. He was at the lowest point of his life, and he took that shit out on me! And after all of that he had the nerve to cheat on me in our house! He shouldn't have fucked me over!" Her chest rose and fell with rapid breaths.

MJ remained calm. "Relax, okay. You're upset, and more than anything else, you're hurt. I understand." His large hand covered hers, and he squeezed gently. "Could I ask you something? You got everything without a divorce. Do you plan on filing for one now?"

Mia's eyes were glossy. She nibbled on her bottom lip and shrugged.

"If you don't, then I'm confused. Why go to these lengths when that's not the plan? If you want it to work out, I suggest counseling for him and maybe you should go too."

"He won't do it. Troy's stubborn."

"If he did, do you love him enough to try to save your marriage? Would you take him back?"

Her brother knew she loved Troy to no end. MJ and their father were huge fans of his too. Finding out Troy was abusing her had to be a shock to them. She decided not to tell MJ about losing the baby or the woman in the video being pregnant. Her plan to expose Troy's abuse never included a mistress or a possible love child. Mia knew that if the woman was pregnant with Troy's child, she was done. It hurt to know that if she stayed, she would be no different from her mother. The tears ran down her cheeks as she looked into the eyes of the product of her own father's infidelity.

Her lower lip quivered as she said, "MJ, I don't think I can."

CHAPTER
28

Khloe stormed into the living room and stood in front of him. After Derrik closed his laptop and placed it on the end table, she tossed the picture from the bookshelf into his lap. "Who the fuck is this?"

"The hell, Khloe. Why were you in my office?"

She ignored his question and began ranting. "How long have we known each other? No, how long have we been doing *this*? Three words, Derrik! You couldn't even say them back to me. Now I know why. Her eyes . . . they're . . . she's beautiful." Khloe glanced at the picture in his lap. "And y'all look so happy."

Derrik knew this day would come. Not that he wanted it to be like this. He'd planned to break things off with her differently. He hoped she would've been in Boston. Doing it over the phone might have been taking the coward's way out, but he knew Khloe wasn't the type to go down without a fight.

She pleaded, "Tell me the truth. Is she the reason?"

Yeah, she is. But he wasn't about to explain who Desiree was and how much she meant to him. It wouldn't help the situation. He placed the picture frame on the end table. "Have a seat, Khloe."

She scowled at him and folded her arms across her chest.

"Klo, will you please sit down so we can talk."

She sat next to him but didn't look at him. Instead, she stared straight ahead with her arms folded and her lips pouting. Derrik exhaled heavily as he shifted his weight and turned to face her. He took her arm in his and softly drew her closer to him. "Look at me."

Khloe jerked away and turned her back.

"Come on, Klo, you don't have to do all of that. You just asked how long we've been doing this. I'm not about to beg you. Now are you going to turn around and look at me so we can talk?"

She turned to face him. Her eyes swam with tears. "Talk about what, Derrik? How I'm good enough to fuck but not good enough to be your woman? How you kick me to the curb when you run into some younger pussy? How I'm only a convenience for you when you're in town?"

Derrik's expression remained neutral. "Are you done?"

Tears streamed down Khloe's cheeks. She wiped them away and gave him a frosty look.

"Dammit, Khloe, spare me the theatrics. Don't we go through this shit every year? Every time you feel threatened by another woman you start this up. 'Who is she, Derrik? Why can't we be together?' Knowing full well how this even started between us and the way we've been doing it. You should know the damn drill."

"You can be such an asshole, Derrik! I know what we are, but I don't deserve you treating me like this!"

"Treating you like what? I give you respect when we're doing our thing. I've never flaunted another woman in your face, have I? No, never. You shouldn't have been in my office."

She sucked her teeth.

"Well, you shouldn't have been, and I stand by that."

"Who is she to you, Derrik?"

"I'm not about to sit here and explain anything that isn't your business."

"This is my business, Derrik! You're my business because we're fucking! I don't expect to see or hear about another woman when I'm around!"

Derrik snorted. "Do you hear yourself, Klo? You didn't see or hear anything about another woman. You're in my house not minding your business. I guess you found what you were looking for, and now you're in your feelings."

"Fuck you!" she spat.

He shook his head while blowing out his cheeks. She wanted more and he couldn't give her that. He loved Khloe but not in the way she deserved. It was the sole reason he never said it. He didn't want it to be misconstrued as anything more than the kind of love a person has for a friend—and she was a special friend. Still, he knew no woman would be able to handle hearing that. It was time to put some distance between them. Without another word, Derrik stood up and began walking away.

There was something more pressing in his world that needed his immediate attention. The phone call from Troy was still spinning around in his mind. He couldn't believe all that Troy had told him. He couldn't find the video online. He didn't bother reading the article on the *Baller Bizness* site and called LaLa instead, but she told him the network executives removed all access to the file. He didn't need to see the video anyway; the screenshots were enough. He wouldn't have been able bear watching her fuck Troy. But he had other questions: Was Troy telling the truth that Desiree was pregnant? Why would she keep that from him? Her initial hesitancy to see him began to make sense. He realized she was probably distraught over not knowing the baby's paternity.

"Where are you going?" Khloe asked, breaking him out of his thoughts.

"I have somewhere else to be. Hodges!"

Out of nowhere she tried to swing on him, but he dodged the punch. "The fuck, Khloe!"

She clenched her fists, her nostrils flared, and her eyes bulged.

"Hodges! Get in here now!"

The petite woman swung her fists at him a few times, but it was in vain. Just as his bodyguard entered the living room area, Derrik grabbed Khloe by the wrists and lifted her from the floor.

"Let me go, Derrik!"

"You know what this is about. Shit isn't going her way, so she's acting like a fucking child. It's time for her to go. She's not about to fuck my shit up again. She can call for a private jet or find a flight, but she needs to go."

Hodges nodded. Khloe tried to kick at Derrik, but his bodyguard handled the small woman effortlessly.

"Nah uh, Hodges put me down!" She tried to squirm free, but Hodges held on tight. She felt misled and humiliated, and her blood was boiling. Khloe's eyes were hot with hate as she spat, "You always do this shit, Derrik! You treat me like I'm one of your hoes, and I'm not!"

He spoke over her shouting, "I have to meet up with Bri about something. I'll text you to fill you in. I'll have Nate come with me. Hit me up after you take care of this."

Hodges nodded again.

"I knew these weeks were nothing but a sham. I've sat around waiting for you like a fucking fool. Not anymore, Derrik! You hear me? Not anymore!"

"When you calm down, we can talk."

She continued yelling as Hodges carried her out. "No, I'm done talking! Fuck you!"

He hated when she got like this. Hodges didn't lie. She wasn't going away quietly. This was another reason he treaded lightly when it came to Khloe. She was violent at times, especially when things didn't go her way. Derrik looked heavenward and exhaled. He would deal with her later. For now, he needed to focus on this situation with Desiree.

An hour later, he and Nate were in front of Brielle's office suite. He didn't wait for Nate to open his door. He jumped out hastily and made his way into the building. Derrik knocked on her door, then walked right in, not bothering to wait for a response. He suddenly remembered the guy slobbering her down the last time he came to her office. He closed his eyes.

"Uhh, Derrik why are your eyes closed?"

He opened them and shrugged. "Shit the last time you were in here getting tongued down by dude. I wasn't trying to see all of that."

"You're too late for that show. But stop busting in my office like that or else you might get an eyeful of my bare ass in the air."

Derrik's mouth fell open.

Brielle laughed. "Come on in and have a seat. I was just finishing up this proposal. I was hosting a conference call earlier. It's why I couldn't answer your call, but I was going to hit you back right after I finished this." She turned her head back to the laptop and started typing.

"Where's Desi? Did she bounce again?"

Brielle didn't look up as she responded flippantly, "No, she's actually been waiting for you to get back. She was looking forward to y'all hashing this whole thing out."

"I want to ask you something, and I need you to keep it a hunnid with me."

She shifted her attention from the laptop and turned to face him. "All right, shoot."

"Why was Desi really avoiding me?"

"She was embarrassed. Imagine getting caught up in a scandal with two men, best friends no less. That's like sleeping with brothers. I wouldn't have bounced, but I get it. So, what's up, Derrik?"

"I got an interesting phone call from Troy a little while ago."

"Ugh, what did that asshole have to say now?"

"Did you know about this video of him and Desi fucking?"

Brielle nodded. "She's hired an attorney to ensure her identity isn't revealed."

Derrik frowned.

"I know, I told her that was a dumb ass move going over there. Mia was not playing about exposing Troy's trifling ass."

"That's not it though—my question." Derrik paused for a beat before asking, "Is Desi avoiding me because she's pregnant?"

Brielle couldn't mask her expression of shock.

"Yeah, that's what I thought."

Not wanting to betray her friend's trust, she attempted to throw him off. "No, Derrik. You caught me off guard with the question."

He stood up and raised his voice, "Dammit, Bri knock it the fuck off!" He leaned forward to look her straight in the eyes. He lowered his voice, "I'm sorry, but come on, Bri. That baby is more than likely mine. I just needed some space to clear my head. Did she think with me knowing this, I was going to walk away?"

Inside she shouted for joy. She knew Derrik would be understanding and step up to the plate. But she was baffled how Troy would have information about Desiree's pregnancy.

"Hold up, how did he know?"

215

"He said Mia told him."

"And how would that heffa know?"

He sat down. "I don't know, but she knows a lot apparently. She's the one with the video of them. She told him she saw us at Rico's funeral."

"That bitch! I bet she was the one that told the cops about y'all too! I told Desi she was up to no good being there with her cameras."

"The cops?"

"That's a whole other story."

He pressured her. "I need to talk to her, Bri. If she's pregnant that's likely *my* baby she's carrying. I have a right to know. Where is she?"

She knew Desiree would have wanted to be the one to tell him, but Brielle was happy and relieved at Derrik's reaction. There's no way this man would leave Desiree's side; his love ran deep. She stood up. "You're right, Derrik. I told her the same thing. I know without a doubt this baby is yours. I'm going too. Come on."

CHAPTER

29

Desiree closed her office door. She plopped down in the chair and leaned back. Even though she had plenty of work to do, she couldn't focus. Derrik hadn't called. Maybe he wasn't back in town. She needed to occupy her mind with something else. Perhaps a cup of tea would settle her nerves. She went over to the other side of the office where the Keurig sat. Without measuring, she scooped a hefty amount of sugar into the cup. "Mmm," she said aloud. "Now this is how you make tea." There was a knock at the door. "Come in."

The door opened slowly to reveal Aaron standing in the doorway. "Hello, Desiree."

She tried to remain poised. "Uhh hey, what are you doing here?"

"Looks like Pryce is ready to move forward. I sent them everything you put together, along with the numbers and my proposal for acquiring these two companies without the red tape. It's just what they were looking for. They're excited and ready to get started. That means we're going to be seeing a lot more of each other over these next few months or so."

Desiree returned a puzzled look.

"I take it you haven't seen the email communications between Samuel and Carolyn?"

"No, I haven't. I didn't get a chance to look at all my emails this morning. Ever since I got in it's been crazy with back-to-back meetings." It wasn't like Desiree to be off her game, but with everything upside down in her personal life, she hadn't

217

been as focused at work. She went to her desk and opened her email. She skimmed the ones Aaron referred to.

"Oh yeah, how did everything work out with your friend?"

"My friend?" she asked lifting an eyebrow.

"Remember your friend who needed legal counsel. I gave you a few names. Were any of them able to help out?"

"Right, yes everything worked out perfectly. She was able to get the advice needed. I appreciate it."

"No problem. Glad I could be of assistance."

"Yes, me too, thanks. Now, I'm looking over the exchange between Samuel and Carolyn. What's changed? It doesn't seem like much, other than he wants to include some stuff we didn't. Why are we moving things ahead of schedule now?"

"That was a summary of their conversation. There's actually quite a bit. Mind if I take a seat?" Aaron sat down, set his small attaché case on Desiree's desk, and opened it. He pulled out a folder and continued, "They liked your proposal, but there were a couple of competitors you didn't consider. It's like you said before—they're positioning themselves in the market for a takeover. Before I get started, could I get a cup of coffee?"

"Yes, of course." Desiree handed Aaron the cup, and they spent the next hour going over the updates their client proposed. By the time he was finishing up, her phone rang. She looked down at her phone and sent the call to voicemail. When she peeked up Aaron was staring at her.

"Nice pic. Who is he to you?" he quizzed.

She frowned. "Who he is to me isn't any of your business, Aaron."

"It is my business if he's someone competing for your attention."

"Excuse me?"

"Desiree, there's something I want to discuss with you." Aaron put the papers back in the folder and slid it into his briefcase. "I'm aware of your situation, and that changes everything between us."

Desiree's eyes narrowed.

Aaron explained that she hadn't mentioned Jamal since LA. He noticed Jamal hadn't called during dinner, when his normal behavior was to call, especially when

218

she worked late. Then he reminded her that she let it slip that Jamal had slept with her deceased friend's sister. "You conveniently tried to deflect when I asked you to elaborate on that."

That little tidbit had come out during dinner when the wine had her relaxed and chatty. She didn't intend to consume as much as she did, but she'd needed to take the edge off. Desiree hoped he hadn't caught on, but it was clear he did. "There was nothing to elaborate on," she said indifferently.

"Hmm, well something told me to check. I know it's been filed. Once your divorce is final, we can take our relationship to the next level."

Desiree couldn't hide her shock. He'd checked into her marital status. It was unnerving to hear him speak as if their relationship were going any further. Aaron had given her reason to pump all brakes on their interaction unless it was work related. "Our relationship? Aaron, what are you talking about? We don't have a relationship."

"Yes, we do," he refuted. "We've always had one, and with Jamal out of the picture, we've got nothing stopping us from being together. Unless *Derrik* is an issue." Aaron got up and moved to her side of the desk. "I should tell you something about me. I never lose. I always win—always. I'm not giving up that easy, Desiree. I want you. I know you want me. You can't deny what's between us."

Desiree squeezed her eyes shut. She wouldn't deny what she felt for him was purely physical, but that was it. She exhaled aloud and pinched the bridge of her nose before opening her eyes. "Aaron, what we have is not what you think. Keeping it real, it was purely physical."

"Come on, you can't be serious," He sounded exasperated. "Okay, you thought your marriage was going to work. That's the reason we weren't pursuing this, right? Now that he's about to be out of the picture, what—or should I ask *who*—else is in the way?" In a swift move, he pulled Desiree from the chair. His gaze burned with such intensity, numbing her to inaction. He caressed the side of her face before lowering his mouth to hers. He claimed her mouth with a savage kiss. Desiree put her hands up and pushed against his chest.

"Aaron, please. Give me a minute."

"No, I'll give you a couple of seconds. We have lunch reservations." He didn't wait for her to object. He picked up his briefcase and went to the door.

219

She blinked. "What?"

"Don't worry. I've already told Carolyn and Tiana we're heading out. Now come on. I know you're hungry. I have another secret location we can check out."

She was left speechless as he walked away. The man was incorrigible. She considered rejecting his lunch offer, but he had a point. She was hungry. Before heading out, she tried to reach Derrik, but the call went straight to voicemail. She grabbed her purse and headed out the door. By the time she made it down the hall, Aaron was standing by her assistant's desk.

"Yes, I heard you're going to be with us for a while. Carolyn had me set you up in the cubicle right over there, so you'll be close." There was no mistaking what Tiana meant by her next statement. "And if there's anything, and I mean *anything* you need, don't hesitate to let me know. I've got you, mmm kay?"

He winked. "Okay, and thank you, Tiana. See you later."

The moment they were in the elevator, Desiree wagged a finger. "You are unbelievable!"

He laughed, forming deep dimples in each cheek. "What did I do?"

"You know exactly what you did back there."

"No, I don't. I haven't a clue what you're talking about. I'm going to be here for a while, right? Tiana wants to help me with getting set up at my desk. What's wrong with that?"

"Nothing, except she wants to help you with more than just setting up your desk. You know full well what she meant about needing *anything*."

The elevator doors opened. As usual, the lobby area was busy with people coming in with lunch deliveries and others heading out for their lunch breaks. The scent from someone's Chinese takeout found its way into Desiree's nostrils. She was about to tell Aaron that's what she wanted to eat, but something else caught her attention. Her eyes widened, and her mouth partially dropped open. Aaron followed her gaze to a couple standing several feet away.

"Desiree, is everything okay?"

Without responding she went over to the pair and stood in front of the woman. "What is this about, Bri?"

"Desi, this wasn't her idea."

She glanced over at Derrik. Her heart was thumping. "Why are both of you here?"

Before he could respond, Aaron came up behind her.

"Is something wrong, Desiree?"

Brielle rotated her neck, "I'm sorry, and you are?"

Desiree turned her head. Her nerves were rattled, but she kept her composure as she made the introductions. "Aaron, these are my friends Brielle and Derrik. This is a colleague of mine, Aaron."

He nodded in her direction and extended his hand, "Why hello, Brielle. It's nice to finally meet the beautiful, best friend I've heard so much about."

Desiree cocked her head to the side and didn't attempt to hide her frown. She hadn't told him anything about her best friend. He was doing the most.

Brielle's eyes swept over the tall man, and she grinned. "Hmm, nice to meet you too, Aaron."

When he released her hand, his tone and mannerisms completely shifted. Aaron looked at Derrik, immediately sizing him up. "What's up, Derrik?"

Derrik returned an unmistakable expression that also challenged the man standing an inch taller than him. "Nothing, what's up?"

Desiree could sense the tension between them. She turned to face Aaron. "Can you give me a few minutes with my friends?"

He nodded without taking his eyes off Derrik. "I'll be over by the security desk." Then he glanced down at her and spoke loudly enough for everyone to hear. "Don't forget we have reservations."

"I'm not sure how long this might take."

He looked back at Derrik and insisted, "I'll be right over there waiting for you."

After what he said in her office, Desiree knew he wasn't going anywhere. "Fine." She returned her attention to her friends once he walked away.

"What's up with your boy, Desi?" Derrik scoffed. "He got a problem with me. Something I don't know?"

Brielle couldn't hide the smirk on her face. Suddenly Desiree felt cornered. She ignored Derrik's questions and squinted. "What is this about, Bri? Why are y'all here together?"

221

Derrik stepped between them with his back to Brielle. "Troy called. He told me about the video and then he told me that you're pregnant. I went to Bri first because honestly, I didn't want you to bounce on me again."

She looked surprised and raised an eyebrow at him. Her eyes went to Brielle who had come from behind him to stand at his side. Thoughts were flying through Desiree's head, but she couldn't find any words. It didn't make sense that Troy would know. She hadn't told him.

"Baby girl, I know what I said. But if you are pregnant, don't push me away, please. I want to be there for you and our baby."

Our baby. She'd heard him correctly. He'd referred to her unborn child as theirs. She took a deep breath and opened her mouth, but nothing came out.

"Well, well, well aren't we lucky to have the trio here together."

Desiree saw two men in suits approaching them. Right away, she knew they were the detectives she'd forgotten to call.

The older man addressed them all, "Mrs. Edwards, Mr. Carter, and Ms. Stephens, we would like to speak to the three of you regarding the homicide of Ricardo Alvarez. Would you mind if we did this at the precinct?"

Derrik asked, "Are we being charged with anything?"

"No, Mr. Carter, you're not. We've only identified the three of you as persons of interest. We need to obtain some information for our investigation. It would be great if you came in without a warrant. Will you be joining us?"

"Yes, but we'll come down on our own, and none of us will speak until my legal team arrives."

"That's fair. So, we'll see you all shortly then, right?"

Derrik nodded. After the detectives walked away, Derrik excused himself to make a phone call.

Brielle chuckled. "I guess you're going to miss lunch with your boy Aaron."

She turned to look and didn't see him by the security desk. He wasn't in the lobby anywhere. Desiree shrugged. Thinking of how Aaron acted earlier, she was relieved to get out of having lunch with him. Her mind was now on the detectives wanting to interview them.

222

Derrik came back. "My legal team is on the way and should be there by the time we arrive." He looked at Desiree. "I suggest we go together."

"I'm okay with that," she said quietly.

On the way to the precinct, he made a few more phone calls. His voice sounded troubled as he discussed their predicament. Desiree did her best to remain calm. She knew they didn't have anything to do with their friend's death.

Just as Derrik had said, within minutes of their arrival, a group with two women and a man came in behind them. He shook the hand of one woman he introduced as Shonda and nodded to the others. Shonda explained that each of them would have someone with them while being questioned.

She advised, "Ladies, we understand the nature of their claim, and it is not to be taken lightly. Let's be sure we provide all the information they need to help in their investigation."

Desiree and Brielle nodded. A few minutes later, the detectives separated the friends to begin interviews. Their fellow detectives questioned Brielle and Derrik while Wallace and Green focused their questioning on Desiree. Janice was the lawyer representing her.

The detectives instructed Desiree and Janice to follow them. Desiree couldn't seem to swallow the lump in her throat. The last time she was inside a precinct was to drop the charges against Troy. The detectives walked on either side of the women, guiding them through a few turns until they reached a room at the end of a long hall. Wallace opened the door. The small room looked just like ones she'd seen on television. There was a medium-sized table with four chairs. Although Desiree wore a blazer, the chill in the room hit her as soon as she sat down. Almost immediately, she began to shiver. Janice seemed unbothered. Desiree wrapped her arms around her body and rocked as she waited for the detectives to begin.

Wallace pressed the button on the recorder in the middle of the table. "Please state your full name for us."

"Desiree Michele Edwards."

The detectives confirmed that Jamal was her husband. She corrected them to inform them they were separated. They asked about her relationship with Rico.

"Rico used to be my personal accountant. I met Jamal through him a couple of years ago."

It was obvious they wanted to focus on the marital problems she and Jamal were experiencing. They even asked if she thought Rico knew about it.

She rocked a little faster as she spoke through gritted teeth, "Yeah, I'm sure he told him about our problems. That was his boy."

Janice touched her arm lightly.

"Sorry," Desiree whispered.

The detectives continued to probe her about the last time she'd seen Rico. She told them it had been more than a couple of months ago when he stopped by to pick up Jamal to play golf. They asked when she'd found out about Rico's sister and Jamal.

Desiree realized what was happening. "Look, detectives, I know what you're doing, and I'm not the one you need to be questioning."

Green repeated, "Mrs. Edwards when did you find out your husband was having an affair with Mr. Alvarez's sister?"

"Jamal's boyfriend called me and told me his trifling ass was cheating on me. It wasn't with just her, but him too. He was living on the DL! That's why we're separated. So, if there's anybody I would've wanted to kill, it would've been Jamal, not Rico. He was my friend, a damn good friend. I didn't even find out that woman was his sister until I went to the funeral."

The room was quiet for a moment as the detectives processed everything. It was obvious they were surprised by the revelation that Jamal was on the DL.

Green broke the silence. "Excuse me, Mrs. Edwards can we go over this again? What did you just say about your husband?"

Desiree blew out a deep breath before she stated, "It wasn't just Rico's sister that Jamal was having an affair with. He had a boyfriend too. Now that I'm thinking about it, I'm sure Rico knew about it. I figured that out after going to his funeral." She paused and mumbled, "I definitely didn't see it coming that both of them were on the DL."

The detectives exchanged looks again. Then Wallace spoke. "Let me get this straight. Your husband's other lover, which happened to be a man, called and told you about your husband's affair with Mr. Alvarez's sister?"

"Yes, well at first, I thought it was a woman. We were going back and forth in messages before he called. He was pissed that Jamal was playing him too."

"Where were you after your husband left that night?"

"Home. I talked to Bri and Derrik to tell them what happened. And then I went to bed."

"What is your current relationship with Mr. Carter?" Green asked.

Her voice was low. "We've been having an affair."

"Mrs. Edwards, we're aware that you and Mr. Carter attended the funeral. Someone saw the two of you in a heated argument afterwards. What was your argument about?"

"Derrik and I weren't arguing. He hadn't seen me in a while. I'd been avoiding him. He wanted to talk about why I left things the way I did. It wasn't about Rico, if that's what you're getting at. We had no reason to talk about him. Neither of us had had any business dealings with him in more than a year. He didn't even do my taxes anymore."

"Are you sure there isn't anything you've overlooked that might help us?" Wallace asked.

Desiree shook her head. "No, I can't think of any reason someone would want to harm or kill Rico."

Janice finally spoke up, "Gentlemen, if you you're not going to charge Mrs. Edwards with anything, this interview is over. She's told you all she knows about Mr. Alvarez and anything that may help you in this investigation."

After they obtained a DNA sample, the detectives escorted the women back to the lobby. Within minutes Derrik, Brielle, and the rest of the legal team joined them. Derrik and his lawyer spoke with each other while Brielle and Desiree stood off to the side. Desiree checked her phone and saw several missed calls and texts from Aaron. At the same time, Derrik walked up to them.

"Listen, we have a situation outside." His eyes seemed apologetic as he spoke to Desiree directly. "I need you to stay close to me when we walk out."

"What's wrong, Derrik?" Desiree asked.

"Somebody decided to tip off the vultures."

CHAPTER
30

Angela became hot all of a sudden. Her palms were dripping wet. She got off the couch and walked into her room. Her mind began to whirl. Angela sat down on the bench in front of the bed, attempting to calm herself down, but her heart continued to race.

Her gaze was drawn to the dresser. She stumbled over to it and grabbed the bottles in a hurry. She opened the first one and popped four tablets without having to chase it down. She was shaking so severely that she dropped the second bottle when she tried to open it. Angela knelt down and snatched up two more tablets, swallowing them whole in a matter of seconds. She crept to the side of the bed, resting her back against it in the hopes that the anxiety episode would pass. She sat motionless, but her eyes were drawn to her hands, which trembled. In a panic, she began rubbing them together. *Shit! Please calm down.*

It hit her she could no longer control the anxiety attacks. They came more frequently as each dose of the medication wore off. She didn't want to use the pills as a coping mechanism, but she had no choice. A few minutes passed before Angela could pull herself from the floor. She looked at the pills scattered on the floor and began taking her time picking them up. She placed the bottle back on the dresser. She took a deep breath and stared at her reflection in the mirror. She smoothed her hair down and fixed her ponytail. "It's going to be okay, Angela. You can get through this," she said aloud.

227

On her way back to the living room, she convinced herself that a glass of wine would take the rest of the edge off. Angela pulled a bottle from the fridge, filled her wine glass to the rim, and brought the bottle back to the living room. She downed a big swallow. Then another. Once she finished the glass, she poured herself another. This time she slowly savored the dryness of the Cabernet Sauv. Suddenly, the silence in the house became deafening. She turned on the television. She sipped and stared at the screen. She thought she heard a voice.

You know you need to stop doing this to yourself.

Angela looked around. "Tré?"

Mi hermana, I need you to be stronger.

She cried, "This is so hard. I miss you so much, Tré. I can't rest knowing your killer is still out there!"

The doorbell rang, startling her.

Clean yourself up, Angela. You don't want to go to the door looking like that.

"You're right," Angela said aloud, wiping her face and smoothing her hair.

She got to the door and slowly opened it to find Mia standing there along with her camera crew. "Mia?" she gasped.

"Angela, are you all right?"

She shrugged and began to cry.

"Come on, let's go inside." Mia guided her back into the house.

As Angela walked in front of her, Mia turned to give her camera crew a signal to start recording. Right before they reached the living room, Angela stopped abruptly.

"What is it?"

Angela sniffled, "Uhh, can you wait here?"

Mia watched Angela as she peeked into the living room. "Is someone here with you? Where's Jamal?"

When Angela looked again, no one was there. Yet, she was sure she'd heard Tré's voice. She didn't want Mia to think she was losing her mind. Angela shook her head. "No, I . . . I was making sure the living room didn't look a mess. I didn't know you were stopping by and bringing them with you. Other than my wine and a couple of dishes sitting out, it's fine. You can come on in."

Mia didn't hide her look of suspicion. "What's going on, Angela? Are you okay?"

CHAPTER 30

"Yeah—I mean no, I just feel, uhh, you know. I honestly don't know how to feel anymore. My heart is empty." Her lip began to quiver. "Mia, Tré is gone, isn't he?" She began crying uncontrollably.

"Aww, Angela, I'm so sorry. I didn't mean to upset you."

Between sobs she responded, "You didn't. Give me a second. I'll be fine. Sometimes it hits me when I think about how we never made up. I feel horrible how things went down and well—"

"No, don't you dare do this to yourself, Angela." Mia spoke firmly to her friend. "I know how you and Tré were. You would fuss and fight about all kinds of stuff but every single time y'all went right back to loving each other like it never happened. I know you would've been speaking again, and you know it too. Don't do this to yourself. It's hard enough to accept that he's no longer here."

"Yeah, I know. It hurts so much right now," Angela said sniffling and letting the tears fall.

Mia rubbed her friend's back and comforted her. A short while later, Angela calmed down and went to wash her face. When she returned, she saw Mia talking to her camera crew. She couldn't make out everything that Mia was saying.

"Mia, why are they here?"

"Filming for the reality show. They have to follow me wherever I go."

Angela heard the front door open and close. Within a few seconds, Jamal walked into the living room. His eyes narrowed and his forehead creased when he saw the cameramen standing in the middle of the room. He turned his attention to Mia. "What's going on here?" he demanded.

Mia rolled her eyes and snapped, "What does it look like? I'm here consoling my friend. Something that you should be doing."

"Really. So why is there a need for all of the cameras?"

"Don't worry about all of that. Where have you been? Out per usual, while my girl is in here alone and upset."

Angela grabbed her arm. "No, Mia, please don't."

She pulled away. With her head held high she rebuked Jamal, "Yes, it needs to be said. Angela knows I've dealt with this kind of behavior. I know you're a busy doctor and all, but really? I've been here multiple times and you're either leaving or nowhere to be found. She's grieving. She needs all the emotional support she can get."

"You think I don't know that? I am her support. You're just visiting, but I live here and make sure she's okay every day. Now again, why all the cameras?" Before she could respond, Jamal addressed Angela, "I told you, didn't I? She's out here trying to make a name for herself and will use anyone to be seen." His eyes went back to Mia. "Are you recording right now?"

Mia returned a menacing glare.

"Are you, Mia?" Angela repeated the question.

"I was trying to tell you before he busted in here. They follow me around for the events unfolding in my life and—"

"Right, you're going to exploit your girlfriend during her time of grief. You've got some serious issues. Sweetheart, look at what she did to her own husband."

"Were you recording everything just now, Mia?"

Mia stared at Angela for a moment and finally conceded, "I was going to ask. I didn't get a chance to. He just showed up."

"I live here, remember? I'm supposed to just show up," Jamal shot back.

Angela walked away from Mia and stood by her man. "I think you all should leave, Mia."

Mia held up her hands. "I came and you were here all alone. I'm trying to show my support."

"Mia, just go. Clearly, this isn't a good time for us to talk. When you don't have them with you, you can come back. And please do not include any of what just happened on your show." Angela moved closer to Jamal. He wrapped his arm around her and kissed her forehead.

Mia rolled her eyes and signaled to her camera crew. As they filed out of the door, Mia turned and looked directly into Angela eyes. "Don't forget what I said about men—"

Jamal closed the door in her face.

CHAPTER
31

"Unbelievable, but I knew something like this was going to happen," Brielle leaned in and whispered to Desiree.

Desiree stared at her blankly.

Shonda advised, "Keep your attention straight ahead. Do not say anything. Do not make eye contact with anyone. We'll handle the circus out there." She turned to Derrik. "I know you're not driving. Where are your guys?"

As if on cue, Hodges strode in with Nate and four other tall, muscular men, all dressed in black and towering over everyone else. Derrik exchanged daps and spoke briefly with them before returning to Shonda. He pointed to the entrance with his hand outstretched, "We're ready when you are."

In front of them, the members of his legal team, led by Shonda, stood side by side. Derrik gave his men a knowing nod. Nate and the other four bodyguards moved in from all sides to flank them. Hodges took his place behind the lawyers, with Derrik behind him and Desiree beside him. Brielle was following closely behind them. Desiree clutched Derrik's hand tightly. With reassuring eyes, he winked at her.

As soon as Shonda opened the door, they were blinded by an assault of flashing lights from the cameras. She approached the crowd, and a pathway opened. The first reporter shoved a recorder near her.

"Was Derrik arrested in connection with the homicide of Ricardo Alvarez?"

"No arrest was made. He was questioned," Shonda replied.

Another reporter asked, "Why question him?"

"You have to ask the police."

"Do they have reason to believe he's connected to the murder?" The next reporter asked.

"My client wasn't anywhere near the victim when this tragedy occurred. The information that connected my client to this murder was from an unreliable source."

Another reporter asked, "So, Derrik isn't being charged with murder?"

Shonda responded coolly, "I don't know where you obtained your information, but my client was not and will not be charged with anything involving the homicide of Ricardo Alvarez."

"Will he—"

Shonda held up her hand as she pushed through the media blitz. "We're done here. No more questions. Thank you."

Derrik heard LaLa's voice from the crowd, "Isn't that the girl from the video with Troy Harris?"

Almost simultaneously the group halted in step. Shonda turned and gave Derrik a look. He nodded to Hodges, and he moved to put more protection on the other side of him where Desiree was standing. They started moving again and picked up their pace as the attention of the media focused on her. The clicks and bright flashes from the cameras continued. Desiree bowed her head and used her blazer to shield her face. She held on tightly to the arm of the bodyguard blocking her from their cameras. As they made their way through the crowd, questions flew from every direction.

"Are you the girl in the video?"

"What is your name?"

"What is your connection with Derrik and this homicide case?"

"Were you having an affair with Troy?"

"Are you trying to extort money from him?"

The group finally maneuvered through the crowd of reporters to the other side of the street where the parking lot was. They made their way over to the three black Cadillac Escalades with black tinted windows. Derrik, Desiree, and Brielle climbed into the first one. Hodges ensured everyone was inside, hopped into the driver's seat, and sped away. After a few minutes of silence, Derrik finally spoke. "I think at this point it's best we go to my house. We can pick up your cars later. Besides, it'll give us an opportunity to deal with *everything*. And don't worry, Desiree, it's going to be okay," he reassured her, putting his hand over hers. "We'll get through all of this together."

Desiree nodded. Derrik's words seemed to ease the nervousness in the pit of her stomach. He wrapped his arm around her, and she snuggled closer, allowing him to hold her as they made their way to his house. They remained quiet on the ride there.

Once they were inside the house, he excused himself to make a few calls. "Please make yourselves at home. I have my chef, Lenny coming with dinner. You know where the bar is, Desi. Wait, no you can't have alcohol. There's juice and sodas in there."

"We've got this, Derrik." Brielle shooed him.

"Okay I'll be right back."

As soon as he left them alone, Brielle went over to her friend and pinched her arm.

"Ow, Bri! What the hell?"

"What the hell? No, what the fuck? Why were you coming out of the elevator with Aaron? I thought he went back to LA?"

"He did. I had no idea he was here until he popped up in my office. He's working on this acquisition that wasn't supposed to happen until next year."

"You conveniently left out the part that he's white, but dayum he's *foine*!" She paused for a moment and smirked. "Now I understand why your ass was acting like that."

"Please, Bri, I want to forget about everything that happened today, especially my run-in with Aaron."

"Well, you can't. It happened."

Desiree's mind was on the reporters and whether any of them had been able to get a picture of her. She sighed as she walked to the other side of the room. Tears formed in her eyes as she thought about the past few weeks. She'd been avoiding everything, hoping it would all go away. She'd thought she could save face by handling things her way, but from where she was standing, everything was unraveling at the seams. "You were right."

"Desi, come on. I don't want to be right. I've only wanted the best for you. That asshole Troy never meant you any good. You see all this drama they're in. You've allowed him to drag you right into this bullshit with his wife."

Desiree remained silent.

"All right, I'm not beating you up about this anymore, but you're going to need to pull it together so you can talk to Derrik."

Desiree turned around, tears falling from her eyes. "How? Why do you think this is easy?"

"Desi, I don't. None of this will be easy, but you're not alone. That man in there truly loves you. Let him show you how much. You deserve that." Brielle held Desiree tight as she cried. After getting through the meltdown, Desiree went to the bathroom to clean up. When she came back, Brielle had a glass of juice waiting. Derrik reappeared at the same time.

"Mind if we talked?"

"Y'all know I can go home. I doubt there will be anybody camped out at my house. Seriously, who am I? It's y'all asses they want on *Baller Bizness*."

They both stared at her.

"Y'all know it's the truth. LaLa is your bestie, Derrik. She's going to want all the dirty deets. Now can Hodges drop me off at my office so I can get my truck? I'm trying to see my man."

"*Your man?*" Derrik and Desiree said in unison.

Brielle's mouth curved into a smile. "Yes, I have a man now. Justin made it official."

"Okay, Peaches!" Desiree teased.

"Heffa!"

Derrik laughed. "Come on, Peaches—I mean Bri."

"You got jokes too, Derrik?"

"Hey, I don't need that nigga coming for me 'cause you at my crib. He shot me some dirty looks that day."

They walked away with Brielle cussing Derrik out for always bursting in her office. While he got her ride squared away, Desiree nervously moved from one chair to the other. Something caught her eye. She went to the end table and picked up the picture frame. She ran her fingers along the side of it and across their smiling faces.

"That's one of my favorite pics. We had a lot of fun that day."

Desiree placed the frame back on the table. "Do you want to be with her?"

"Huh? Who?"

She spun around. "Don't play dumb, Derrik. I saw the awards show. That skank you were with in Miami."

He snickered at her reference to Khloe.

"I don't find it funny. I bet it was her calling that night you were at my house. After that, you were rude and short with me. I saw how y'all were, laughing in each other's face. Is she your little girlfriend now?"

Derrik moved from the other side of the room to stand in front of her. His eyes locked onto hers, and he shook his head. "No, Desi she's not. I thought you were going to be my girl."

She dismissed his statement, "I'm not stupid. I know she's your type."

"No, you're my type and always have been," he confessed.

"Just stop it, Derrik! I know you fucked her!"

"And you fucked Troy!" he shouted back.

Desiree flinched. She hung her head. "There's nothing else to talk about at this point. You'll never forgive me for what I did. You already said you were done."

"I was pissed that day, and you know it. I needed time. I still do, but there's plenty to talk about—like this baby."

Tears she didn't know were there came rushing. "I don't even know if it's yours, Derrik! God knows I want it to be so bad. What if it's not, then what? I don't want to lose you!"

He wrapped his arms around her and pressed his lips on the top of her head. "Shhh, you won't. I'm here for you."

Derrik was treading in uncharted territory. She'd asked a valid question: what if the baby wasn't his? He honestly didn't know how to feel about it. "Can't we get a paternity test done sooner?"

She sniffled. "Yes, I thought about that. I'm far along enough for them to do one."

"How far along are you?"

"Next week I'll be twelve weeks, and I go back for the ultrasound to see the baby. I can ask for it then."

"I'm coming with you."

The corner of her lips curved upwards as she glanced up. "Yes, I want you to." When he released her from his arms, Desiree took his left hand and placed it over her heart. "No matter what happens from here on out, believe that my heart beats for you and you only. I love you, Derrik."

"I'm sure I love you a little more." He pulled her back into a tight embrace. Derrik closed his eyes and inhaled her perfume: Gucci Guilty. He needed to cherish the moment. When he opened his eyes, he gazed down at Desiree smiling back up at him. He could see specks of gold dancing in her irises. He was hypnotized staring into the warm, hazel eyes of the only woman that captured and imprisoned his heart.

In a swift, effortless move, he lifted her from the floor. She draped her arms around his neck. He leaned in. The tips of their noses touched. Her soft lips brushed across his and they shared a short, sweet kiss. Desiree closed her eyes and tilted her neck. She wanted more, but they were moving. She opened her eyes. Derrik's eyes never left hers as he walked through the house. He reached the master bedroom door and motioned for her to open it.

He placed her in the middle of the bed and knelt beside her. Derrik lifted her chin. His eyes searched hers. Her heart skipped when he leaned forward and covered her lips. Unlike their kiss downstairs, this kiss lasted longer. When his tongue touched hers, Desiree's insides short circuited. She needed him. Her moan was deep as she reached for him, trying to tear away the clothes that were a barrier between them.

Derrik pulled away from their kiss long enough to undress her. As he removed her clothing, he planted kisses on every part he exposed. He squeezed and suckled her breasts, noting that they were fuller than before. He moved down to her belly and rested his head there a moment. Desiree caressed from the top of his head to the back of his neck, pressing him closer. Derrik splayed his fingers across her stomach and silently prayed the baby growing inside was his. He placed a kiss there before moving down to her mound. Desiree gasped and spread her thighs wider when he kissed her button through the lace material. He yanked her thong off. He kissed and licked the plumps lips open. "Hmm," he moaned. "I've really missed her."

Derrik's oral skills were unmatched. He did something with his tongue that sent two chills up her spine. She arched her back as his tongue swirled around her pussy. He teased, nibbling and sucking her clit. Desiree let out a hoarse groan when his tongue flicked rapidly on the swollen nub. She vibrated within from the orgasm that took over. Her stomach muscles contracted. She clutched the sheets and curled her toes tight as she released. Derrik slurped up her juices and sucked even harder. She tried to squirm away, but he kept sucking until she came again. Her legs trembled uncontrollably. He lifted his head and smiled. Her cheeks began to flush hotly seeing his face covered in her juices. She bit into her bottom lip and reached down to touch herself.

"Carmen needs you, Derrik."

"Oh, she does?" He didn't waste another minute in removing the rest of his clothes. Desiree's eyes grew big when she looked below his waist. He was rock hard and at full length. He gripped the thick, veined shaft in his palm. Precum spilled from the tip as he pulled, stretching his dick an additional inch. "You have no idea how much I've missed you both."

"Show me, babe," she coaxed as she opened her thighs and spread her folds revealing the pink flesh.

Derrik rubbed the head of his engorged dick back and forth across her pussy until she erupted. He worked his hips with short pumps, inching into the heat until the full length of his shaft disappeared inside. He pulled out and pushed back inside with such force, it made her squeal. She observed his smug grin as he realized he'd tapped a delicate part of her pussy. He took a minute to pause and appreciate her beauty before beginning to slowly and steadily pump into her. She watched as his eyes traveled down to where their bodies connected. He eased out halfway. Desiree could see her arousal glistening on his shaft. She lifted her hips to meet his next stroke. She rotated in slow donuts around his cock. Derrik pushed himself deep into the heated crux of her body. Desiree crossed her ankles against his back, pulling him closer to her.

They were perfectly matched in rhythm as he picked up the pace. Pelvis to pelvis, they grinded against one another, trying to meld themselves into one being. Her walls clenched around his dick like a vice grip. She shook uncontrollably, her nails digging into his back. Derrik forced himself to slow down, fighting the sensation rising in his lower abdomen. It was proving difficult to maintain stamina. He wasn't ready to bust. He reluctantly withdrew.

"Come here," he whispered. He attempted to change positions, but Desiree had something else in mind. She wasted no time in scrambling to get to the long, thick chocolate bar. Desiree cupped his balls as she swallowed his shaft. Derrik's head snapped back when he felt his helmet go past her tonsils. He grabbed a fistful of her hair and fucked her face. Desiree took every inch like a pro. The slurping and gurgling sounds coming from her mouth sent him over the edge. "Fffffuck!" he bellowed.

Desiree pulled it out and kissed the tip before shoving it back in. Derrik shuddered watching it disappear in her hot, wet mouth. Her head bobbed up and down. He knew he was going to lose it. He tried to push her away but the suction around his shaft tightened.

"Oh shit, Desi!" he cried out.

She ignored him and continued sucking with one goal in mind.

"I'm . . . I'm about to . . ." His words were lost. Derrik's body went taut. Desiree felt his dick swell and pulse at the roof of her mouth. Seconds later hot, creamy fluid filled her mouth. She gulped, swallowing all of it and continued sucking until Derrik convulsed. "Okay . . . okay . . . okay. Stop!"

Desiree released him from her mouth. Derrik's breathing was heavy as he squeezed and pulled, draining the rest of his cum from his dick. She happily licked him clean. Then she kissed the tip once more and scooted back toward the middle of the bed. He smiled big as she licked her lips.

"You have no idea how much I've missed you, Derrik."

He knew she enjoyed giving him oral pleasure as much as he enjoyed receiving it. It'd been a while and long overdue. He laughed heartily. "Yeah, well I think I might have an idea."

She blushed but relished knowing she'd successfully snatched her man's soul. Derrik joined her in the middle of the bed and propped up one of the fluffy pillows. She snuggled into his arm after he leaned back. He kissed her forehead. There was a brief moment of silence before Desiree shook her head.

"What?"

"Remember that day in my apartment, you know after he dumped me?" She was careful with her words since she didn't want to ruin the moment, but she had to tell him.

Derrik smiled, admiring her efforts to avoid saying his name. He lifted her chin and spoke gently, "Of course, I do. How could I forget? He hurt you that day, Desi. And I promise you, I'll never put my hands on you or do anything to intentionally hurt you."

She nodded. "Recently you reminded me of what you said. Do you remember?"

"No, what did I say?"

"You said the right man was going to come along and treat me the way I'm supposed to be treated. I know you're that man, Derrik. You've loved me more than any man could ever love me. I made a stupid mistake for a man who didn't know me and certainly didn't love me. I never meant to betray you or take for granted what we have." She paused for a moment to caress the side of his face and plant several kisses on the lips she'd missed. "I know I hurt you, babe. I swear I never meant to. And although I can never change what's happened, I will do everything in my power to make it up to you. I'm truly sorry. I love you so much. Could you ever forgive me?"

"I already have, baby girl. Now come here." Desiree shrieked as Derrik playfully rolled them over onto her back and spread her thighs open. "We've got a lot of making up to do."

CHAPTER

32

"I can't believe she would do something like that."

Jamal shrugged, "I can. The woman has no couth."

"Jamal."

"No, Angela, she doesn't. I know it was your decision to let her come to your brother's funeral with those cameras. And I get that you felt it might have helped get it out in the media, but it didn't. Can't you see she's trouble?"

"No, I can't. You shouldn't think that about my friend."

"But you should," he retorted.

"Well, I'm not. Mia's been there for me all these years, especially when I needed someone to have my back the most."

"Okay, then she should have enough respect for you not to expose you in a delicate situation like this. Like she said, you're grieving. The last thing you want—no, *we* want, is for you to end up on national television behind her desire to be famous."

Angela shook her head in disagreement, but instead of responding, she poured another glass of wine and gulped it down as Jamal eyed her.

"You know you—"

"Don't start. I'm fine, I just needed a sip."

"No, I am going to start because that was far from a sip. I'm not going to sit by and watch you become an alcoholic."

"Really, Jamal? An alcoholic? That's what you think?"

"Well, what do you think is going to happen at the rate you're going?"

"At the rate I'm going? I've always drank like this."

"No, Angela you were never *like this*. Now listen, I've been thinking about this buddy of mine. He helps people get through their grief and shows them how to manage life after a tragedy. You and your brother were close, so his loss has been more devastating for you than any of us could imagine. It's his job to help you find healthier ways to cope with it."

"No, we are not going to a shrink. You can forget that."

"He's not a shrink, Angela. He's a grief counselor that can and will help you get through this. I'm not going to let you talk me out of it this time."

"Jamal, I think—"

He held up his hand. "I love you too much to watch you go through this kind of self-sabotaging behavior. As your man, it's my job to take care of you. It's time to heal. Let me help," he pleaded.

Angela glanced back without saying anything. She continued to sit quietly, brooding over his suggestion. Suddenly she started fidgeting as her breaths quickened.

"What's wrong, sweetheart? Are you having an anxiety attack?"

Angela stared back at Jamal while rubbing her hands across her thighs in an attempt to dry her sweaty palms. She began rocking back and forth, mumbling.

"What's the matter?"

She stopped moving and tears formed in her eyes. "Did you hear that?"

Jamal rubbed his temples, an uneasy feeling rising in the pit of his stomach. He peered into her eyes and softly gripped her shoulders. "Sweetheart, what do you hear?"

Angela closed her eyes as she wiped her face.

Jamal moved from the couch to the floor and knelt down in front of her. "Angela, open your eyes and look at me, sweetheart."

She reluctantly opened her eyes, and as she tried to focus on him, a few tears ran down her cheeks. "I . . . I miss him . . . so much."

CHAPTER 32

He wiped her tears away, leaned forward, and kissed her cheek. "I'm so sorry your brother's gone. I really am, sweetheart."

She tried to look away, but Jamal cupped her chin again making sure to keep her attention on him.

"Noooo, Jamal! He's not gone. I—I heard him," she cried. She jumped from the couch and went out into the hall shouting, "Tré!"

Jamal followed her. He grabbed her hand and tried to pull her towards him, but she snatched her hand away. "Angela, please," he pleaded.

She began to feel faint. She pressed her hands to her cheeks. Her breathing became labored. Jamal reached for her again, but she swatted his hand away. Her vision became blurred. She spoke in short breaths, "Babe . . . I think . . . I think I need to sit down."

Jamal wrapped his arm around her waist and guided her back to the couch. "I'm going to get you some water."

"Ok," she whispered.

When Jamal returned, Angela was speaking into thin air. "I heard you earlier. Please come back. I don't want him to think I'm crazy."

Jamal put the glass of water on the coffee table and went into the bedroom. When he returned, he handed Angela a double dose of the medication. "Here, take these. They'll help you calm down and get some rest." He handed her the glass, and she downed the pills quickly.

Jamal went to take a shower. When he returned to the living room, he saw that Angela's head was lobbing forward. He caught her just in time before she fell off the couch. Jamal knew he shouldn't have given her the medication after she'd been drinking, but the dose he'd given her wasn't enough to cause this kind of change in her demeanor. Something else was wrong.

"Angela, sweetheart, can you hear me? Open your eyes for me. Angela?" He leaned her back and checked her pulse and eyes. She was unresponsive. Jamal got up, threw on a pair of sneakers, and grabbed Angela's shoes. He got Angela into the car and sped out of their subdivision, calling the hospital while they were in route. He got there in less than an hour. When they arrived, Jamal rushed inside to get help from the nurses.

"What's going on Dr. Edwards? Who do we have here?" the triage nurse asked.

Jamal explained that Angela was a friend who took an extra dose of her prescription medication. He added that she had been drinking.

"Is this for an overdose then?"

Jamal nodded. "She lost her brother recently and has been self-medicating to cope with the depression."

"I see," the nurse replied quietly as she and another staff member helped get Angela out of the car.

Jamal gave specific instructions to the nursing staff and informed them he'd put in a call to his colleague, Dr. Mitchell. "She's going to be under his care. If she wakes asking for me, please call me." He handed over a Ziploc bag with her medications. Here's what she's been taking."

The nurse took the bag and went over the rest of the paperwork with him. The staff finished updating Angela's admissions chart, and Jamal watched as they rushed her to the back. He decided to go to the waiting area. He sent a text to Christian to let him know he was at the hospital for an emergency. He'd been on his way to visit Christian when he decided to stop by the house and check in with Angela. Jamal was fortunate he arrived when he did since Mia was there with her cameras. He wasn't prepared, though, to deal with Angela and the possibility of an overdose.

After thirty minutes, they were able to stabilize her. They admitted her for a forty-eight-hour psychological evaluation. Jamal called her mother and brought her up to speed on what had happened. He sat for a while longer thinking what might happen next. He'd spent the last few days pondering all the ways he could let her down. But he was concerned about her mental health; he couldn't leave her right now while she was so reliant on him. Still, he wasn't sure how long he'd be able to keep up his relationships with both her and Christian. He'd have to figure it out eventually.

For the time being, he needed to be where he could get away from the mess he'd created. Jamal left the waiting room and walked out the exit doors.

CHAPTER

33

Troy limped towards the bathroom. It had been a rough day at practice. Before they'd even made it onto the field, the team had heard about the debacle at Mia's event. His usually rambunctious teammates seemed more reserved, and he sensed indifference from his head coach. Troy was convinced the offensive coaching staff had it out for him. They kept setting up plays he'd never run before. He couldn't get into a rhythm with his teammates, and he missed easy catches. To top it off, his knee hurt.

"Fuck!" Troy snatched the prescription bottle from the cabinet. He'd spent most of the evening elevating his knee, hoping the pain would ease up. The strain from the day's work on the turf had irritated it. He'd psyched himself to believe the discomfort he felt would lessen with continued strengthening and conditioning, as his rehabilitation specialist suggested. *Things will get back to normal in a couple of weeks. My knee needs time to readjust, that's all.* He threw the pills back and swallowed the glass of Hennessey in one gulp. That combination seemed to do the trick, and he felt better within half an hour. Wanting something—or rather someone—to occupy his time, he thought about the Jamaican honey pot. He decided to give her a call.

"Troy, wat a gwaan?"

"You tell me, sexy. Where you at?"

Her patois was thick, but he could hear the concern in Sadé's voice. "Eh, yuh wife, she loud up di ting. I tink she may 'ave a black heart."

245

"Girl, you know I don't speak that shit. What did you just say?"

She chuckled. "I saw di stuff about yuh wife on IG. She airing out yuh dutty laundry. She messy, eh? I'm saying she cold hearted."

Troy rubbed the front of his boxers. It was something about her accent that turned him on. "Yo, fuck her. She's mad at me right now. Can you come through? I need to see you . . . but only you."

"I'll be deh when I get off work. Make sure yuh pop one. All night long, yeah, mon!"

"Hell yeah! Call me when you're on the way. See you later, sexy."

"See yuh."

After hanging up, he opened the drawer where she'd left the pills. He popped one and finished off the glass of Hennessy. He leaned back and smiled as he thought about his last session with Sadé. He could still taste her pussy on his lips. She tasted as sweet as honey. The thought of her riding his dick made it pulse. He yanked his boxers down. He massaged the length of his thick tool, running his hand from the helmet down the base. Troy imagined it was her mouth sucking the tip. He pulled at the head and grabbed his balls. His arm jerked up and down. He kept rubbing his dick thinking of how he was going to fuck the shit out of her. Minutes later he felt the sensation in his lower abdomen. "Shit!" he exclaimed.

He stroked his dick and convulsed. The thick, milky substance shot from his pee hole and trickled down his fingers. He rubbed until he was drained of cum. She needed to hurry up. He wanted to feel her pussy, not his hand.

Troy realized must've drifted off to sleep. The ringing from his cell phone startled him awake. Disoriented, he answered.

"Wat a gwaan?"

"Where the fuck you at? You were supposed to be here getting my dick up."

"I'm not dat far."

He murmured, "Yo, what's in them pills? I feel kinda weird."

"How many did yuh take?"

Troy chuckled. "Just one. Your accent is sexy as fuck. How long before you get here?"

"Thirty minutes or suh. I need di code for di gate.

"Shit, umm, yeah. It's 4734 and press the pound sign."

"Make sure yuh unlock di door."

"Okay, and if I'm sleep, you know how to wake me up."

"Yes, I do."

He hung up and went downstairs to unlock the door. He ended up dozing off again, but this time he awoke to complete darkness and her mouth around his helmet. She suctioned his dick in and popped it out. The slurping and burping sounds she made had his dick stiff at attention.

"Damn, you sucking this dick like you really love it."

"Hmm mmm," she moaned while licking and sucking on his head. The way she tried to swallow the shaft, pulling it down her throat, made Troy feel as if he was going to bust. He eased his dick from her mouth gently.

"Come sit on it," he commanded. He heard her opening the drawer. "Yo, you gettin' a pill too?"

"Uhh . . . uh huh."

"Hurry up, 'cause this shit got me good and hard."

A moment later she straddled him, eased down, and impaled herself on his dick, taking every inch. He gripped her big ass and buried himself deeper. He filled her completely and began thrusting his hips up. She hissed as her walls put his dick in a chokehold.

"Shit, girl you coming already?"

He smacked her thick ass and felt her double bubble bouncing on his thighs as she rode him like a bull. The sensual sounds of her wetness in response to his assault on her pussy echoed throughout the room. She cried out as Troy went deeper. He flipped them over and pulled her underneath him. He pushed her knees up, repositioned himself between her thighs, and grinded his pelvis into hers. He slid his hands under her ass, bringing her hips in to meet each of his long, hard strokes.

"Ooooh shit!" She tried to squirm away as his dick hit a sensitive spot.

"What you moving for? Take this dick."

She cried out again.

"Shit, girl your pussy is so fucking wet!"

He went deeper and grinded harder into her pelvis. She dug her nails into his back as Troy's relentless thrusts rammed into her. The tingling sensation crept into his abdomen. "Oh shit, I'm about to come."

She moaned, "Yes!"

"I'm coming!" he growled in response.

Troy jerked repeatedly. He didn't pull out. His last thrust was deep, and he released his seed within Sadé's walls. Without saying a word, he rolled off and onto his side, passing out instantly. When he awoke the next morning, he reached over for round two, but she wasn't there. He was drifting back to sleep when his phone rang. He yawned, "Yeah, hello."

"Wat a gwaan?"

"Girl, how you put on a show like that and bounce? I was trying to fuck a minute ago. Shit, the least you could've done was cook some of that good-ass breakfast for your boy."

"Wat show? I don't know wat yuh talking 'bout."

"Last night, and I know I wasn't dreaming."

"Yuh must've been."

"Girl, I'm laying here in your nut and mine."

She chuckled, "Yuh party too haad, eh? Troy it must be anneda gyal. Your door was locked. Check yuh phone. I called, but yuh never ansah. I can come now, if yuh want."

He sat up and looked around the bedroom. He checked his phone for her missed calls. She wasn't lying. *The fuck?* He inspected his dick. He knew he hadn't been dreaming because the telltale signs were crusted on his groin and in between his thighs. "I could've sworn . . . you know what, never mind. Yeah, get your ass over here now."

"Ok 'den, I'll see yuh in a few."

Troy got up and went to the shower. His thoughts replayed the previous night, but he found it difficult to recall much. He could've sworn that Sadé was there with him, and they had sex. He was sure of it. He considered the side effect of the alcohol with all the pills he'd taken. Perhaps he'd been dreaming about her while masturbating. That had to be it. After he showered, he changed the sheets and tidied up the bedroom.

He was at the foot of the stairs when his doorbell rang. By the time he reached it, the bell had rung a few more times. He swung the door open. He was about to shout when he realized it was Mark. "What the hell? Why you ring my bell so many times?"

"You didn't answer my calls. I hoped you weren't out. For a minute I was worried."

"Nah, you told me to stay put, so I have been. I just got out the shower."

"Are you alone?"

"Yeah, why? What's going on?"

Mark didn't answer. He walked past him and went into the living room. After Troy closed the door behind them, Mark turned around. "Troy, there's no easy way to put this." He paused before announcing, "I'm really sorry. We did all we could, but they've released you."

"What! Are you fucking serious? Come on, Mark, no."

"They've been pretty quiet about all of this stuff with Mia. I reached out to the owner and GM last week to let them know everything was under control. Buddy, you were out of control at Mia's event. A few of your teammates' wives reported and complained about what happened. We couldn't avoid the blowback from that situation."

He clasped his hands behind his head as he groaned. "Fuck!"

"Relax, buddy. I'm working on getting you signed somewhere else. I've been on the phone with New York, San Fran, and Miami. It looks promising. They all want you, but you'll have to do some counseling in an anger management program."

"I don't wanna play for none of them. And why I gotta do all that?"

"Do you want to play at all?"

Troy glared at him.

"Okay then. You'll do whatever they ask and play wherever we can find you a home. And listen, Troy, there's something else. You need to hear this."

He watched as Mark pulled his phone out, keyed in the passcode, and placed it on the coffee table.

"Heeey Mark, how are you doing? Are you getting those press releases ready? I hope so because I have some interesting info on your precious wide receiver. I'll cut straight to it: I think Troy lied about his knee. I'm almost certain he paid that rehab specialist to sign off on his release. I watched him at practice yesterday, and Mark, it was brutal. That's not the Troy I remember, 'cause he sucked out there. Then I thought maybe it's all this stuff I've been doing that's getting to him. I wanted to talk to him, to encourage him to get out of his funk and stop letting all of this get in his head. So, I stopped by to see him last night. But as you can imagine there was no talking with us. And Mark, let me tell you. He was on more than just Henny. I was looking for a condom, but I found ecstasy pills in his drawer. They must've given him some kind of boost. I've never seen him like that. He was an animal. Better than ever before. But then I got to wondering, did you know about this? How long has he been popping pills? I just hope his next piss test comes up clean." Her maniacal laugh echoed from the speaker.

Mark picked up the phone. He looked up to see Troy's face contorted and tears shining in his eyes. He dropped to his knees. "She's ruining my life, Mark."

CHAPTER

34

The detectives had been keeping a close watch on Jamal since Desiree revealed his double life. Their theories of what might have happened that night didn't match up. They'd gone over everything from forensics in an attempt to link Jamal to Rico's death, but they had nothing and were unable to come up with a clear motive. They kept surveillance on Jamal, hoping he would slip up.

"It's really disturbing to know he has that beautiful young lady at home mourning the death of her brother, his own friend, while he's out here living on the low."

Green nodded. "She's a front like his wife was. That's how this works, Wallace. These men have been doing it for years, especially here. We're known as the capital for them."

Both men returned their attention to the front entrance of the club just as the pair went inside.

When Christian reached for the door handle, Jamal gently grabbed his hand. "Wait. I'm not so sure about this."

Christian leaned in and whispered, "What's wrong, Jamie? There's nothing for you to be shy about. This time follow my lead, and you'll be fine."

One of the bouncers standing at the entrance spoke, "Y'all keep it moving. You're blocking the door."

"You'll have fun. Trust me. Come on, let's go."

As soon as they walked in, Jamal was captivated by the strobe lights and décor of the night club. Christian hadn't lied when he said it was just like the other clubs in Atlanta. The DJ had people bobbing their heads and twirling all over the dance floor, while go-go dancers snaked and gyrated in cages above. Jamal looked around and watched the patrons of different ethnicities enjoying themselves. The anxiety he'd felt about coming to a gay club started to dissipate as they maneuvered through the crowd into another area where people were sitting at tables eating.

Jamal and Christian enjoyed a light dinner with heavy drinks. They sat around talking, laughing, and watching as the party crowd grew. After his fourth glass, Jamal felt the alcohol taking over and his inhibitions waning as he watched his lover talking. "I have to tell you I really love your lips."

"You do, eh?" Christian asked coyly before licking them.

"Yeah, they're one of your best features." Jamal smiled and leaned over, sharing a sensual kiss with him. "I can't get enough of you."

"I know. The feeling's mutual, Jamie. I've really enjoyed spending time with you over these past few weeks. I don't want it to end."

"And it won't."

Christian got up and led Jamal to the dance floor where they began grinding against one another. Their bodies were entwined and swaying to the rhythmic sounds filling the room. Then they switched positions. While Christian gyrated against his hips, Jamal teased pushing up against him with the thickness of his package. Christian bent over, touching his toes while Jamal smacked his ass. As they freaked each other on the dance floor, they laughed, enjoying the moment. A few songs later, after they'd had enough dancing, they went back to their table for another round of drinks.

"Damn, Jamie, I didn't know you could put in that work on the dance floor."

"It's been a minute since I've danced like that, but with you it's been easy to let myself go."

"Have you ever swung an ep in public?"

"What do you have in mind?"

Christian motioned with his finger, "Follow me."

Jamal followed him out of the night club. "Have you done this before, Chris?"

"No, but it's something I've always wanted to do. Come on, there's too much light over here. We need to be away from anyone leaving the club."

"I'm still following your lead."

Unbeknownst to either man, they'd positioned themselves directly in the view of the cops sitting in the tinted, unmarked truck.

Christian wasted no time unzipping the front of Jamal's pants and releasing his long, thick rod. With Jamal's back pressed against the brick wall Christian squatted in front of him and began sucking with vigorous passion.

"Yes! That's it," Jamal whispered as he watched Christian swallow the full length of his dick and pull it back out, then repeating it over and over again.

He couldn't take anymore of Christian's deep-throat action on his dick. He gently pulled him away and brought him to his feet. They shared a quick kiss before Jamal turned him to face the wall and assume the position. Christian unbuttoned his trousers and bent forward, pulling them down to his ankles. Jamal spread his cheeks and spat right into his hole before guiding the head in. Christian rotated his hips until Jamal was halfway in.

"Oooh Jamie, spit on your dick, baby. Lube us up."

Jamal snorted before he spat a good load of mucous right on his dick and into Christian's tight hole. It gave them the lubrication they needed. He buried himself deep inside, feeling the tightness of the forbidden space. "Fuck!"

He started probing the inside of Christian's ass, loosening it with each stroke. He spit on his dick for more lubrication, and the familiar sounds from their shameless lovemaking began to fill the alley.

"Ahem, excuse me gentlemen."

Startled, the lovers split apart and hastily pulled their clothing back up to cover their nudity. The detectives shined flashlights in their faces, blinding them momentarily. They held up their hands and covered their eyes to protect them from the bright lights.

"You're both under arrest for indecent exposure and engaging in a lewd act in a public place. Please turn around and place your hands behind your back."

Jamal stared at Christian in disbelief as he turned around. He dropped his head in shame. Wallace removed his cuffs and placed them on Christian while Green placed cuffs on Jamal. As they guided the men back to their truck, Wallace made the call to the precinct. Jamal looked up at the detective guiding him into the backseat, and he recognized him instantly.

"Good evening, Dr. Edwards."

"Uhh, good evening."

Green closed the door, and before getting inside, he looked over at his partner who returned a knowing grin. Once they arrived at the precinct, the detectives processed the two men, then they pulled Jamal into an interrogation room for questioning. Wallace closed the door as soon as his partner was seated at the table. He stared at Jamal as he grabbed the chair next to Green and sat down.

"Dr. Edwards, we meet again, eh?"

Jamal wouldn't let his eyes make contact with the detective's. Instead, he kept his head lowered.

"Would you mind telling us why you were in that alley engaging in such an act? We knew your friend Mr. Alvarez was homosexual, but we didn't know you were."

Jamal looked up and responded defiantly, "I'm not."

"Perhaps you're not ready to, as they say, come out of the closet, right?"

Jamal bit into his bottom lip and fidgeted in his seat.

Wallace continued to probe. "Eh, Dr. Edwards we just need to clear the air here before we get started. You know, clean the slate and be honest for once."

Jamal glared back at him. "I'm not gay."

Wallace nodded at his partner.

"Dr. Edwards, I have to say this before we go any further." Green proceeded with reading Jamal his Miranda rights.

The seriousness of the situation hit Jamal at that moment. He wasn't sure what would happen next, but all of a sudden, he felt nauseous. "I don't feel so good, guys."

"Hey man, are you about hurl?" Wallace asked.

Jamal hiccupped. "I think so."

Green jumped from the table, grabbed the wastebasket from the other side of the room and placed it next to where Jamal was sitting. As soon as the detective moved away, Jamal leaned over and expelled everything he'd consumed that evening.

The detectives went to the other side of the room and turned their heads as he continued vomiting. A few minutes passed before he finished heaving.

When he heard the heavy breathing, Green turned and asked, "You done?"

Between dry heaving and spitting, Jamal whispered, "Yes."

Wallace left the room and returned a few minutes later with a janitor who removed the wastebasket and mopped the area where the bile didn't make it into the can. He placed an empty wastebasket next to Jamal. He also put paper towels and a cup of water on the table in front of him.

They sat back down at the table and, as if nothing had happened moments earlier, Wallace continued, "Shall we?"

Jamal nodded.

"We've spoken with your wife, Mrs. Edwards."

Jamal remained silent. He knew he needed to maintain his story if they'd spoken with her. The alcohol was still affecting him. More effort was necessary to remember the details he'd already shared with them.

"Can you tell us again where you were the night Mr. Alvarez died?"

Jamal remained poised as he stared into the eyes of the detectives. "I was with Angela for most of the night. I went to the hospital to make rounds. After that, I went home. My wife and I got into an argument about me cheating. She told me to get out, so I went back to Angela."

Wallace leaned forward. "You know what I think, Dr. Edwards. You're hiding something. You don't want to admit you're gay, but we know you and Alvarez probably covered for one another. Did he know you were sleeping his sister?"

"No, because I didn't even know Angela was his sister until after he died," Jamal insisted.

At that moment there was a knock at the interrogation room door. Green got up to answer it. When he opened the door, there was a woman from forensics standing there. She whispered something to the detective and opened the folder in her hands, showing him a few documents. He looked at Jamal and smiled. "Wallace, you won't guess who we brought in with him."

CHAPTER

35

The detectives took up the chairs across the table from Christian. Wallace pressed the button on the recorder and read his Miranda rights before beginning the interrogation. The detectives told Christian they wanted to speak with him regarding a different case they were working on.

At first, Christian didn't respond to the detective. He remained quiet and kept his gaze on the wall behind them.

Green chimed in, "Mr. Hilcrest, do you know Ricardo Trevor Alvarez?"

Christian glanced over at the detective and rolled his eyes.

"Mr. Hilcrest, if you wish to remain silent and not continue with this interrogation, please let us know. We can proceed another way. Now I'll ask you again. Do you know Ricardo Trevor Alvarez? He's also known as Rico or Tré."

"No—I mean yes," he finally responded. "I connected with him on this dating site, DaBoyzClub. I never even met him. We were supposed to meet, but he reneged."

Green pressed, "You sure about that?"

"Yes, I am," Christian snapped back.

"You know Mr. Alvarez is dead right?"

Christian nodded quietly.

"Would you happen to know anything about that?"

He shook his head. "No."

Wallace nodded to his partner. Green pulled out the folder that the forensic scientist had brought into the room earlier that evening. He opened it and removed a few of the photos. He spread them out across the table.

"Mr. Hilcrest, would you like to explain why you were coming out of Mr. Alvarez's apartment on the night he was murdered?"

Christian couldn't hide the shocked expression on his face as he stared at the pictures lying in front of him. He remembered that night. It went against everything he'd done in the past, but Ricardo had persuaded him they were consenting adults. Christian was supposed to meet him at his house for drinks before their date, but when he arrived, Ricardo didn't answer the door or answer his phone calls.

"Mr. Hilcrest?"

He blurted out, "Okay, yes, I was there, but I never went into his house. We'd been talking for a few weeks, and normally I don't ever go to anybody's house, but Ricardo piqued my interest. I got there, knocked on the door a few times. I even called, but he never answered. He stood me up. Of course, I didn't bother calling back, and I never heard from him again. A few days later, I saw it all over the news about his death."

"Why didn't you come forward?"

"Come forward about what? I never even met the man in person."

Wallace asked, "Is there anyone who can corroborate your alibi of where you were afterwards?"

"Yes, everybody and their mama at the club you just busted me and my guy at. I was in there until daybreak. Ask the barmaid, Yancy. We became very acquainted talking about her husband, John. She wanted me to check if he was on the DL."

"When did you meet Dr. Edwards?"

"About a month ago or so."

"Did you know he was married?"

"Yes, I did know." Christian was proud Jamal had come clean. He leaned forward and informed them arrogantly, "They've separated because of me."

Wallace glanced over at his partner. Green shrugged and continued with the questioning. "Did you know that Dr. Edwards was friends with Mr. Alvarez?"

Again, Christian was happy that Jamal had shared everything when he did. He proudly announced, "Yes, he told me Ricardo passed away tragically, and y'all didn't know how. Clearly, you're thinking I had something to do with this, but I'm telling you I never met him."

"Can you think of anything that might help us?"

Christian sat back in the chair and shook his head. "No, that's why I didn't call in the first place."

The detectives had nothing else to go on and couldn't charge him with anything. After obtaining a DNA sample, they took Christian back to a holding cell.

The following day, the detectives received a call from Angela. She was calling from the hospital to find out if there had been any breakthroughs in her brother's case. The detectives were curious why she had been admitted, especially since Jamal was in custody. When they arrived at the hospital, they discovered that Angela was in the psychiatric ward.

The seventh floor of Northside General Hospital was calm and noiseless with very little activity in the halls. The walls were brightly painted with murals of the sun, fields of flowers, and palm and peach trees. A smiling nurse escorted the detectives down the corridor to Dr. Mitchell's office.

"This is going to be interesting," Wallace mumbled.

"Why do you think she's here?" Green asked.

The nurse chimed in, "The doctor will be meeting with you first and can answer all of your questions." She knocked on an office door, and a voice from the other side told her to come in. She motioned for them to enter. "Dr. Mitchell, here are the detectives that wanted to meet with Ms. Washington."

A balding man in his late fifties to early sixties got up from his desk and cleared his throat before extending his hand. "Hello, how are you doing? I'm Dr. Mitchell."

"Good, I'm Detective Wallace."

"And I'm Detective Green. Doing well, thanks."

When they finished greeting one another, Dr. Mitchell motioned for them to have a seat. He returned to his chair behind the big mahogany desk. "So, what can I do for you gentlemen?"

Wallace responded, "We're handling the homicide investigation of Ms. Washington's brother who was murdered last month. She called us for an update on the investigation into his murder. Can you tell us how long she's been in here and why?"

"She was brought to us a few nights ago after she'd been drinking with her medication. She'd been hallucinating, claiming to have heard voices. Dr. Edwards felt it was in her best interest to stay under my care, and I would have to agree. I'm still in the process of evaluating her, but from my initial analysis, it's clear she's not ready to come to terms with her loss."

"Dr. Edwards brought her here?"

"Yes, and I'm glad he did." Dr. Mitchell leaned forward, his expression earnest. "She could've overdosed. It's evident she's self-medicating to deal with her brother's death."

Wallace addressed the doctor, "Uhh, hey Dr. umm . . ."

"Mitchell."

"Right. Is she lucid and able to speak with us for a few minutes?"

Dr. Mitchell cleared his throat again. "At the moment, Ms. Washington is stable. How about we go down to the conference room, and I'll get her for you."

They followed Dr. Mitchell a few doors down to a room that had a large table in the center of it and a flat screen television on the wall. The detectives went inside, and Dr. Mitchell motioned towards the nurses' station for one of them to come over. He and the nurse spoke briefly. A few minutes later, Angela appeared dressed in a light blue hospital gown.

"Hello, Angela. How are you feeling today?"

"I'm all right, Dr. Mitchell. And you?"

"I'm well, thank you. Come on in. You have some visitors."

The doctor guided her into the available chair across the table from the detectives and sat down next to her. Wallace and Green shared the recent developments in their investigation. When they finished, Angela didn't seem to fully understand what they were saying about Jamal's relationship with her brother.

"If they'd met, I'm sure Tré would've been cool with him. Sure, he was a bully and scared my other boyfriends off, but Jamal is so different. He's sweet, kind, funny, and loving. They would've gotten along. I'm sure of it."

"Ms. Washington, Dr. Edwards already knew your brother," Green stated.

Angela argued, "No, he didn't."

Wallace explained, "Dr. Edwards is married to a woman who was also friends with your brother. She confirmed their friendship."

Angela looked at her doctor in confusion and then back at the detectives, "I-I don't believe you. He would've told me."

The detectives probed her to confirm Jamal's timeline the night of her brother's murder. She rubbed her forehead gently and bit into her bottom lip. "I umm, I think—well, no. He got a phone call and said he had to go the hospital. He might have been gone for about two or three hours. I don't remember. I was just happy my man was home and for good."

"Are you sure Dr. Edwards never mentioned his relationship with your brother?"

"He didn't know Tré," she responded with annoyance.

Wallace held his hand up. "Okay, Ms. Washington, that's all I have. Thank you for your time. We'll be in touch with you as soon as we learn more."

Angela nodded. Dr. Mitchell escorted the detectives to the door, and a nurse walked them back to the lobby. As soon as they were in an area where he could get reception on his cell, Wallace made a call in to the precinct. "Make sure you hold Jamal Edwards until we get down there."

"Sorry, Wallace, we couldn't hold him. After you guys left, he made bail. Matter of fact, him and that other guy y'all brought in are gone."

CHAPTER
36

Her divorce wasn't final, and she wasn't one hundred percent sure Derrik was the father of her unborn child, but neither mattered. They were officially together. Derrik wanted her and believed the baby was his. Desiree knew his love and support would ensure a happy and healthy journey for their bundle of joy.

She returned to work with confidence. Her professional image wasn't tarnished, and her identity remained anonymous. After the fiasco at the police department, Atlanta's attention shifted to Troy's release from the Falcons. He was no longer a factor. It should've felt as though her world was getting back to some normalcy.

Yet as she sat in the conference room, there was a loose end sitting quietly across the table from her. She and Aaron were in the middle of a stare down. He was upset she'd kept him out of the loop. Desiree didn't feel he had a reason to be upset, and she was over it. She frowned and stood up.

"Sit down, Desiree."

"You're sitting there not saying anything."

He lowered his eyes. "If you hadn't kept this a secret, I wouldn't have to handle things in this manner."

She cut her eyes as she sat down. "I didn't keep this a secret. It was none of your business."

"None of my business? Desiree, you came to me, and I helped you. This is all of my business now."

"I'm not trying to downplay what you've done. I had no idea you inserted yourself in this. I don't know why you bothered. I called your friend. She'd already handled everything."

"No, she hadn't. Once I found out what was going on, I checked and she hadn't done half of what I would've. I realized she wasn't thorough enough. She was sloppy, missing several key details that would've left you with inadequate representation. Trust that it was in your best interest I got involved."

Desiree was tempted to go off. She was irritated to find out Aaron had been snooping around once again, but it was clear he'd gone to great lengths to guarantee her name would never be exposed. Aaron informed Mia's lawyer that if Desiree's identity were ever revealed, they would face a revenge porn case. He took a sealed envelope from his briefcase and passed it across the table.

"Thank you, Aaron. I really appreciate this. You have no idea how much—"

"Yes, I do. And for the record, you didn't have to lie about any of this."

"I didn't lie."

"You did, Desiree."

She eyed him in confusion.

"Remember you asked for help on behalf of a *friend* that was in trouble. Which friend might have that been? Brielle or Derrik?"

Instead of responding, she averted her eyes, embarrassed.

"Right. You led me to believe I was helping a friend. Come to find out that friend was you. I don't like being lied to, Desiree. We've been upfront with each other this long. Even though the foundation of our relationship was based on complete deception, I'll overlook this. Perhaps it's what you're used to."

She glared back but held her tongue.

"Don't be upset, sweetie."

"I'm not. You didn't have to say that though."

"No, I did. Isn't that the case here? You were married, right? You were lying and sneaking around on your husband with not one, but several men. You've lied to all of us because one just isn't enough for you."

She frowned. "What are you getting at, Aaron? I don't appreciate your tone or these accusations."

CHAPTER 36

"Accusations? No, these are the facts. Do you have any idea what I've done for you? The people I had to talk to and ask for help without revealing too much? I want you to understand how much I had to do to ensure that woman didn't slander your character behind her husband, your ex."

"Aaron, I know what you did, and that's not what I meant. What I'm saying—"

"No, let me finish, Desiree. I don't think you fully understand. Knowing this could've potentially ruined your career and reputation, I wasn't about to trust anyone else to help you. I had to step in to protect what's mine. When it comes to you there's nothing I wouldn't do. I hope you understand I'm not about to lose you. If that means going to the ends of the earth, I will."

It hit Desiree that Aaron was serious. An uneasy feeling settled in the pit of her stomach. Just then, she was startled by her phone ringing. Her phone was facedown, but she knew it was Derrik. She kept it cool. "I have to take this."

"Hey, you." Derrik was calling to let her know that his meeting had gone longer than expected and that he would be late. As he explained the changes in their plans, Desiree got up and went over to her desk. She moved some things around, fumbling to find a pen. She opened her Louis Vuitton day planner and began scribbling a note. "Yes, of course . . . Now why would that be a problem? I've ridden with him by myself before. Did you forget that day he brought me to work after I left your office? . . . Right. We'll be fine." Aaron got up and came over to her desk. Desiree held up a finger. "I'm finishing up my last meeting now. I have to run by my house first. I'll see you then." She giggled, "Okay, bye."

"Was that *Derrik*?"

Her poker face activated. She looked directly into his eyes. "No, I have to meet up with Bri in an hour. I promised I would help her with this event."

Aaron stepped around the other side of the desk to stand in front of her. "Desiree, I hope we have an understanding. Don't ever lie to me again." He lifted her chin, forcing her to look at him. His eyes fixed on hers. "Are we clear?"

He stared at her with such intensity, Desiree felt her soul shiver. She whispered, "Yes."

CHAPTER
37

Desiree slipped her hand into Derrik's and intertwined her fingers with his. In her heart, she knew it was Derrik who would go to the ends of the earth for her. Not Aaron. Derrik's eyes met hers, and he smiled as they entered one of their favorite restaurants. It was neatly tucked away on a side street in the Virginia Highlands. She wasn't divorced yet, so Derrik understood they needed to keep their relationship low key and out of the public eye, even though he was ready to show her off as his woman. This particular establishment catered to celebrities and respected their privacy. They wouldn't have to worry about being photographed; the restaurant had a no-photo rule and no paparazzi allowed. The delicious aromas wafting in from the kitchen hit Desiree's nostrils. Her stomach growled loudly.

"I believe my boy's hungry."

"Goodness, you heard that?"

Derrik chuckled. "I think everybody in here heard that." He nodded towards the hostess. "Didn't you?"

Desiree playfully punched him in the arm and pouted. "You're not funny."

"No, but you're sexy pouting like that." He gave her a peck on the lips.

Desiree flashed a smile and sighed happily, leaning against his chest. After a few minutes, the hostess guided them to their booth in the corner away from the main floor. Once they were seated, they continued with small talk.

"Sorry about switching up our plans, but I had to finish my meeting."

"It's all good, babe. Believe it or not, I got Hodges talking for the first time. I didn't know he was so country."

"Yeah, he's from Louisiana. When he does talk, everything's 'my Mama said.' He's the real-life Bobby Boucher."

"Oh, my god yes!" They both laughed for a few minutes about the bodyguard and his different 'Mama said' sayings.

"So, tell me about your day. How did things go with this acquisition you were working on?" Derrik asked.

She didn't want to talk about it, considering Aaron hadn't focused on anything regarding the acquisition. She responded dryly, "It's coming along fine. We should be wrapping things up in a couple of weeks, if not sooner."

"You know I meant to say something about your friend the other day."

"My friend?"

"The white dude."

"Ahh, Aaron."

"Yeah, *Aaron*. I peeped how he was acting. He gave me this vibe. As if he has a thing for you."

Her laugh came out sounding nervous. "No, I highly doubt that."

"I know what I saw. You better tell that vanilla wafer to watch it. He tries that shit again, he's likely to get his chin checked."

Aaron's behavior was somewhat unnerving. Desiree didn't want to downplay it as nothing. She appreciated him taking care of Mia trying to expose her with the video, but Desiree didn't owe him anything. She didn't want to be with him, and he couldn't force them to be together. She decided if he tried to come at her again with the crazy talk, she would have her man chin-check him.

Desiree acknowledged the seriousness in Derrik's promise. "You don't need to worry about him. And babe, it's hella sexy to think you'd check his ass for me."

"I'd chin-check any nigga thinking they can try me when it comes to you, baby girl."

"Oooh, so sexy," she said, grinning at him.

He put an arm around her shoulder, and they settled into a comfortable silence. Derrik lowered his gaze to study her heart-shaped face in detail. She didn't have prominent cheekbones, but when she smiled or laughed, her round cheeks reach her eyes. He loved the way her tiny nose wrinkled, and he enjoyed her full, luscious lips that were made for kissing. He cupped her slightly pointy chin, lifting her head. She raised her amber gaze to meet his, leaving him spellbound. "There's something I need to do."

"What's that?"

Desiree watched as he slid out of the booth and got down on one knee. He flashed her the biggest smile.

She whispered, "Oh my god, Derrik, what are you doing?"

"Something I should've done a long time ago. After those walking papers are signed it'll be official with us. I'm not about to lose you to any other man again."

Everything around them fell silent as other restaurant patrons ceased their conversations to focus their attention on the couple. Desiree's eyes welled up with tears as Derrik drew a purple suede box from his pocket. A few women gasped when Derrik opened the box. Desiree could hear the compliments on the huge, sparkling diamond cluster, but she was unable to glance down at the ring. Her gaze was fixed on Derrik's brown eyes.

"Desiree Michele Thompson, I've wanted you since I stepped on the back of your heel and first laid eyes on you. I've loved you for just as long. A friend of mine's mama said when it comes to love we can't control when it happens or where it might lead us. The heart, after all, is a compass. It just knows what it wants to feel and how to get there. It wants what it wants, and there ain't nothing you can do about it. No matter where I've gone, my compass has always led me back to you. I was a fool all these years letting others have what's rightfully mine. Never again. Tonight, in front of all these people, I profess my love and devotion to you and you only. Please do me the honor of saying yes. Will you marry me, baby girl?"

Desiree blubbered through her tears, "Yes! Yes, of course I will!"

He stood up and lifted her up into his arms. Desiree clasped her hands around his neck. His lips settled on her mouth, and he kissed her slowly. Derrik's kiss set fire to her soul, melting away all doubts and fears. There was no other man for her. With him, she felt safe, protected, and adored. She heard the applause, cheers, and congratulations coming from everyone around them. When they withdrew from the kiss, Derrik released her from his embrace long enough to slide the ten-carat ring onto her slim finger.

Desiree's eyes grew wide. "Derrik, this ring is beautiful!" she gushed.

"Not as beautiful as you, baby girl."

She blushed and admired the diamond, squinting as the light hit it at the right angle. "Damn, now this is what you call bling bling."

"I know," he said proudly, "and my future wife deserves it."

She blushed again.

After thanking the people that stopped to give them their well wishes, the pair cuddled and quietly basked in the moment. A few minutes passed before Derrik finally spoke, "Before you get under way with the wedding plans, have you thought about what we're naming him?"

"Him? What makes you think we're having a boy?"

"You're right. But just so you know, we have a lot of twins in my family," he boasted. "You might be carrying my twins."

"We'll find out soon enough. I can't wait for you to meet Dr. Logan. She's amazing. You'll love her."

"I don't think so. The only woman I'll ever love is you."

Desiree's heart fluttered. She gave him a quick peck. "I love you too, Derrik."

They spent the rest of dinner discussing plans for her to move in with him. He told her she had free reign of the house to pick out the baby's room and could hire a designer to help remodel it. Desiree couldn't help but get caught up in her new life as she saw it. She smiled at the thought of being Derrik's wife and the mother of his babies.

After dinner, they walked through the neighborhood to check out the scenery and shops. By the time they reached his truck, Desiree felt exhausted. She waited for Derrik to open the passenger door. As he closed it, she tilted her head back and let out the loudest yawn. He climbed inside. His hearty laughter echoed throughout the truck.

"What's funny?"

"You."

She gave him a strange look.

He pointed at his watch, "You're sleepy this time of night. He's already wearing you out." He started the engine and checked the rearview mirror to see if Nate was behind him. Derrik put the truck in drive after Nate gave a signal with a flash of his high beam. "Let me get you home."

"According to Dr. Logan, our baby is doing the most growing right now. I'm going to be tired and especially after eating a meal like that, then walking. I'm stuffed and sleepy."

She cradled her abdomen. He moved his hand over to cover hers.

"I'm looking forward to seeing your stomach swell. You want to know what else I'm really looking forward to?"

"What's that?"

"Your titties being full of milk and that round ass spreading." He moved his hand between her legs. "They didn't lie about pregnant pussy. It stays so gushy."

She bit into her bottom lip and slouched down in the seat. She opened her thighs wider. Derrik massaged her clit through the taut material. She needed to feel his fingers inside. She started fumbling with the button on her jeans. She slid them down and pulled her thong to the side. Derrik licked two fingers and slid them in. Desiree moaned.

"I can feel your pussy opening up."

He slipped his ring finger in. Desiree gyrated her hips as he plucked her G-spot. She shuddered as the first orgasm took over. She gripped his arm, her head tilting back. "Derrik!"

He felt the muscles tighten around his fingers. He pushed them in deeper. "That's it, baby girl. Come for me."

Desiree thrusted her pelvis against his hand. She felt the sensation ripple through her. She was on the verge of unraveling. Derrik withdrew his fingers.

She whimpered, reaching for his hand. "That was the spot, babe. Why did you stop?"

"Hold on." He frowned and turned his head to look behind them. "What the hell is wrong with this asshole? I have someone following too close. They've been riding my bumper for a minute."

She turned to look back, only seeing the bright lights of the car behind them. They flashed their high beams. She covered her eyes. "Why don't you let them go around. They're being a road hog."

Derrik complained, "The fuck? I wonder if Nate sees this asshole riding me. Let me speed up and get up around this bend. He can get between us." He accelerated, and as he made his way around the bend, Desiree's neck jerked. The truck jolted forward. They began zigzagging sideways towards the oncoming traffic. Derrik pushed the brake pedal to the floor of the truck. It didn't slow up. He slammed his foot into the pedal again, but the acceleration continued.

Desiree screamed. "Derrik!"

"The brakes!" he exclaimed. He tried to gain control of the steering wheel and turn it in the opposite direction to bring them back on their side of the road. The truck starting spinning and skidded a few feet before flipping over several times.

A bright light flashed. It disappeared. It reappeared and disappeared again.

Desiree tried to move her head. It was then she realized she couldn't shield herself from the blinding light. *I can't move!*

Every attempt was useless. She couldn't feel anything other than the hands over her face and fingers forcing her eyes open. The bright light finally went away. She tried to open her eyes on her own, but they were unusually heavy. She couldn't speak. Her throat was obstructed with something. The distinct noises of an oxygen machine could be heard nearby.

She mustered the strength and willed her eyes open as wide as they could. Her blurred vision came into focus. She saw her best friend standing next to a man she didn't recognize, but there was no mistaking who he was.

"Please be honest, Doc. Will she ever come out of this? Is there any chance for her?"

"Yes, absolutely. Considering the minor injuries sustained—a concussion, chest contusions, and a broken arm—she's healing considerably well. She's not the first pregnant woman to have gone through this type of trauma. We'll continue to keep them as comfortable as possible, which is all we can do. Her body has to do the rest. It's great that you've been here every day sitting with her. She'll wake up soon enough. Just keep talking to her. Patients respond better when they hear their loved ones."

Desiree's eyelids were too heavy. Even though she wanted to keep them open, she stopped fighting and closed them.

"Doc, did you see that? Were her eyes open just now?"

"Hang on, let me check something here."

The bright light flashed in her eyes again.

"Remarkable. A few minutes ago, there wasn't any response to the light."

"What does this mean?" Brielle probed.

"It means we have our first sign she could be coming out of this coma."

"This is great news, Doc!"

"Whoa, Ms. Stephens, let's not get ahead of ourselves. Yes, this is a sign that she might be improving, but she's still unresponsive and hasn't shown any signs of voluntary movement. I'm going to have the nurse schedule some more tests. As I mentioned, our job at the moment is to keep her comfortable for the babies' sake. Unless you have any other questions, I have to check on a few other patients."

"No, at least she did something. I'm not losing my faith she'll pull through."

"That's the positive attitude to keep."

"Thanks again for everything, Doc."

"You're welcome. I'll talk to you soon."

The door closed. Desiree felt a soft hand caress the side of her face.

"Hey, diva, I don't know if you heard that, but the doc here says you're improving. We finally have some good news. Listen, keep fighting. Do you hear me, Desi? Fight like you've never fought before. You have two babies to live for."

There was a knock on the door.

"Ahem, umm, hi Brielle."

"Hey, Aaron."

Aaron? What is he doing here? Where's Derrik?

"Everybody at the office is worried about her. I told Carolyn and Tiana I would stop in to see how she's doing. Any change?"

Brielle nodded. "She might be coming out of this coma. The doctor said to keep talking to her. They respond to their loved ones talking to them."

"Yes, the love of friends and family has the power to heal. She's going to pull through," Aaron reassured Brielle.

"I have to believe that." There was a moment of silence. "Hey, I'm sorry I wasn't much for conversation when you were here last time. I didn't expect to see you, and with this happening I just . . ." Brielle's voice faded.

He chuckled. "No sweat. I understand. I guess I was supposed to stay a secret from everybody."

"Right."

Another moment of silence filled the room. Aaron finally spoke, "Listen, Brielle I'll be in town for a while to finish up this acquisition we were working on before this happened. I plan to keep visiting until she wakes up. I wanted to let you know I'm here for you as well. If you need anything, don't hesitate to ask."

"I appreciate it, Aaron, and I know Desi does too."

"It's no bother at all. Perhaps we can catch up with coffee or lunch. That's if you don't mind and would like the company."

"Yeah, yeah, that'll be good. Well, no—not today."

"I didn't mean today but whenever you're free."

274

"Right, okay let's do that."

Aaron handed Brielle his cell, and she keyed in her number. He sent her a text so she would have his number as well.

"Thanks again."

"No need to thank me. I'll see you soon, Brielle."

Brielle leaned down, kissed her friend's cheek, and whispered, "Remember what I said. Fight. I'll see you later, okay. Love you, diva."

Desiree heard the door close. Moments later his lips brushed against her ear.

"She said to talk to you, so I hope you can hear me, Desiree. You really had me worried here for a minute. When I came the first night, you were in pretty bad shape and hooked up to more machines. I wanted to hold your hand and let you know I was here, but they wouldn't let me come in." He paused, but Desiree could still hear his breathing. "God, even lying here like this you're still so beautiful. I thought I was going to lose—" He paused again. His tone was stern as he continued, "Desiree you lied to me again. You were supposed to be with Brielle. Why were you in his truck?"

Her heart rate began to increase. She wanted to scream but couldn't.

"I can't believe he managed to make it out of that mangled mess. Brielle has way more faith than I do, that's for sure."

The noise coming from the machines was deafening. Yet, his words could be heard over it all.

"I doubt he'll make it if he goes through another surgery. Once he's out of the picture, we don't have to worry about anyone else coming between us. I told you I never worry about the competition because I never lose. I always win. I get what I want. I love you, Desiree, and you're mine."

Her body stiffened for a brief moment before starting to jerk rapidly. Desiree arms and legs flailed across the bed. The machine's alarm blared. By the time Aaron made it to the door, the nurses were rushing in.

"Sir, please, you're going to have to wait outside."

That was the last thing Desiree heard before everything went silent.

Afterword

Whew! That was an unexpected ending, right? I didn't see it coming either. I know, here I go again leaving my readers on yet another cliffhanger. Yes, *One Ain't Enough* sparked questions, and while most of those have been addressed, *One Still Ain't Enough* has prompted new ones. I can promise this time I won't keep y'all waiting for more than a decade. The final installment of this series, *One Is Enough* (Spring 2023) will address some of the topics raised in this book. However, for a few of the sub characters, their stories will be resolved in later books.

Now I don't know about y'all but, Desiree was getting on my last damn nerve acting immature about her situation with Derrik. Now, I can admit back in the day I got caught between two lovers, but I had nowhere to run. How lucky was she to be able to hop on a plane and run from her problems? I wanted her to face Derrik sooner than later, but she kept focusing on everything else except talking to him. I couldn't blame her, but she only prolonged the inevitable. She ultimately had to accept Derrik's initial response. I thought for a moment she'd lost him to Khloe, but in the end, Derrik chose Desiree and stepped up to the challenge. I had a feeling he would. He loves her. Besides he was already talking about Desiree being the mother of his babies.

Hold up though. We still don't know who her baby daddy is, but I guess we have a clue, right?

I'm sure it was unexpected to introduce another love interest for Derrik, but I thought it was unrealistic to think he wouldn't have someone else. He couldn't have been pining over Desiree for all these years and not have other women on his roster. The man is rich and fine! I enjoyed bringing Khloe into the picture as she adds a different side to who Derrik is and where he came from. This wasn't explored in book one, and from what was seen, he had some unfinished business with her. That's why I don't think Khloe's going away that quietly. I'm pretty sure we'll be seeing her again soon.

This situation with Mia and Troy is toxic as hell. When I write for them, there's one song that stays in rotation – Love the Way You Lie. Troy has done the unforgivable, and despite his attempts to disguise it behind his hard exterior, Mia has finally brought him to his knees. All I can say is, they will not let any of us tell them what to do about their relationship. They are like moths to a flame. They'll likely reconcile, but not before Mia exacts her revenge. She has a plan and is going to execute it by all means necessary.

As for Jamal, his story is just beginning. He was able to walk away without being punished for his treacherous behavior. This doesn't mean it won't get resolution, but the Atlanta detectives didn't have enough evidence to charge him. As he becomes more self-aware, he realizes that everything he sought to hide—including the motive behind his friend's murder—is who he really is. Now that he's met Christian, there's no hiding his true identity.

I truly hope you enjoyed this second book of The Enough Series. It's taken years for this work of art to reach some of your hands. I can't thank you enough for your continued patience and support. I poured my heart and soul into continuing the drama of Desiree Edwards while introducing new, unforgettable characters, creating unexpected plot twists, and ultimately, adding more scandal to this cast from Atlanta. I ask whether you liked it or not, to please take the time to leave a review on Amazon, Bookbub, and/or Goodreads.

While in the writing lab, there's always music playing. There are some dope R&B and rap tracks that kept me inspired throughout penning this story. You can check out the playlist for this book on Apple Music and Spotify, under the same title.

Please keep up with me on Facebook @mo.flames, Instagram and TikTok @ moflames_author, Twitter @moflames

Please subscribe via my webpage for updates and sneak peeks of upcoming releases https://moflames.com

Join my Facebook group, Mo's Corner at https://bit.ly/3BO3dL7 for live discussions, inside information on upcoming releases and giveaways.

Also by Mo Flames

The Enough Series
One Ain't Enough

Girl, He Don't Want Your Ass,
The 10 Signs He's Not Interested (Non-Fiction)

About the Author

Mo Flames is an avid reader, writer, wine lover and a super fan of The Office. She pens contemporary romance stories with complex characters, controversial topics and unpredictable plot twists. Mo's experiences and creativity fuel her written words. She's never been bashful about racy relationship topics. She's unashamed and unapologetically real. It echoes with her tagline, 'leaving that fire between the sheets, literally.'

When she's not writing, she enjoys playing the Sims, reading romance and suspense, binge watching The Office, Snapped, Criminal Minds or any crime television shows. She resides in Atlanta, GA with her husband and daughter.

www.ingramcontent.com/pod-product-compliance
Lightning Source LLC
Chambersburg PA
CBHW021004260626
47169CB00006B/1930